Karen Woods was born and raised in Manchester, where she still lives. Karen left school without any formal qualifications and obtained her inspiration from attending an adult literacy course. Since then she's written twenty novels as well as adapting some of them for the stage. Karen works in education and is passionate about introducing people of all ages to the power of storytelling.

VICE

KAREN WOODS

Harper
North

HarperNorth
Windmill Green,
Mount Street,
Manchester, M2 3NX

A division of
HarperCollins*Publishers*
1 London Bridge Street
London SE1 9GF

www.harpercollins.co.uk

HarperCollins Publishers
Macken House, 39/40 Mayor Street Upper,
Dublin 1, D01 C9W8, Ireland

First published by HarperNorth in 2022

3 5 7 9 10 8 6 4

A catalogue record for this book
is available from the British Library

ISBN: 978-000-852864-5

Printed and bound in the UK using 100% renewable electricity at
CPI Group (UK) Ltd

This novel is entirely a work of fiction.
The names, characters and incidents portrayed in it are the work
of the author's imagination. Any resemblance to actual persons,
living or dead, events or localities is entirely coincidental.

MIX
Paper | Supporting
responsible forestry
FSC™ C007454

This book is produced from independently certified FSC™
paper to ensure responsible forest management .
For more information visit: www.harpercollins.co.uk/green

For Christine Price and Maureen Orman,
the Golden Girls forever.

Darren Woods, a legend always. Remembering you is easy
I do it every day and missing you is the heartache that
never goes away.

Dale, good night God bless x

Chapter One

Jenny Johnson sat staring at the calendar, running her fingers through her long dark hair. Dark circles shadowed her eyes. She had saggy pale skin and she looked stressed. She was away with the fairies, staring at a date circled in thick black ink. The fourth of July was only one week away. For crying out loud, she thought, she was nowhere near ready to go back to her old life. She was enjoying her freedom too much. She closed her eyes and inhaled, deep breaths, calming her speeding heartbeat. He'd be back then, back in her life, ruling it, making every day a complete misery. The punches, the kicks, the mental abuse, not a minute's peace, always having to answer to him. It would all return along with him.

A chill passed over her body. She rubbed her arms as the small blonde hairs stood on end, fear filling her body. Should she up and leave before he came out of jail? Could she? Go and start again, find somewhere new to live where nobody knew her name, her past?

Who was she trying to kid? She would never leave him. She'd never had the guts before – why was now any different? Time after time she'd planned her escape, but still she was here. Instinctively, she looked for her cigarettes. She needed to curb her smoking. This last week or so she'd been chain-smoking, and now her chest was rattling and her purse was empty. But this was what she did when she was stressed: smoke, smoke and smoke.

'I'll cut down tomorrow,' she mumbled as she stared at her fags.

Already it sounded like another failed resolution. Every time she had a minute, she would grab a smoke. It was second nature to her and, as she lit up now, for a brief moment she relaxed, pushing aside the fear coiled inside her.

The living room door swung open and her son, Danny, shot a look at her as he walked in. He could tell straight away something was wrong and came over to where she was sat. He patted her shoulder.

'Mam, what's up?' he asked as he bent slightly to see her face fully. He'd towered over her since he was a teenager, and now in his twenties, his broad frame made her look smaller and more fragile than she was. He'd become a real heartbreaker – tall, dark and handsome, and a magnet for girls who liked bad boys. If only someone had warned her off those kind of men when she was young, thought Jenny. Her life could have been different – really different.

She blew out a mouthful of grey smoke with a laboured breath. The face of a thousand cuts, the look that told him she was on one.

2

'Your dad's home soon. Life will never be the same again, will it?' She wiped her nose on her hand.

Danny perched next to her, his eyes following hers to the calendar. He gripped her knee with strong, warm fingers, trying to tell her everything was going to be OK.

'Mam, we need him home. He's been stuck in the slammer for over three years now. You're just spooked, that's all. You know once he's home you'll be fine. You and my dad are sorted, right?'

Danny watched her expression, checking for any signs that she was having second thoughts. He couldn't tell. Danny had never really spoken to his mother about her marriage: he simply took it for granted his parents were fine. He had his own life to lead, and was too busy to care about what happened behind closed doors. Anyway, why wouldn't they be fine? His old man was a top geezer, you could ask any of the lads down the boozer. Who wouldn't want to be married to the main man round here? Charley Johnson was a local legend. He was always buying everyone drinks, laughing, joking. So Dad would have a few beers at night and maybe get a bit gobby when he was steaming drunk, but that was a man thing, wasn't it? Nothing to end a marriage over. And yes, his dad moved in dangerous circles – but that was the price you paid for a bit of money and respect round this side of Manchester.

Danny had grown up with his dad running this part of town – clubs, protection, dealers, all roads round here led back to the Johnsons. Until this latest time the law had caught up with his old man. He'd got a longer stretch than usual and it hadn't taken long for other families to try to move in on their turf. Worst of all were the Bennets – there was bad blood between the families and Danny knew it wasn't just for the money that they were trying to take streets of his family while Big Charley was inside. Danny and Paul had tried to keep business ticking over, even his mam had stepped in, but each day was a battle to keep their influence and reputation intact. He needed everyone to fear the Johnson name – needed his dad back visible again. So what was his mum doing wishing him longer in jail?

Jenny rubbed at her arms again – she couldn't shift the goosebumps.

She spoke in a low voice, still staring at the calendar. 'People change, Son. Your dad has been in and out of prison for most of our marriage so I've been like a single woman half the time. He's never been here for the important things in your life, if I'm being honest. It's me who brought you up, not him. And it was hard, let me tell you.' She flicked her hair over her shoulder as she continued, proud to have been a solo parent much of the time. 'I don't know if I'm cut out for this life anymore. I've changed, Danny. I used to wait for him to get out, but I've learned waiting gets you nowhere. I have a life now when your dad is locked up. I go where I want, come in what time I want. I'm my own keeper.'

Danny was having none of this. He knew what his old man would say: she was a wife and a mother so she should be happy with her lot: what else did she want? She was a woman and her place was at home, cooking and cleaning and looking after the place. Clearly caretaking some of the family business while his father had been inside had gone to her head. He didn't want her getting ideas – the Johnson crown was his to inherit – he wasn't sharing power with anyone, not even his own mother.

He moved his hand away from her. 'Mam, stop waffling. You go on like you've had a great time while my dad's been in the big house, but you've been miserable. Go on, admit it?'

She stubbed her fag out with a sour expression. 'Don't make me bleeding laugh, Son. You don't know the half of it. I'm just saying it's going to be hard adjusting when he's out, that's all. How can I have him telling me where and when I can go out? The man is a control freak, and you know it. I only missed his allotted phone call the other night and you should have heard him ballooning down the phone at me, threatening to shave my hair off and put me in a body bag. I'm not putting up with all that shit anymore just because he's paranoid. Like I said, I've changed. I'm not being anyone's doormat anymore. I'm sorry I even mentioned anything now. Like you would give a shit about me having a life. You're a chip off the old block.'

That was it, she'd said her piece. She looked around the front room at the state of it and sighed. That's all she was to the men in this house: a bleeding slave, fetching and carrying.

Danny rolled his eyes. His mother must be on the rag or something. She was always feeling sorry for herself when it was that time. Before she could start her usual lecture about the house being a shit-tip, he changed the subject. 'It's not my dad I've come to talk about. You know who I'm after. Have you seen that shady fucker this morning, or is he on the missing list again?'

Jenny hunched her shoulders and sighed. She knew who he meant. Paul was her youngest son and there was always some kind of beef going on between the two brothers. 'Nope, I've not seen sight nor sound of him. He's probably in that bird's bed who he's been going on about. You know what he's like. He'll stick it anywhere, he will. He's a dirty bastard.'

Danny stretched his arms above his head. 'He's had his hand in the till again. It's only a few hundred quid this time, but how many times does he think he can have me over, the silly twat? He's getting bombed on the minute I see him. I'm not asking any questions. I'm going to waste him. I know it's him taking it, Mother, no matter what lies roll off his tongue.'

Jenny looked at Danny. She was sick to death of the arguing between her sons. It was like they were still ten years old. They always wanted whatever the other one had. But then their father had encouraged that – he always said you had to fight for anything you wanted. 'Come on, give the lad a break. Bloody hell, every time anything goes missing, you're all over him like a rash. Maybe he has taken money in the past, but you can't keep knocking on his door every time the count is down.'

Danny was fuming now: she was protecting Paul again. Sonny boy, golden balls, that kid could do no wrong in her eyes. 'Why do you always think the sun shines out of his arse, Mam? You always stick up for him. You need to see the guy for who he really is, a thieving lying bastard who has no family loyalties.'

Jenny bit hard on her lip and started to clean up before she said something she regretted. She threw clothes that had been left lying about onto the back of the sofa, mumbling, 'Like I need any more shit in my life. Don't you think I've got enough on my plate without you two at loggerheads?'

Danny couldn't make out what she was saying. She'd often talk to herself when they'd had words, snide comments under her breath. He was safest changing the subject. 'Any brekkie, Mam? I'm starving. A few bacon butties will see me right, if you're making any?'

Jenny's face went beetroot. She stood facing him with her hand on her hips, 'Piss off and make your own. I'll have enough of being a servant when your dad gets home, so get off your backside for once. I'm not your skivvy. And, for your information, your dad will be getting told the same thing, too. You can all kiss my arse and start doing things for yourself. I'm going to start looking after me for a change. Doing things that I want to do.'

Danny chuckled to himself and reached for the TV remote. 'I'll take that as a no then. Bloody hell, I was only asking.'

Jenny stomped around the front room, no eye contact whatsoever. She paused as she came to a big box of trophies, a tangle of golden figures of boxers, all with small plaques mounted on the base: *Awarded to Charley Johnson*. She booted the box and snarled at it as if it could hear her. 'And you lot can piss off, too. I don't want all this crap scattered around the living room.'

She couldn't face the thought of yet another trip down Memory Lane once Charley was home. Many a night he would sit down with his family and tell them the story of his boxing career. He could have turned professional, he could have won a world title, he would tell them. Who knew if he was telling the truth or not? Whichever it was, the shine had long since come off the trophies, just like their marriage.

———

Jenny sat in the quiet of the kitchen after Danny realised there was no grub coming, and no little brother either, and finally cleared off. This pine table had heard so many stories over the years. If it could have spoken, half the Johnson family would have been six feet under by now. Secrets: even if you never wanted to hear them in the first place, you were stuck with them, carrying them around, feeling them dragging you down. Jenny was running her fingers over a gouge in the wood when her friend, Gina, came in through the back door. She never knocked. Gina had bright-red hair and there was no doubt she hammered the sunbed. Laughter lines were etched deeply into her face. 'Bleeding hell, cheer up – it might never happen. What's up with your mush today?'

Jenny lifted her cup and sipped her coffee. 'Nowt, just a bit pissed off, that's all. Same shit, different day.'

Gina sat down at the table and peeled off her black leather jacket. She pulled a twenty deck of fags from her coat pocket and placed them on the table with a grey lighter perched on top of them. Just one look at her friend and she knew this was going to be a long day. She raised her eyes. 'So, come on then, what's up?'

Jenny shook her head. 'You know what's up. It's the same as it was yesterday and the same as it was the day before. I'm counting down the days but nothing's changing.'

Gina rolled her eyes and rested her elbows on the table. 'So, like I said, pack up and leave him. I can't understand why you stay, why you've always stayed. The guy is a bully, a wife-beater. You do my head in sometimes. You're such a strong woman in every other way, but when it comes to Charley you let him walk all over you. He's a wanker and you should kick his arse to the kerb.'

'Gina, I've told you that I will never leave my kids.'

'Kids?' Gina shouted. 'The lads are men, Jenny. Danny's twenty-seven and Paul is twenty-five. Even "little" Rachel is nineteen now and she can look after herself, so I don't understand your problem. Just tell him you've had enough and bin-bag the fucker.'

Jenny reached over for the cigarettes and picked one out of the packet. It was like banging her head against a brick wall. 'No one will ever understand my situation. Until you've have walked a mile in my shoes, you can't say anything. It's so hard.'

Gina gritted her teeth and faced Jenny. There was no way she was listening to this bullshit again. She was sick of it, sick of seeing her friend scared and upset. 'Right, so what's the real reason? Tell me straight, do you still love Charley?'

Jenny was taken aback by the question and hesitated.

Gina stared at her friend. 'Just answer the bloody question. I'm trying to help here.'

'I do and I don't. He's the kids' father. We used to have dreams, plans. A part of me still remembers that. When he's nice he's very nice, but when he's drinking and he switches, he's an evil bastard. Honest, you don't know the half of it, nobody does. But I know it's no use me looking back. I need to do something about the here and now. I feel trapped, suffocated.'

'So, speak with someone then. Go to people who can help you get away from him, Women's Aid or something.' She paused and her eyes widened. 'But you know as well as me that Charley will never stop looking for you as long as he has breath left in his body. You're his world. Don't think you can stay here in Manchester. You would have to do a proper moonlight flit. Maybe even emigrate. A place in the sun, that's what you need.'

Jenny took a long hard drag of her cigarette and ran a single finger around the rim of her cup, all the fight had gone out of her voice. 'I'll see what he's like when he comes home. If he kicks off again then this time I'll start making plans. I can't just up and leave him before he gets out of jail, can I?'

Gina slammed a flat palm on the table. 'Dead right you can. That's your problem, Jen, you think too much about other people when you should be looking after yourself. If my Dave was being a wanker he'd be out through the front door, let me tell you. Gone are those days when women put up with all that shit. Let the wanker crash and burn. See how he likes it getting by on his tod.'

Jenny had to hold her words back; it would have been so easy to remind Gina about some of the men who had knocked ten tons of shit out of her in the past. Her friend had forgotten about the black eyes, the thick lips, the bruises she'd had in the past. All the late hours she'd landed on Jenny's doorstep heart-broken and barely able to stand up. All the men she dated who were just after a quick leg-over and a place to get their head down.

Gina checked behind her and whispered in a low voice. 'What about, you know, can't he help you out? For old time's sake?'

Jenny's eyes were wide open, panicked. 'Shut up, will you? For crying out loud, how many times do I have to tell you not to mention his name in my house? Walls have ears, Gina; you never know who is listening.'

The words had barely left her mouth when the back door swung open and in wobbled Paul. He looked rough and the reek of stale beer surrounded him. He was still dancing, shaking his arms in the air. Gina covered her mouth with one hand and started laughing as she clocked him.

'Oh, to be young again, not a care in the world,' she said to Jenny, then turned to Paul. 'My god, you look as rough as a bear's arse. Have you even been to bed yet?'

He stumbled over to the table and plonked down on the chair at the side of her, still steaming drunk. 'Nar, I was drinking until six this morning. I've had about two hours sleep. I'm still twisted, Gina, if I'm being honest. I can't wait to get in my pit. But, if you're up for partying, I'm ready when you are.'

Gina adjusted her blouse, raising her eyebrows. 'It's too early for me, Paul, maybe another time.'

Jenny sat back in her seat and folded her arms tightly across her chest. 'You better go to bed and get some sleep because Danny is gunning for you. He was round here earlier. Said you've nicked money again. He's fuming and I wouldn't want to be in your shoes when he gets his hands on you.'

'Me? What the fuck, Mam?' His voice was high-pitched now. 'I swear on anyone's life that I haven't taken a penny. Why does he always think it's me who's nicked something?

It does my head in. Honest, it's always me who gets the finger pointed at them. Dickhead.'

Gina watched her son closely, never taking her eyes from him. His eyebrow started twitching and he was flexing his fingers. She knew then he was lying. He'd always been the same when he was trying to pull a fast one: his body language gave him away.

She came right back at him; she couldn't stand the lying. She started to interrogate him, eyes all over him. 'So where did you get your money from to be out all night then? Because, as far as I can remember, you were skint when I asked you for your keep money.'

He sniggered and nearly fell from the chair. 'A few of the lads got the beers in, Mam. Just like I do for them when they're on their arses. I'm a top lad, aren't I, and the boys love having me out with them. Don't tell me you think I've took it, too? Wow, this house does my head in. In fact this fucking family does, too.'

Gina leaned back, well used to the drama. She was always one of the first here whenever she spotted a cop car outside the Johnson house.

Jenny knew she was pissing in the wind; he'd never admit anything to her. A born liar. 'You need to sober up. Go and get in that bleeding bath. And put some Dettol in it. God knows whose bed you've been in. I can smell you from here: you stink.'

Paul stood up and staggered towards the door. He turned and winked at Gina. 'You can come and wash my back if you want, Gee, or better still you can jump in with me and give me a good scrubbing.'

Gina blushed. 'Oi, cheeky balls. Keep that filthy talk to the streets.'

Jenny shouted after him. 'And get that bed changed too. It's crusty, and I'm not going near it.'

Gina was still laughing, and Jenny shot her a look. Maybe, if she hadn't been here, Gina would have taken Paul up on his offer. Her friend had always had the eye for a younger man. Cougar. But these were her children, her boys, a no-go area for any of her friends. Jenny sighed and rolled her eyes. 'He's disgusting, I swear to you he'd shag anything with a hole. How dare he think he can hit on my mates. I'll knock his bleeding block off.'

Gina fanned her fingers in front of her face, loosening her blouse and wafting her chest with it. 'Oh, I've come over all peculiar. The thought of a young man all over my body,' she chuckled.

Jenny's mouth rose at the corners. She could see the funny side of it now and playfully punched Gina in the arm. 'Leave my son alone, you slapper. You'd eat him for breakfast.'

'Correct. I would ruin him, Jen. I've not had sex for three weeks, you know. Dave's been working nights and he's knackered all the time. He'd better watch out, because I'll be looking elsewhere if he continues. I'm gagging for a bit of slap-and-tickle.'

They both burst out laughing and Jenny's mood lifted. Her sex life had been a big, fat zero with Charley banged up but, if she was honest, she would much rather have a nice glass of wine instead of her fella rolling about on top of her whispering sweet nothings. Sex was a distant memory for

Jenny and not something she craved any more, or so she told Gina.

Jenny caught her breath, the laughter subsiding. 'I've got to drop Rachel's key off at work before we go shopping. The dizzy cow has left it on the side again. It's a good job her feet are in her socks otherwise she would bloody forget them too, the numpty.'

Rachel was Jenny's youngest child. She had never given the family an ounce of trouble. She was a quiet girl who hated that her family was involved in the local underworld. She couldn't handle that the police were always booming their front door down in the early hours looking for drugs or looking for one of her brothers for questioning. She just wanted a quiet life, normality.

Gina stretched her arms over her head and yawned. 'Come on then, we'll drop the key off at the café and grab some lunch. I love the cheese and tomato toasties from there. I'm starving.'

Jenny stood up. A day of retail therapy might help – but she knew she'd be spending blood money.

Chapter Two

Charley Johnson lay on his bed with his arms looped over his head. He was a tank of a man –ripped, hench and hairy. Looking over at his pad mate he nodded his head slowly. 'Not long left now, Son, before I'm out of this shit-hole. I'm getting too old for this jail life, Jezz.'

The man in the next bed was of similar stocky size to Charley and his arms were covered in tattoos, sleeves of black ink. He rolled onto his side. 'Yeah, I get where you're coming from, pal. This is the second stretch I've done and it's breaking my back. I think when you're young it's a walk in the park, but it's hard graft now I'm older.'

Jezz had another month to serve and the two had been padded up with each other for over a year. They knew each other from the outside and had worked together a few times. Jezz had even kipped at Charley's house when he had nowhere else to go. Being good mates on the outside had meant Jezz was one of the few guys Charley trusted on the inside. There was no doubt that when Charley finished this sentence he would keep Jezz close. Maybe put a bit of graft his way, keep him in the good life.

Charley stared at the ceiling. 'The Mrs has been a bit quiet lately. I hope she's not been fucking about on me, because if I hear one whisper that she's been at it, I'll end her. I had enough of hearing shit about her the last time I was in here. She's lucky I never carted her then.'

Jezz sat on the edge of his bed and cracked his knuckles. 'Nah, Charley, you're overthinking it. Jenny is alright. She never misses a visit, does she? And she's always on the end of the blower when you ring her. Come on, mate, if she was banging someone else you would be able to tell, you'd sense it. Stop tormenting yourself.' He fidgeted about on his bed and turned his eyes to the TV, wanting to change the subject.

Charley gritted his teeth – the thought of his wife having sex with another man – his fingers rolled into tight fists by his sides. 'I just hope you're right, mate.' His anger turned to silence for a few seconds. 'I don't know what I'd do without my Jenny. She's my world. There was a time when I nearly lost her, you know.'

Jezz sat up straight, waiting eagerly for him to continue: his cell mate had never mentioned this before. Charley dropped his head and played with his fingers. 'I've given her a few belts, Jezz. It's not something I'm proud of but she pushed me too far. You know what women are like when they're down your ear going on and on and not shutting up. I can't handle it. I lose the plot.'

Jezz blew out a laboured breath and raised his eyebrows. 'Tell me about it, mate. That's why I'm on my lonesome. I can't hack a relationship, it's too much stress. Women. They want to know the ins and the outs of a cat's arse. Fucking crackers, they are. Look at the last one I was involved with: a brass, she was, I found out in the end. She'd been lying to me every bleeding night, telling me she worked late shifts in a care home.'

Charley chuckled. 'Tough pill to swallow, that one, Jezz. I mean us men just want a quiet life: nice food, a bit of sex a couple of times a week, watch the footy and we're sorted. It's not a big ask, is it?'

Jezz clutched his crotch and squeezed his nuts. 'Don't even mention sex to me. I'm dying for it. I was even looking at that female screw the other day. Honest, pal, filthy stuff running through my mind. The woman is rough, too. I must be desperate,' he smirked over at Charley.

Charley roared laughing. 'Jezz, she's about fifty years old, if she's a day. Nar, mate, she's grim. Stay well away.'

'You don't look at the mantlepiece when you're poking the fire, pal. And plus I'm attracted to the older women. Just something about them that turns me on.'

Charley sniggered and sat on the side of the bed facing his pad mate. His look changed; ears pinned back. 'The clock is ticking now for those fucking Bennets. They will know I'm due home and I bet their arses are twitching. It's nearly D-Day.'

Jezz nodded and licked his bottom lip slowly. He knew about the war between the two families and had already said he'd back Charley in the future if he ever needed some muscle to sort them out. 'I know, you keep saying, Chaz. I hope the fuckers get what's coming to them for stitching

you up. Bad that, lower than a snake's belly grassing someone up.'

'It's happening, don't you worry about that. Archie
Bennet is a dead man walking. He's living on borrowed
time. Honest, I can't even explain to you the things I've got
planned for that prick. I just need to get my act together. It's
this place sucking every bit of life out of me. But once I'm
out, they'd better be ready.'

Jezz scratched the side of his head and piped up. 'Did I
hear you right when you said he used to be a good mate?'

Charley ragged his hairy fingers through his thick dark
hair. 'Yeah, we was, back in the day, but he went behind my
back. Snidey fucker, he is. He makes my blood boil and this
time it's gone too far – I know he got someone to grass me
up. I'm going to rip his head off. He's always been jealous
of me, ever since I won that boxing match when we were
younger. Honest, I've thought about it a lot since I've been
in here and it always comes back to that boxing match.
Don't get me wrong, Archie was a good fighter, but I was
better. When we were sixteen, we fought for the Collyhurst
and Moston title. A big fight in the area and lots of top
geezers were there, people from the professional world.'
Charley was lost in this story and telling it like it happened
yesterday. 'I knocked Archie on his arse a few times, but he
kept getting back up. I'll give him that, he had guts. But in
the ninth round I gave him a right hook that nearly snapped
his jaw. A proper knockout punch it was. He fell to the floor
like a sack of spuds. He never got back up, knocked out,
sparkled. For a minute, I thought he was a goner. Now I
think it might have been better if I had ended him that day.'

Jezz was hanging on his every word, squeezing the newspaper he'd been reading tighter in his hand.

'The medics were around him and everything. Anyway, he was alright in the end. He came round and I won the title. He never even congratulated me.' Charley chuckled. 'He just sat with his head down as the presentation took place. He couldn't even look at me. He hated that I won, and he never got over it. On my life, if I offered him a re-match for that same trophy, he would bite my hand off for it. Even after all these years. He always told everyone it was a lucky punch. Bullshit, and he knows it. We never really got on after that.' He sucked in a large breath. 'And other shit happened. The man is a wrong-un. Not to be trusted. Don't let anyone ever tell you different, Jezz, mate.'

The cell door swung open, and a male officer stood smirking at them. He deliberately didn't step inside the pad. No, he made sure he was safe and the men couldn't get their hands on him. He'd made that mistake in the past and the scar on the left side of his eye was a constant reminder that he could never take his eye off the ball again. These guys were dangerous, never to be trusted, the dregs of society, he reckoned. Charley was well known on the wing to be a snapper and he'd already assaulted members of the staff. 'It's time for dinner, lads, if you're coming out.'

Charley shot a cool look at the officer and snarled, 'Fuck off while we are talking. We'll be down when we're ready.'

The screw stood tall, a quick look behind him to make sure he could escape if Charley ran at him, and tried to stand his ground. 'Listen, cocky balls, who do you think you are talking to? Carry on and you'll be down the block again.'

Charley bolted up from his bed, eyes wide open, the vein at the side of his neck pumping with rage. 'I said jog on, you fucking weapon.'

The officer swallowed hard and eyeballed the inmates. 'Just remember I am the one who holds the keys to this door. If I wanted to, I could make every day you spend here a fucking nightmare, so think about that, gobshite, before you put your mouth into gear.'

Jezz knew it was going to kick off and there was no way he wanted another lockdown. The last one had been for a month: no TV, no privileges, it was a joke. He blocked Charley with his arm stretched out fully. 'Right, we'll be down in a minute, boss.'

The officer glared at Charley, knowing he'd rattled his cage. 'Good lads,' he sniggered, proud that he had earned respect from at least one of the inmates.

Charley watched him leave and punched his clenched fist into the pillow, imagining it was the screw's face. 'That shit-for-brains knows what he's doing. If I ever see him on the outside, he's getting tuned in. On my life, I'll put him on the missing list. The clown.'

'Calm down, Charley. You're out of this place in a week. Don't give the prick any reason to nick you. Take it on the chin and relax. He's a wanker. Fucking jobsworth.'

Charley hung his head low; prison life was really getting to him. The sleepless nights, missing his family, being locked behind a door all day long was all too much to take. This stretch had finally changed him, he felt, proper broke his back. 'Who the fuck does he think he is, Jezz? He treats us like we are nobodies behind these walls. We have rights. We're not animals, are we?'

Jezz agreed, aware that if he added fuel to the fire Charley would one-bomb the officer the next time they spoke to him. Strangeways was notorious for a reason. There were murderers behind these walls, sex offenders, armed robbers. As for the staff: they were just people doing their jobs, in the main. But there was a handful of the screws who loved seeing the inmates suffer, loved having control over them. Charley stood up, walked to the door and smiled. 'I'm calm again now, mate. Come on, let's go and see what shit they're serving us today. That prick will keep for another day.'

Charley's presence was felt as soon as he walked into the canteen. An eerie silence descended as he made his way to the servery. Whispering amongst the inmates, officers nudging each other. Charley's shoulders pulled back and he made sure he could see all around him. Men like Charley were open targets at this time of the day. All it took was some nutter to run at him with a blade and plunge it deep into his body and he would be a goner. Attempts like this happened often in this place and the deep scar on Charley's left arm was a constant reminder that he was never safe, always had to look over his shoulder, sleep with one eye open.

Charley sneered at the server as he put one blob of grey-looking mashed potato on his plate. He kept his plate there and looked at the inmate serving the food with his eyes wide open. No words needed. Another two dollops of potato were placed on the plate. Charley reached over and grabbed a sausage from the silver tray in front of him and shoved it in his mouth. He was a law unto himself in this place and the prisoner knew not to mess with him. Stories about Charley's antics circled the jail endlessly: graphic accounts of how brutal he could be if you got on the wrong side of him. The man was sick in the head, twisted – everyone said so. Plenty of prisoners and screws alike said Charley should have been in a high security jail, one where he was constantly watched and kept in line. One where specialists could get inside his head and see what was going on. Charley had turned down endless sessions with therapists. Nosey bastards, he called them, trying to discover his weaknesses.

Jezz stood behind Charley now and whispered into his ear as he shoved a small package into his pocket. As he moved along the queue, Charley took the package out and quickly placed it in the hand of the man serving him. It all happened so fast. Most of the inmates were like magicians. Now you see it, now you don't. The server smiled and just like that, whatever it was, was gone. There were more drugs in jail than on the streets of Manchester. That's what the inmates said, anyway. You could get anything you wanted in this nick if you had a stack of money and the right network. There was always a bent screw out to make a few quid and from the moment Charley stepped foot into jail he sussed out who that was and made sure he had him on-side. It meant Charley was still earning money from behind his cell door. After a few power plays, he now ran the jail when it came to drugs: any gear that landed there had his name on it. If anyone even thought about taking over his role, he was in their pad smashing them up, making sure they never attempted it again. The last idiot who thought they could have Charley over had boiling sugar water poured over him. He'd been in the burns unit for months.

But running the joint didn't mean he'd made his peace with the place. Charley had witnessed some things during his sentence, things that he didn't like to talk about. And it took a lot to get under his skin. Many a night he would lie on his bed tossing and turning and unable to sleep. In the small hours, visions tormented his mind. But jail was a dog-eat-dog world and only the strongest survived. He'd never admit it to his fellow prisoners, never show weakness, but he knew he'd seen too much.

Charley carried his food away and sat down at the table at the back of the room. He could see everything from here, just the way he liked it. The screw from earlier was walking up and down, making sure there was no trouble. Charley watched him patrolling with his colleague. He knew the officer would be bearing a grudge, but it would take time to work out if he was a genuine threat.

Prison Officer Sam Sullivan did have his eyes on Charley. He and a colleague stood a little way off from Johnson, feeling the tension in the canteen crackling with energy. Whispering, Sam covered his mouth enough so he couldn't be heard by anyone but his workmate.

'Charley Johnson is a prick and if he carries on with his attitude, I'll have him, honest. He's walking a thin line with me. I'm just waiting to nick him.'

His pal shot a look over at Charley and made sure he couldn't hear him. He was just here to earn a wage, he didn't want any beef with anyone, especially a man like Charley Johnson. 'Are you tapped in the head, or what? He's gone soon. Do yourself a favour, Sam, and back off. They don't pay you enough in this place to confront the likes of Johnson.'

Sam Sullivan's nostrils flared, and he knew his colleague was right. But it still wound him up, still made his blood boil that this inmate had no fear of him. But Sam was clever: he knew he could hurt this man by stopping his phone calls, taking away the things that he loved. Charley needed to be careful, very careful indeed – and he'd let him know that.

Later, Charley sat in his pad and made sure the coast was clear to use the mobile phone he had stashed. Jezz gave him the nod and Charley quickly unscrewed a pipe running along the wall. His large fingers dug deep inside, pulling a bag out. Once he'd pulled the plastic wrapper off, he turned the power on. Mobile phones were like gold in jails, and it wasn't unheard of to pay upwards of eight hundred pounds to get a working iPhone into the jail. Phones meant uncensored contact with the outside world: a call, a quick text, or, if you timed it right, even a video call. Sure, they kept the contraband moving, but more often than not the forbidden calls were used not for dealing but to give inmates a taste of home, something that helped the cons rest at night.

Charley lay flat on his bed to FaceTime Danny. Danny was the apple of his eye. A chip off the old block, Charley told everyone. When the line connected, he smiled as he saw his son on the screen.

'Are you OK, Son?'

But Danny didn't reply, instead turning to speak to whoever he was with then flicking the screen towards them. Another man appeared on screen now, smiling when he saw Charley.

'Yo, how you doing, big C? Long-time, no see. When you out?'

Charley was glad to know he'd been missed on the outside. 'Not long, Steve, just a few shits and a shave left. How are you keeping?'

'You know me, pal, ducking and diving, wheeling and dealing, still earning a crust though.'

'That's how we like it, lad.'

Danny moved the mobile phone screen back to himself and he was eager to discuss a few issues with his old man. 'Got a few grows ready for chopping down next week, Dad, so we'll be able to bung you a few quid when you get out.'

Charley huffed. 'I don't need money from you, Son. Stop worrying about me. I'm sorted. Been raking it in from in here. Anyway, what's new?'

Jezz popped his head in the door: the coast was still clear. He gave him the nod to continue.

Danny filled his father in on changes that had happened in the area. Danny and Paul were still locked in struggles for turf – fighting off the Bennets' dealers, nicking their crops. But it was all going to get easier once Charley was out.

They laughed and joked, then Charley paused. 'How's your mam been acting lately? She was pissed off when I spoke to her last night. I know we had a few words, but she usually calms down faster?'

'You know Mam. Talks a good game but never does anything different. Everything is fine.'

Charley sighed. Yep, his son was right: his Mrs was a nightmare when she had a bee in her bonnet about something, even threatening to throw him out sometimes, but she never actually did. This was enough to settle Charley down.

After a few more minutes Jezz whistled in to Charley, 'Say your goodbyes. Sully is on the prowl.'

The call ended quickly, and the phone was stashed away. Charley flopped back down on his bed and lay twisting his fingers, restless. 'Jezz, do you think I'm a paranoid guy, or what?'

Jezz wanted a quiet time tonight and the last thing he needed was his pad mate stressing all night long. He swallowed hard. 'Nah, you're sound as a pound, you are, Chaz. It's this place that messes with your head. Everyone has a few setbacks in here. Look at me last week when I thought the screws were setting me up. I was adamant the bastards were planting stuff on me.'

Charley yawned and sniggered. 'Yeah, you were on another planet, mate. I told you to stop blazing the bud, didn't I? It's no good for you. It fucks your head up when you're locked up in a small room like this.'

Jezz agreed. 'Yeah, I suppose it does, but it chills me out each night. I'd be climbing the walls if I didn't have a zoot.'

Charley scratched his head, still overthinking. 'Maybe Jen's met somebody else. You hear about it all the time when you're banged up in here, don't you? Look at him next door. Ten years he'd been with his woman and she sent him a bleeding Dear John telling him she'd met someone else and it was over. Fuck me, he cried every night for months he did, none stop. I had to bang on the wall to tell the wimp to get a grip.'

Jezz sighed. He'd lost track of how many times they'd had this same conversation. 'Wow, Chaz, mate. I've told you a thousand times that Jen is a diamond. She loves you to death. Stop worrying and bang that TV on so we can watch a bit of *Coronation Street*. I think there's a new girl in the street that might be worth putting in my wank bank.' He looked over at Charley and knew he would have to tell him again to put his mind at ease. 'I would give a kidney away to have someone like your Jen on my arm, mate. Honest, she's mint.'

Charley rolled on his side looking at the wall where his photographs were. He stroked a single finger slowly over his wife's image. His words were low and Jezz looked away, pretending not to hear. 'You know if I ever found anything out, Jen, that would be us done. Honest, love, I would hurt you. I mean seriously hurt you.'

Chapter Three

Rachel sat gazing out of the window when Dorothy Jenson wobbled to the café entrance. Frail and weak, the poor lady struggled to open the door. Rachel jumped up from her seat.

'Dot, hold your horses, give me a second and I'll help you,' she shouted across the room. Rachel held the door open as the pensioner trudged passed her. Dot was in her seventies and every day without fail she would come into the café for a cup of tea and a piece of toast. Always the same order, it never changed: lightly toasted bread, two sugars in her cup of tea. Rachel never charged her, though. No way. She was an old dear and needed looking after. And Rachel wasn't sure if the old lady had any money to pay for it, anyway.

'Good morning, lovely,' Rachel said.

Dot lifted a gentle smile and held Rachel's arm as she steadied herself. 'Good morning, sweetheart. Oh, I've had a bit of a fall on my way here. Look at my hand: it's swelling up already. I'm a right clumsy cow sometimes.'

Rachel helped the woman to her usual spot facing the window and pulled the chair out for her. 'Come and sit down. Bloody hell, Dot, it looks like it's bruising already. You need to be more careful.'

This wasn't the first time Dot had injured herself. Every other week she had some scrape or bruises from where she had fallen.

'Thanks, Rachel, you're an angel. Let me sit down before I have another dizzy spell. It must be those new tablets the doctor has given me for my blood pressure. I've only been on them for a few weeks, and I've had a constant headache with them. My ankles have swollen up, too. I'm sick of it. I rattle when I walk, I'm on that much medication. Our John has told me to stay inside and wait for him to take me out, but I can't do that, he's never home, that boy. I love getting out to the shops; it's the only enjoyment I get these days.' She sniggered, 'But what he doesn't know can't hurt him, can it? As long as I'm back before he gets home, he'll never know I've been out.'

Rachel looked concerned as she made sure the woman was seated properly. All she needed was another accident. 'Let me go and get a cold cloth or some ice to put on that hand, Dot. Hopefully it will ease the pain.'

Dorothy sighed as Rachel left her side. She should have stayed indoors today and rested, but loneliness had got the better of her. She looked forward to coming to the café each day just so she could see people, talk to them, have a bit of company. Ever since she'd lost her husband just over a year ago, she could not stand the thought of sitting in the house every day looking at four walls. She would have gone loopy, she knew it. Of course, she had a family, but they didn't come and visit that often, Christmas and birthdays, if she was lucky. Dot still had her son John living at home, and he was meant to be the one looking after her. But he was out all hours of the day and night. When he did show up, he was usually pissed, and when he was like that she didn't want to be in the same room as him. So she soldiered on – alone.

Rachel returned and examined Dot's hand in more detail. The skin was thin and transparent: you could see the purple veins through it. These were the same hands that had dried a child's tears, the same hands that had picked him up when he fell, the ones that had cuddled him when he was upset. The hands that had cooked and cleaned for years. Hands always have a story to tell, Rachel thought. She pressed the ice pack softly on Dot's hand and wrapped a tea towel around it. She knew exactly what she was doing. She'd done it for her brothers on numerous occasions when they'd been fighting or had punched walls in temper. Maybe she should have been a nurse: she'd seen enough, and nothing shocked her anymore.

'I'll go and get you a cup of tea, lovely, and a piece of toast. You look very pale, Dot, and a warm cup of tea and something to eat might be just what you need.'

Rachel went back behind the counter and started to brew her a drink.

Katie, the owner's daughter, stood watching her. 'You have such a big heart, Rach. On my life I wouldn't have the patience you do with these old codgers. Dot's alright, but half the time they stink of cats or I can't understand a word they say.'

Rachel popped the piece of bread into the toaster. 'Don't say that! The lives some of them have led, you wouldn't believe it. You just have to take a moment to listen. I mean, what about our lovely Dot? I love talking to her; she has great stories to tell, you know. I love hearing about the old days and how her life was.'

'No offence, but maybe you need to get a life, Rach. I can think of a hundred things better than talking to a pensioner. What happened to your love life, anyway?'

Rachel stirred the hot cup of tea and pulled the tea bag out, placing it on the side. 'I've not got one! But me and Hannah are out on the razzle on Friday, and we're going clubbing, so that might all change if I meet Mr Right.'

Katie giggled and rolled her eyes. 'Good luck with that, love. Mr Right doesn't exist around these parts. Trust me, I know. I've already met Mr Skint, Mr Dickhead, Mr Druggie, and, last but by no means least, Mr Wife-Beater, so don't hold your breath. The men around here are dickheads, only after a leg-over.'

Katie had had a few boyfriends over the last year or so and every time she thought he was 'the one' they showed their true colours and left her either heartbroken, bruised or broke. But Katie always went after the bad boys, the players, so what did she expect? Rachel, on the other hand, was a hopeless romantic. Her dream world was fluffy and full of sparkles and diamonds. It was probably why she was always single: she wanted a perfect man, one who made her heart beat faster and swept her off her feet. Not a 'wham bam thank you mam' like Katie seemed to find all the time. She wanted a grand passion. She thought of how Dot talked about her husband. Yes, 'til death do us part' was what she was looking for. She got Dot's tea tray ready and made her way back to her table. She was due a break anyway and the café was quiet. Placing the cup carefully on the table, she patted Dot's arm.

The old lady nearly jumped out of her skin. 'Oh, you scared the life out of me! I am so jumpy lately, honest. The slightest noise and I'm having a heart attack.'

Rachel chuckled. 'There you go, get that down your neck. I'll just get your toast.'

Dot's hands shook as she lifted the cup up to her thin lips, spilling some of the drink over the table. Rachel was back, spotted the spillage straight away and quickly wiped the mess away with a serviette. 'It's been pretty quiet in here today, Dot. I —'

Before she could finish her sentence, cold wind rushed in from outside and they both looked over at the open door. Rachel's jaw dropped. There he was. Her heart skipped a beat, her palms hot and sweaty, and she felt like her windpipe was closing up. She could feel her cheeks burning up. Niall Bennet. The man oozed confidence, and why not? He was drop-dead gorgeous; tall, dark and handsome. Rachel heard him behind her, ordering his food from Katie. Her body trembled and she was glad she didn't have to serve him.

Dot reached over and touched her hand softly. 'You know you should just talk to him. Every time that young man comes into the café you fall to pieces. I've watched you for months now. Don't let chances pass you by.'

Rachel stuttered, aware Niall might hear her, 'Dot, he's a Bennet. Our families are at war. I could never be with Niall.

My brothers would never speak to me again and my dad would disown me.'

Dot kept her voice low and double-checked no one could hear her. 'Go with your heart and you'll never go wrong. When I was younger there was a man I idolised and, just because my family didn't like him, I let him go. I'm not afraid to say that I never stopped thinking about him. Even when I met my Ted, who was a lovely chap, in the back of my mind Albert was always there. Don't end up having regrets, love.'

Rachel nodded and smiled. These were wise words from an old lady. She could speak to Dot and pour her heart out, tell her anything without being judged. But Dot didn't know the depths of the feud. She opened up. 'I've fancied him for like forever. Honest, every time I see him, I go weak at the knees. I can't think straight when he's about and my body goes boiling hot.'

Dot chuckled. 'So, there's your answer. Strike whilst the iron is hot.'

Rachel had never told anyone about her feelings for Niall before. She had a great relationship with her mother, but she could never speak to her about the Bennets. If she so much as mentioned their name Jenny would go ape, so she'd learned some things were better left unsaid. But she couldn't get Niall out of her head. She'd always noticed him but, until recently, she'd only ever seen him surrounded by the rest of his clan. Niall had four brothers: Nathaniel, Cruz, Arlo and Dalton. He was the youngest of the five and they were a close-knit family. You would always see the brothers together, strength in numbers. But over the last few months,

Niall had started coming to the caff by himself. She was still blushing every time he came in, and she'd never even served him: Katie always stepped in. Rachel stood up now and walked back into the main part of the shop. She could feel his eyes checking her out, burning into her as she edged behind the counter.

'Can I have a can of Fanta too, please?' Aware that, as he was asking a direct question, she couldn't blank him, she gulped to steady her voice. 'Yes, I'll get Katie to bring it over with your food.' Was she still blushing? She felt like it.

'I'd much rather you brought it over.' He smiled.

Rachel was too taken aback to answer. But she needed to hurry up and reply before the moment had gone. 'I'll see what I can do, then,' she purred in what she hoped was a soft voice. She made her way to the back room. She could have kicked herself: why on earth didn't she reply with something better? 'Keep wishing,' she could have said, something to show him she had confidence. Taking deep breaths, she looked over at Katie and quickly filled her in on what had been said and rubbed her hands together in excitement.

'Just be cool, don't be desperate. Play it by ear and let him do the chasing.' Katie grinned. 'It's do or die time. You need to be calm.' Katie was her wingman now. She passed Rachel the order she'd been preparing for Niall.

Trying to act casual, Rachel placed the food on the table in front of Niall. Already her heart was beating like a speeding train.

'So, do you go out round here, or what, Rachel?'

This was amazing! He'd called her by her name, he knew who she was: he must have been doing his homework on her.

'Yeah, when I can. Why are you asking?' She tried to look straight at Niall. Was he winding her up?

'Just curious, that's all. Where do you go?' He smiled and Rachel felt all pretence of acting cool vanish in the heat of the moment.

'Well, this evening I'm going to Crystals. The music is good in there and it's always a top night.'

Niall picked his fork up and started to scran his food. Rachel wondered if that was it – conversation over. Just as she was about to walk away, lost as to what to say next, he put his fork down.

'I might see you in there then. So it's a date, right?'

Rachel remembered what Katie had told her. 'You might, you might not.'

She walked away and forced herself not to look back.

Katie nodded at her when she returned to the kitchen. 'So, what did he say? Come on, spill.'

'He asked where I go out drinking and said he will see me there.'

Katie playfully punched her in the arm. 'You go, girl. What did I tell you? Treat them mean and keep them keen.'

At last, the ice had been broken. The ball was in Niall's court now. But what about her family? She hadn't crossed any lines just by talking to him, had she? She remembered Dot's words about following her heart. Usually, Rachel was the sensible one, but this time she felt a pull that was hard to resist. One thing was for sure: if her family found out, this would get dangerous, very very fast. She was playing with fire.

Chapter Four

Danny sat in the front room scrolling through his iPhone. His Facebook account had been busy, and he smiled as he looked through his friend requests. Girls, pretty little things, all trying to get on his arm, to be his woman. It had been a day since he'd last seen Paul and he knew the wanker was dodging him. He was like that when he knew he'd been rumbled. But today was D-Day. Sooner or later Paul would turn up here at his mother's house, and when he did Danny would be ready for him. The snide was getting it big time. How dare he think he could have his brother over and get away with it?

A sound interrupted his thoughts. Danny held his breath, put his ear to the door to listen. It was showtime. He sprang behind the door, shoved his phone in his back pocket and clenched his fist ready to attack. Rustling in the hallway, footsteps getting nearer. The door swung open and in walked Paul. There was no time to think. Danny pounced on him like an animal and wrestled him to the floor in a death grip.

'I knew it was only a matter of time before you turned up.'

Paul was trying to break free. Punching, kicking, blood spraying from Paul's nose. The door swung open again and Jenny froze as she saw her two boys rolling about on the floor.

'Fucking turn it in, will you? Danny, get off him! For crying out loud, like I need this. Bleeding stop it!'

But Danny was in the zone and this lad was not in the mood to let it go. He dragged Paul up from the floor and pinned him against the wall, nose to nose.

'Did you think you could dip the till and get away with it, you prick?'

Paul's nose was busted, and bright-red claret streamed down onto his top lip. His bottom lip was swelling up, too. Danny was getting ready to steam in again, so Jenny jumped in between them and made sure he couldn't swing another punch.

'Are you right in the bleeding head? You're brothers. Stop it now, Danny, and let him talk.'

'Talk? Get a grip, woman. He knows what he's done, look at him, you can tell by his boat-race.'

Paul was struggling to breathe, his windpipe being squeezed by his brother's thick-set hand. Jenny gripped Danny's fingers and bent them back, dragging and pulling at them desperately. Paul finally fell to the floor, gasping for breath. Danny was still trying to get to him, but Jenny blocked him.

'Go over there and let the kid breathe. Then he can talk,' she yelled.

Danny backed off, fuming, sucking in large mouthfuls of air. 'Go on then, let's hear whatever bullshit he's got to say.'

Paul staggered as he got to his feet, his mam by his side, protecting him like a lioness protecting her cub. Jenny led Paul to sit down, her eyes still on Danny, making sure he didn't steal one on him.

Eventually, Paul rasped out, 'You're barking up the wrong tree. Go and see Pat. See where he's got his money from. You've heard him, talking about the Jimmy Choo shoes he's just bought his bird, and what about the Gucci handbag he got her?'

Jenny opened her eyes wide, waiting on a reply. So another grafter in their team was flashing the cash about. Why wasn't he in the firing line? Why did Danny always blame Paul first?

'Pat isn't a thieving bastard like you,' Danny sneered. 'If you wanted cash, you should have asked me. If I can't trust my own flesh and blood, who can I trust?'

Jenny put her hand on Paul's shoulder and passed him a tea-towel from the corner of the sofa to dab his nose.

'I've just told you, it wasn't me. Go and see the boys. Ask them if they bought my beers when I was out. And if I wanted money, I would have taken my cut, so shut the fuck up chatting shit.'

Danny's nostrils flared; he would run at him in a minute and knock the prick out. Paul pulled his mobile phone from his pocket with shaking hands and found a contact number. The phone was ringing, the call on speaker. Paul held it out – half like a shield, half a peace-offering.

'Yo, Tez, it's me, Paul. You're on loudspeaker. Just tell our kid you paid for my beer all night. The prick thinks I've nicked money from him.'

'Yeah, mate, I sorted you out all night. You owe me big-time. Plus, you ticked the Charlie in my name, too.'

Paul tried to speak over his mate, feeling his mother's eyes all over him. 'Right, no worries, Tez, catch you later.' Too late. She'd heard alright. He might have bought himself a moment from Danny but now his mum would be on his case.

As the call ended, Jenny dug him in the ribs: 'Fucking drugs now! Oh my god, you are getting worse by the minute. Since when have you had a habit?'

Danny dipped his head low; this wasn't his argument. Of course, he'd sniffed when he was out in the clubs – everyone did – but there was no way he wanted his mam on his back giving him a lecture about how drugs wreck lives.

'Mam, give it a rest. I don't have a habit. I had a bit of a pick-me-up, that's all. A bump.' Paul's bottom lip started to tremble. 'I was missing my dad. I felt down. It's hard for me knowing my old man is locked up behind bars. I miss him, Mam. You believe me, don't you?' Paul dropped his head slightly.

Jenny's voice softened. 'Oh, Son, he's home soon. I know it's been hard for you – it's been crap for all of us – but it'll be over soon.'

Danny sucked on his gums. His brother was such a great actor, and he was giving a performance to be proud of. He, however, wasn't buying Paul's sob story for one single second. He sat back and lit a ciggie up: he needed to calm down.

Paul doubled-down on his performance. 'It feels like forever waiting for his release date. He's an old man now, freaks me out thinking about him in nick.'

Jenny looked over at Danny, a look that told him his brother was suffering and needed him to make friends. Danny sucked hard on his fag and stared at his mother. For crying out loud, she was buying his brother's shit, and now Danny was the bad one yet again. Ever since they were small children, Paul had always been a mard-arse. It was always somebody else's fault, never his. The neighbours would knock on the door complaining about Paul being nasty to their sons and all Jenny used to say was they must have deserved it. Her youngest son was not a violent person, she always insisted, and something must have happened for him to act the way he did. She was still the same mother today, protecting him, making excuses for him. He was a mummy's boy. Danny knew it was pointless even trying to change his mother's mind. Jenny would sit there all day long trying to prove his innocence. If she hadn't come in when she did, he would have got a confession out of him, he knew it. He'd have got the rat to admit that he'd nicked the money.

Jenny launched into her usual lecture about brothers and family loyalties. 'You two have to stick together. You are blood and you should be tight-knit. I bet them Bennets aren't fighting between themselves, are they? Oh no, they all stand by each other.'

Paul looked over at Danny, still dabbing his nose, playing the victim. 'Our kid, I would never have you over. My mam's right: how are we going to get back in the game if we're fighting between ourselves?'

Danny squirmed, stubbed his cig out in the ashtray next to him. How the hell had this happened again? Why was he feeling guilty?

Mam was watching him, urging him to speak.

'Listen, if money goes missing then I'm going to come knocking on your door because you know where it is – you always do. If I've got it wrong and it was Pat, then sorry. But come on, you've admitted taking stuff in the past. Do I have to remind you about your track record?'

'Bro, that was yonks ago. I thought we were over that. See what I mean, Mam? He always throws the past in my face. It should be forgotten about, shouldn't it?'

Jenny nodded, defending him again. But she knew more than anyone that the past could never be forgotten. She jumped up and pushed her hair from her face. 'Right, can we put this to bed? I've got things to do. I need to go down to Blossoms soon and sort the girls out. Danny, say you're sorry and then we can move on.'

'Fuck off, Mam. Money went missing and his name is in the mix for it. I just can't prove it, that's all.'

'So, until you have evidence that Paul took it, keep your bleeding hands off him. Look at the state of him now. Fucking hell, if your dad was here, he wouldn't have this shit going on.'

Danny knew he was fighting a losing battle, but she could kiss his arse if she thought he was going to grovel to his younger brother. No way was he apologising. He stormed out of the front room and marched down the hallway.

The front door opened and banged shut: he was gone.

Paul looked over at his mother and she growled, 'Don't even go there. I know you took the money. You're a lying, thieving bastard. You're lucky I came in when I did, otherwise he would have done you in good and proper.'

Paul staggered to his feet, pointing out his wounds, after some sympathy. 'Oh, I might have known you would turn on me. You heard the phone call like that dickhead did, so stop going on.'

'I know you of old, Paul. You can never hide your lies. I'm your mother and I know you better than anybody. I stuck up for you because I didn't want you getting your head kicked in. And now I find out you've been blowing it all on sniff.'

'Do one, Mam, you're as bad as Danny. I'm innocent here and look at the state of me. I mean, if he'd asked for a straightener, I would have been ready for him, but instead he was shady and pounced on me when I come in. Come on, Mam, do you agree with that?'

Jenny sat down on the sofa, reached over and gripped her Benson and Hedges silver, popping one out of the twenty deck. 'Are you for real? Give your head a shake and wake up and smell the coffee beans. He would have knocked ten tons of shit out of you. And sniffing cocaine?' Her voice got higher. 'What, you've turned into a druggie now?'

Paul screwed his face up. 'And you think Danny doesn't have a line when he's out clubbing?'

Jenny swallowed hard. 'So you're telling me Danny is a sniffhead, too? Make sure you answer this right because, as soon as he comes in through that door, I'll have him. So don't make stories up if you're not willing to back them up.'

Paul was grassing, putting his brother in the frame, too. He panicked. 'I'm saying most people have a bit of Charlie when they're out, that's all. It's a social thing, not a habit.'

Jenny folded her arms tightly and shot a look over at Paul as he edged past her to the door. 'Sick of all this shit. We're meant to be a family to be respected round here – now look at us.'

Paul left the room, and Jenny was alone. She took one last drag from her cigarette and squashed it into the ashtray with force. She reached over to the coffee table and picked up her phone.

'Gina, what are you up to?' she said when she reached voicemail. 'I need a night out if you're up for it. I just need to pop into Blossoms first to sort the girls out.'

Charley had set Blossoms up over five years ago and it had been up to Jenny to look after it while he was in the big house. At first, she had been against it and told her husband straight that women selling their bodies did not sit right with her. But, as usual, he pressured her and told her, if she wanted the life she was used to, she had no other option. The brothel had always been a good money-maker, and since Charley had been locked up it was Jenny's main income. She ran a tight ship and she made sure she looked after her girls. If she was going to run a knocking-shop, she decided it would be the safest, classiest one in town. One the girls wanted to work at. They all had regular tests to make sure they didn't have any sexual diseases. They had top-of-the-range security cameras, plus Charley's boys were always nearby in case any idiot started to give them trouble – which happened quite a lot, especially at the weekend.

Some of the stories the girls told would curl your toes. There were some twisted people in the world.

Jenny grabbed her things. She always looked forward to seeing her girls. It was the one place in her life where people listened to her, respected her. Being the boss made a change. It was the kind of thing she could get used to.

Chapter Five

Jenny parked up in the side street next to Blossoms. The area was dimly lit, and it was a dodgy place to park, too secluded. The night shadows always freaked Jenny out. You never knew who was out, and she hated that she couldn't see properly. Anybody could be lurking here. The business was tucked away nicely on the streets of Moston in North Manchester, discreet. But you paid a price for that privacy. She turned the engine off and quickly scanned the area, eyes wide open, checking every nook and cranny.

Her black heels clipped along the pavement as she rushed down the back-street, always looking over her shoulder, never feeling safe. The traffic was quiet tonight, just a few cars passing. It was Friday and everybody was most likely at home getting ready for the weekend. Jenny held her car key sticking through her fingers in her fist. If anyone pounced on her, she would gouge their eyes out with it. Charley had told her to get a rape alarm but she knew she would never have time to get it out of her bag if somebody was attacking her. Attacks were quick, a victim unable to shout or scream, everybody knew that.

Once she reached the front of the shop her heartbeat slowed down. The night was cold, and the wind was picking leaves up from the ground, circling them around and throwing them up in the air. Jenny pressed the intercom, then stood back so they could see her face on the camera.

'Hi, Paige, can you let me in please?' The sound of the buzzer drilled her ears as the door opened. Jenny headed up the stairs with her black leather bag draped over her shoulder. She looked nice tonight with all her glad rags on. She'd made an effort: black skinny jeans and a bright-red shirt. She swung the door open at the top of the stairs and was greeted by a young woman. She had waist-length blonde hair, and she was tanned, with such a pretty face and heart-shaped lips.

'Hi, Jen, just give me a minute to get the girls together and I'll be with you.'

Jenny sat down on the white leather chesterfield sofa. This place was top-notch; glittery wallpaper, classy décor. Not one of them seedy brass gaffs you saw in and around some parts of town. She crossed her legs, looking at her bright-red nail polish. She loved having her nails done and she was never without a set of acrylics. Jenny had always liked to look after herself, but over the last few months she'd let herself slip. She had too much on her mind to worry about how she looked. But tonight was different; she was on point, a woman on a mission.

Paige was back and she sat facing her. Jenny gave her the once over and smiled. She always made the effort, Paige did: black lacy underwear and a black silky dressing gown that just slid from one shoulder. Paige had worked at the brothel for over a year now. She was a favourite with the punters, always fully booked. Sometimes Jenny wondered what had led her down this path to selling her body, but she had never delved into her personal life. Business was business, after all.

Paige waited until the other girls on shift were seated and gently smiled over at Jenny. 'Madge isn't working tonight, Jen. She's got a lot of shit going on at home and she's a mess. Social services are threatening to take her kids from her and she has to sort her head.'

'Bloody hell, that woman never has a quiet life. I'll try and have a chat with her when I get a minute. That's all she needs is social services on her back – trust me, I know.' Jenny dropped her head slightly, ashamed. Her kids were only young when the police had always been knocking at her door for Charley. The authorities said her children were in danger and it was only by the skin of her teeth that she was allowed to keep them at home. Charley's sister worked in social services and pulled some strings for them.

Paige sat forward in her seat, eager to get back to work. She sat pushing the skin at the side of her nail.

Jenny cleared her throat; she had everyone's attention now. 'Right, nothing much new to run through tonight. Just be extra careful who you let in through that door. I've heard a few heavies have been rushing gaffs and taking money from the girls. I'm not sure but I think the younger Bennet boys are behind it.' Jenny didn't have any names really; she just threw the Bennet name in the mix because she knew the girls would listen then.

One of the newer girls, Paula, played with her jewellery as she spoke. 'That's the last thing we need here, isn't it? I just want to come to work and earn some money.'

Paige agreed. 'Yes, Paula, we all do, so we have to be extra careful who we are letting in. We know most of our punters – regulars we can trust – but if we get someone who looks a bit suss tell them to piss off.'

The women looked anxious. And Jenny knew it was her job to make them feel safe. They could hardly make the punters relax if they were nervy themselves.

'Girls, chill out, nothing is going to happen. I'm just letting you know what is going on in the area. There are some shady bastards out there who wouldn't think twice about having you over, so be extra careful, that's all I'm saying.'

Paula reached over and picked up her glass of wine. She was an older woman; thin, high cheek bones and raven-black hair. 'I've heard a few stories about Archie and his boys lately. Ruthless they are, sick in the head.'

Jenny inhaled as a rush of adrenaline kicked in. The mere mention of her husband's rival made her stomach churn. 'Charley is home next week, and things will be changing around here. We all know about the beef between our families, so the shit will hit the fan soon, trust me. And the Johnsons always come out on top – so you're safe, you'll be looked after.'

Paula voiced her opinion. 'He needs knocking down a peg or two, that Archie Bennet, and his wife Andria. I seen her last week in the town centre and she looked at me like I was a dollop of crap on her shoe. So what? She's got false tits too, but I earned mine myself, no man bought them for me. She's a money-grabbing bitch and we all know what her game is. You can't polish a turd, that's what I say.'

The girls started laughing. Even Jenny cracked a smile. 'Anyway, this is only a flying visit. Big Larry will be locking up tonight, so any problems ring him because I'm having a well-earned night on the tiles before Charley gets home.'

The girls all cheered. They knew how hard it was sometimes for Jenny. They'd seen the bruises on her arms, the shiners that even expert make-up couldn't fully hide. They didn't need to ask where they were from, her face had said it all. Jenny stood up and gripped her handbag. She glanced at her wristwatch and raised a smile. 'Like I said, any problems give Larry a call. Enjoy your evening, ladies. I'll bob in tomorrow to see you all again and have a proper catch up.'

That was it, the meeting was over. The girls stood up and wandered about the room. Before Jenny left, she eyeballed Paige. 'Remember what I said: be careful and double-check who you're letting in. Some of the newer girls aren't used to the drill, but you know they listen to you. Queen of the Night, you are.'

Paige giggled and escorted her to the door. 'I've got a big baseball bat ready for them if they think they can come in here and take our money, love, don't you worry. I've used it before, and I'll use it again if necessary.'

There was more to this woman than met the eye. Jenny knew what it was like to have a core of steel. It was the ones you never suspected that had real strength.

Chapter Six

Rachel stood in front of the full-length silver mirror and twirled around in her candy-pink dress. Her make-up was perfect and her hair silky and bouncy.

Hannah sat on the edge of the bed fanning her fingers out, admiring her fingernails. 'You look amazing tonight, Rach. I love that dress.'

'I loved the colour as soon as I spotted it. You know what I'm like for bright colours.'

Rachel and Hannah had been best friends for as long as she could remember. Hannah lived two doors down from her and they had always played together growing up. Even through their school years, these two were as thick as thieves. If one fought, they both did.

'I haven't been out in ages. I hope a good crowd is out tonight.' Rachel didn't mention the one person she really wanted to be out.

Hannah replied with a chuckle. 'Stop worrying, you stress-head. Come on, neck some of that vodka and let's get the party started.'

The bedroom door swung open, and Paul popped his head inside. Rachel covered her mouth with her hand when she clocked the state of his face. 'Bloody hell, what's happened now?'

Paul edged into the room and sat down on the bed next to Hannah. He winked at her, trying to act hard, like the wounds he had never bothered him. He inhaled deeply. 'You smell good enough to eat, Hannah. What's that perfume you're wearing?'

She went red and replied in a timid voice. 'Erm, it's only a cheap one. I forget the name of it. I can't smell it on myself, though.'

Rachel watched her brother flirting, and stopped him dead in his tracks. Cheeky he was, hitting on her mates, he'd overstepped the mark. 'Oi, back off, lover-boy. I've told you a hundred times that my mates are a no-go area for you. Anyway, what's up with your face?' She turned away from him, not really bothered by the cuts and bruises she saw. Her brothers' fighting was part of her life. Every other day, one of them had a scar or an injury.

Paul patted Hannah's thigh and replied to his sister, 'Just a bit of beef with our kid. You know the score. We're friends now, it's sorted. The guy's a prick, and next time he needs to get his facts right before he tries chinning me.'

Rachel turned back to face the mirror.

Paul was still checking Hannah out. 'Where you girls off to? I might pop in and have few beers with you.'

Rachel spun around and spoke to him directly. 'Not happening, Paul. We want a fun night out. Every time you're pissed you start ballooning, so do one and find your own friends.' She was right, too. Paul was a headache when he'd had a few too many. He was a trouble-causer, one of those people you would swerve when they were in the boozer; loud, wind-up.

He sniggered; he knew she was right. 'Oh, is it like that?'

She snapped at him, making sure he knew the crack. 'Yes, I don't go out that much and I don't want you spoiling it.'

He smirked at her friend. 'Hannah, what do you think? You wouldn't mind me joining you both, would you? I'm a good laugh when I'm out.'

Hannah was stuck for words, put on the spot. 'Erm, if Rachel says you have to stay away then I back her.' Girl power.

Rachel nodded at her friend and sniggered at her brother. 'Stay in and watch a film with my mam. Save your money,' she joked.

'Mam's out on the piss, too. There is no way I'm being the only one left in. Sack that, I'm getting ready and getting on it.' He stood up and danced out of the bedroom. Before he left, he said, 'See you girls later.'

Rachel threw a hairbrush at him and shouted after him. 'Don't even think about it, Paul! I swear to you now, if you turn up, I'm coming straight home. I'm not babysitting you all night like the last time.'

Hannah was blushing. The door closed behind him and she kept her voice low. 'He's gorgeous, you know. Even with a split lip. If I didn't know what a womaniser he is, I'd defo make a play for him. In fact, both your brothers are mint.'

Rachel grabbed her silver handbag from the chest of drawers and gripped the door handle. 'Since when have you had a thing for my brothers? Yuck! Stay well away from the both of them. We have a pact, remember. Plus it would only end in tears. You know they're both players.'

Hannah took one last look in the mirror and followed her out of the room. 'I know, but once that vodka gets in my system you know I have no control of my body, so don't blame me if you find me in one of your brothers' beds in the morning.'

The two girls entered the night club, bright-coloured lights spinning around the room. The music was booming, and the clubbers were out in force. Rachel wasted no time scanning the crowd.

She nudged Hannah. 'OMG, he's here. He said he would come and see me, and there he is. My heart's beating ten to the dozen. What am I going to do if he comes over?'

Hannah turned to see where Niall was standing. 'What, Niall said he was coming to see you?'

Rachel placed a hand on her hip and tried to sound breezy. 'What's up with you? You know I've fancied him for like forever.'

Hannah shrugged. 'I thought he was forbidden fruit, what with being one of the Bennets. But if you say he's come to see you, then who am I to question you? Let's get our drinks and go and stand near him, see if he notices.'

Rachel was in a panic. 'No way, I'm not going near him. I'm not begging for it. If he wants me, he should come over and make himself known. Just look at him over there with all those girls hanging around his neck. He loves the attention, doesn't he?'

'And that's one reason why you should give him a wide berth. Plus, if your family found out you were sniffing around one of the Bennet boys, either you or he would be six foot under for mixing with the enemy. If you don't want him enough to go over, then do yourself a favour and walk on.'

Rachel's voice was low, her smile dropped. 'Tell me something I don't already know, Hannah. Still, it doesn't stop me from wanting a piece of him, does it? And it's not just because I can't have him. Look at him, he's drop-dead gorgeous.'

Hannah looked at her best friend in more detail. There was more than lust in her eyes when she looked at Niall Bennet; the girl was mesmerised by him. Hannah got the attention of the barmaid and ordered drinks. 'Two double vodkas and lemonade, please.'

Rachel was still gazing at Niall, in a world of her own. Hannah tapped her arm. 'We are getting our drinks and hitting the dance floor. These legs of mine haven't danced in ages. Stop looking over at him. If it is meant to be, he'll come and find you, won't he? Stop looking desperate.'

Hannah was right and Rachel knew it. She quickly turned back to the bar. The music was loud, baseline pumping throughout the club. The two girls held their drinks above their heads as they made their way to the dance floor.

The song changed and Hannah screamed at the top of her voice, 'Tune! Let's dance.'

They placed their drinks on a nearby table, she grabbed Rachel by the hand and dragged her onto the dance floor. For a while, the girls were lost in the song, free. Rachel was shaking her hips, twerking. She'd shown her mother the same dance once and Jenny had gone ballistic.

'That's not a bleeding dance,' she'd screamed. 'It's bloody dirty. Don't ever let me see you dancing like that when you're out. Only scrubbers dance like that.'

But Rachel hadn't listened. All the girls were dancing this way, why should she be any different? The music seemed to take control of her body and she was feeling the relentless power of the music when she felt a hand on her bum. She quickly turned around ready to confront anyone who had dared to touch her precious body. And it *was* precious: she'd not slept with anyone. She'd fooled around a bit with some lads from the estate, but up to now her virginity was still intact. She swallowed hard when she met the eyes of Niall Bennet. And where the hell had Hannah got to? One minute she was with her and the next she was dancing with some guy on the other side of the dance floor. Despite the heaving club, Rachel suddenly felt alone with Niall.

'Yo,' he chuckled. 'A bit of a mover, aren't you?'

She smiled back at him, and her words seemed stuck behind her teeth. 'I'm good at a lot of things,' she finally replied.

Niall gripped her by the waist and started to dance with her. She could smell his aftershave, a clean fresh aroma, soapy. It was all happening so fast. When she'd imagined this in her head, there was a proper date, a restaurant some-where away from here where no one knew them, talking for hours to each other, him taking her hand and kissing her fingertips. But instead, right here, in front of countless club-bers, Niall planted his hot red lips onto hers and she didn't just let him. She leaned in. For years she'd waited for this kiss, dreamed of it, wanted it, craved it. All the films she'd watched, they'd all told her one day a man who made her feel this way would show up. She just hadn't expected it to be one of the Bennets.

Rachel pulled away from him and looked deep into his eyes. 'Oi, ask if you can kiss me next time,' she giggled.

'Niall Bennet never asks a girl for a kiss when he knows she wants him,' he said in a cocky tone. 'Do you want to sit down for a bit? I'm not much of a dancer. I only got on the dance floor to get a grip of you.'

Rachel burst out laughing. 'Oh, did you now?'

He smiled and took her hand and guided her through the crowd of clubbers. Rachel could feel the looks of other girls burning into her, jealous that she had only gone and bagged a kiss from the one and only Niall Bennet. He found a table and sat down.

'I'll get my mate to get us some drinks.' He waved to a lad stood at the bar and shouted over to him to get his atten-tion. He nudged Rachel. 'Quick, what are you drinking?'

'Vodka and lemonade, please. But I've got a drink already. It's on the table over there,' she pointed to the table.

He ignored her. 'Mate, get us a double vodka and lemon-ade and a Jack Daniels and coke for me.' He gazed at Rachel. 'I've fancied you for as long as I can remember, you know.'

This was really happening, and Rachel smiled broadly. She could feel her cheeks burning up with embarrassment. 'Really? Well, you've never said. You kept that one quiet, didn't you?'

Before he could answer, Rachel felt someone standing behind her. She twisted round in her seat. A woman stood there with her hands on her hips. She was undeniably gorgeous: long brown hair, big eyes the colour of chestnuts. 'And what the hell do you think you're doing? I thought me and you had a thing, Niall?'

Niall looked unruffled. 'Miranda, we had a few drinks together, that's all. Wow, I can't even believe you're stood here going on at me. Jog on and stop making a fool of yourself.'

The girl gulped a mouthful from her drink and swilled the rest over Niall's head. 'You're nothing but a wanker, mate. Don't come knocking on my door when this one here gets sick of you. And you will. He's like a dog on heat. I'm so out of here, you can do one. Enjoy my sloppy seconds, love.' She stormed off, barging past anyone who stood in her way.

The cold, sticky cocktail ran down Niall's face and you could see he was fuming, but he held himself back. 'I'll send you the dry-cleaning bill,' he shouted after her. 'Tramp!' he mumbled under his breath.

'Bloody hell, are you alright?' Rachel asked.

'Yeah, the girl is off her nutter. We're not even an item. I had a bit of a thing with her the other week and that was it as far as I'm concerned. Some girls are not right in their heads, I swear to you. Off her rocker, she is.'

'What, is that what I am, too?' She put him on the spot, instantly regretting it.

'Nah, I told you, I've fancied you for time. Honest, on my life, that girl means nothing to me. I'm single and ready to mingle.'

Rachel's emotions were battling inside he. Sure, she'd secretly lusted after Niall for ages, and yes, that kiss had felt like nothing she'd known before. But this guy was so full of himself and not how she thought he would be. She had to protect herself, protect her heart. 'I'm not into guys who sleep with anything that has a pulse, you know. If I wanted somebody like that, I would get back on the dance floor with my mate Hannah and grip a guy for a one-night stand. I'm not a slag and I don't want someone like you thinking you can bed me then walk away.'

Niall's eyes were wide open, realising he had to back-pedal. 'Rach, honest, I'm a good guy. I would never do that to you. I've had my eyes on you for years and I don't want it to be ruined by some slapper thinking we were a thing when we were clearly not. I mean, I've never come near you before because, well you know why. But if you feel the same way I do, then…' he trailed off, leaving Rachel wondering what he meant.

At least she could see by his body language that he was sorry. He looked deep into her eyes and smiled. 'Can I take you out, maybe get some food and a few drinks through the week?'

Rachel flicked her hair back, looked over to the dance floor and slowly replied, 'Maybe, let's see how the rest of the night goes.' She got the feeling no girl had ever given him the run-around before. He was used to being the one calling the shots.

Niall's friend brought the drinks and jerked his head over at Rachel. He was going to say something, but Niall stopped him dead in his tracks. Rachel followed the man's gaze, and stared, eyes wide open. Paul was in the club, on the other side of the room. If he spotted her sat with one of the Bennet boys, nothing would stop him kicking off. She had to think on her feet.

'I'm going outside for some fresh air. It's boiling in here.' She stood up and looked at him, hoping he would escort her.

'I'll grab our drinks. We're not wasting them. Prices are sky high in this joint.' The two of them headed towards the exit, Rachel checking over her shoulder. She reached into her handbag and quickly sent Hannah a text message:

Am outside with Niall. Paul's in club.
Nightmare! Txt me when yr coming out & I'll
come find u

This was the good girl code: always let your friends know where you are. Rachel and her friends knew lots of clubbers made the mistake of ignoring this code when they were out and ended up alone, drunk in a ditch somewhere, or worse, being attacked. She and her friends knew it shouldn't have to be like this – always watching out for being spiked, always telling someone when they were walking home – but you couldn't be too careful. She pressed the send button and rammed her mobile phone back into her handbag.

There was a cold chill in the air tonight, a slight breeze. Niall and Rachel headed to a brick wall at the side of the club. There was a girl not far from them, spewing, a man stood behind her holding her hair back. Niall chuckled.

'That's love that, isn't it?'

Rachel smiled. So, this guy did have a heart after all. Maybe his player image was only a front. He seemed to have lost his cocky attitude now there was no one else to see it. He leaned back and stared upwards.

'I like looking up at the stars,' he said. 'How far away they are. They say some of them will have exploded by the time their light reaches us. It baffles my head when I think about it.'

Rachel looked up into the night sky. 'I like stars, too. When I'm in bed I always start counting them through my window. The moon is my favourite, though. I find it soothing. I always have. It's mystical.'

Niall snuggled in closer to her and touched her knee with his warm hand. 'Can I have a kiss then?'

'So, you're not stealing one now, you're actually asking me?'

He cupped his hand behind her neck and slowly pulled her nearer, so her lips met his. This time the kiss was deeper, longer, meaningful. To say he'd taken her breath away was an understatement. She'd never been kissed like this before. Pushing all thoughts of their families from her mind, she decided there and then that, whatever happened, she would remember this kiss for the rest of her life. Nothing seemed to matter anymore. She was in his arms and lost in the moment.

Chapter Seven

Jenny sat in the pub, more than a few glasses of wine in, her cheeks like two rosy-red apples. It was nearly two in the morning, but the landlord was always having lock-ins. Like most folk round here, if there was money to be made, he was here to make some, and people were happy to look the other way to make that happen. Jenny was looking over to the vault where Archie Bennet stood at the bar with a few of his boys. She stared at him a lot longer than she needed to and it was only Gina's voice that brought her back into the present moment.

'Jen, I swear to you that guy over there is all over me like a rash. He's not taken his eyes off me all night. If my Dave was here, he would knock him out, the creep.'

Jenny looked over at the man. Gina was right, he was still looking. But she quickly glanced back at her bag. Her mobile was ringing.

Gina snarled, placed her hand on Jenny's shoulder and rolled her eyes. 'Is that Charley again? Oh my god, does the man ever bleeding sleep? You've told him where you are, so what is his problem? Tell him to piss off and leave you alone.'

'I can't even be arsed with that anymore, Gina. I'm letting it ring. He'll be belling my phone out all night long. I'll speak to him when I get in. You'd have thought he wouldn't be able to bother me from inside his cell, but there's no let up.'

Gina switched the small button on the side of the phone to silent and rammed it back inside Jenny's bag. 'Shall I get us another round in? Pointless going home yet, isn't it? I mean Dave will be fast asleep and you're going home to an empty bed.'

Jenny scoffed. 'Cheers for that, Gina. Rub salt in the wound, why don't you?'

'You know what I mean, babes. I'll sneak in next to my old fella, he won't even know what time it is. He'll be snoring his head off. Us ladies gotta stick together. And that means another round!'

Jenny considered this and nodded. 'OK, you go to the bar and I'll nip to the toilet. I'm bursting for a wee.'

Gina stood up and headed towards the bar. The man who'd had his eye on her followed her. Jenny watched him stand behind Gina. He was probably one of her rejects. Or maybe even an ex she didn't remember. Stories about Gina behind the pub for a quick knee-trembler were never far away.

Jenny caught a glimpse of herself in a mirrored frame. She barely recognised the woman looking back. Would she even find another fella if she gave Charley the heave-ho? It was crap getting old. She hurried past, anxious to go to the loo then get back to make sure Gina wasn't stuck with a letch.

Suddenly, a large hand gripped her back. Jenny had never clocked him, he'd been hiding away in the shadows. Shocked, she turned to him. His face was still in shadow but there was a familiar swagger in his manner that set alarm bells ringing in her. 'What the fuck! Take your hands off me, you idiot.'

'I only want a quick word. Relax, woman. Breathe.'

She knew the voice immediately, and the face came into focus. But there was no relief. She turned her head one way then the other, hoping nobody spotted them talking. This was all she needed: someone gossiping, putting two and two together and coming up with six. Word could get back to Charley, before she'd even got back to her seat, that she'd been seen in the shadows with another bloke. But talking to *this* bloke? This was dynamite. She had to nip it in the bud. 'I've got nothing to say to you, so piss off and move yourself out of my way.'

Archie Bennet sniggered and let go his grip on her. 'I see you've still got attitude; some things never change, eh? A little warning for your hubby: tell him I hear the messages he's sending out and I'm ready for whatever he's got to bring to the table. He's a has-been.'

Jenny backed off, but before she got to the toilet door she spun around and looked him directly in the eyes. 'Fuck off, Archie. You're the has-been. Leave my family alone and crack on with whatever you're doing. Charley will always be twice the man you are, and you know it.'

'Your family!' he cackled. 'Less said about that the better, eh, Jenny?'

He stared at her for a few seconds and walked back into the vault. She sprinted into the toilets and ran straight into the cubicle. She sat on the toilet trying to keep her cool. Once she'd finished, she still sat there staring at the door, fanning her face. A hot flush had taken over her body. Recently, she'd been waking up some nights rolling in sweat, and they seemed to be getting worse. Maybe she needed a visit to the doctor. She was probably hitting the menopause, or maybe it was stress-related. Her fingers gripped her knees, the skin turning white, as she closed her eyes.

'Bastard, Archie Bennet. Nothing more, nothing less,' she said to herself. She'd faced down worse threats in her time.

She heard voices outside. The door handle shook, someone wanting to come in. 'Hold your bleeding horses, will you! For crying out loud.' She straightened her clothes and yanked the door open. A busty woman stood there eyeballing her, fuming that she'd had to wait. Jenny stared back and jerked her head. 'Any problems, love?' She was in the zone and if this cake-muncher wanted an argument, she was more than ready for her.

'You've been in there forever. Have you finished or what? Because, if you have, can you move out of the way? You're blocking the door.'

Jenny went nose to nose with her, ready to scratch her eyes out. 'Fuck off out of my face, you daft bitch. Trust me, the day I've had, you're cruising for a bruising.'

The woman stepped back immediately, drained of colour and quiet as Jenny barged past her.

Jenny paced over to the mirror and straightened her hair. Because she was small, people often thought she was a soft touch. She wasn't having it anymore. Deep breaths, and more deep breaths as the rage left her body. She grimaced at her reflection and whispered, 'Fuck you, Archie Bennet. Carry on with me and I'll rip your family apart. Go on, test me and I will show you what I'm all about.' Her words were powerful, and she meant every syllable. He'd rattled her cage, for sure. Her phone started vibrating again. She pulled it out of her handbag and sneered at the screen. 'And you can fuck off as well, Charley,' she sighed as she dropped the phone back into her bag.

Chapter Eight

Danny sat in the driver's seat with his head dipped low, cracking his knuckles, constantly looking from left to right. Shit had just got real. He was ready to take people down if needed, no fucking about, straight in and straight out, job done. Paul was next to him and there were two others sat in the back of the car. These two looked dodgy as anything. The kind of men you would hate to meet on a dark night. Danny was edgy, his eyes all over the place.

'Keep your eyes on that door, lads. Once that light goes off we're in there like rats up a drainpipe. You know the score. You two upstairs, and me and our kid will sort out the downstairs. If we've done our homework well, two of them at the most will be in the gaff. We do what we need to do, alright, to knock the fuckers out?'

The air seemed to change, and they all knew that tonight heads were going to roll. Paul patted his brother's leg and winked at him. He was still brown-nosing, sucking up to him to get back in his good books. Words had been scarce between them for a couple of days now and it was Paul who had to break the ice and try and make amends. 'I'm ready for this, our kid, you just leave it to me. I'll slice the fuckers up if they start any funny business. You know me. When I'm in the zone, I'm ruthless.'

Danny gave him no eye contact, still concentrating on the house, ignoring him. 'Ethan, are you tooled up ready for 'em?'

One of the men in the back smiled at him through the rear-view mirror. 'Born ready, Dan.'

'Jack, I know you always come prepared. I don't even know why I'm asking you,' Danny chuckled.

'I'm ready willing and able, mate. I'm on the bones of my arse, so I need this job to come off and pay some of my debts off. I'll put the fear of God into them, trust me. I'm here for a good time, not a long time,' he joked.

Danny gripped the steering wheel and squeezed it, knuckles turning white, adrenaline pumping. This grow they were after was ready for chopping down and if this job came off it would be a good pay out for all involved. At least twenty grand. The word on the street was it was the finest weed, stardog, a great seller on the streets. The yellow light coming from the window facing them faded. It was show time. Danny licked his lips frantically, grabbed his crowbar, a quick look at his boys in the back and he was out of the car and ready for action.

'Ready, remember, no mistakes, we all know the script. Right, lads, let's have it.'

These boys were like soldiers on a mission. They all knew their roles, their places in the group. The four of them sprinted towards the door. This had to be precise. The door needed to be boomed in on the first go, knocked from its hinges. With all his might, Danny wielded the big crowbar and rammed it into the door. A good clean shot, the door sprung open. Screaming, shouting, two upstairs, two downstairs. Danny ran into the front room, dropping the crowbar and pulling his machete from its sheath. Where were they? He couldn't see anyone. He sprinted one way then the other, nothing. He heard shouting upstairs, footsteps running about, and without pausing for breath he ran through the doorway and headed upstairs.

Paul hovered over a man, was already giving him a good hiding, blood spraying, body shaking. This man would give them no problems. Jack had the other man gripped by the scruff of his neck. He jerked the bloke's head back, and nutted him. He fell to the ground like a sack of spuds.

'Get the fucking grow and let's get out of here!' Paul shouted.

They worked like a team, fast, every movement getting the job done. But this was too easy, the last man had seemed to go down without a proper fight. Danny clocked the guy on the floor and saw a mobile phone in his hand. Too late, he'd already dialled a number and now he bawled down the phone before anyone could get to him.

'We're being had over! Hurry the fuck up and get here,' he pleaded.

This was a bad move. Paul ran at him and booted him right in the face, ripping the phone from his hand and stamping on it, smashing it to pieces. Danny's ears pinned back. Any other time he would have put these two scrotes in the hospital, nil by mouth. But there was no time to spare. They all used the bags they'd brought and yanked the plants from the dark soil. Danny kept looking out of the bedroom window: they were living on borrowed time. Whoever really owned this grow, not just the lads employed to tend it, they would be on their way, team-handed, ready for war. Paul ran in and out of the rooms, dragging, pulling at the plants. Jack was sprinting down the stairs loading them into the car. Each in turn bombed it down the stairs to get as much as they could before it was too late. Danny looked around the room. It was time to go, they'd done what they came to do.

Before he left, he gripped the man on the floor and dragged him up by the scruff, eye to eye with him, his hot breath spraying into his face. 'Next time, you'll be in a fucking body bag, mate.'

The man crumbled to the floor as Danny gave him one last dig to the jaw. There was no mercy here today.

Chapter Nine

Charley Johnson stood at the small window in his pad and felt the soft breeze from outside on his face. He'd often stand here and look outside at the world. Thinking time he called it, getting his head around everything that had gone wrong in his life. It was a time when the life he'd chosen played heavily on his mind. He licked his lips. He could almost taste the freedom, feel it in his bones. A pigeon landed on a wall near his window and he stuck his hand out from the bars, clucking to try and befriend it. But not even the birds trusted him; maybe they sensed something about him. Today he would be a free man. Time to say goodbye to this shithole for good.

It was early and Jezz was still asleep. Charley looked at him enviously. What he would give for a good night's kip. He'd never had a full night's sleep since he entered the jail. The noises kept him awake – men crying, screaming, shouting – how could anyone sleep through that? He looked over at his packed bags and nodded slowly. He'd waited for this day, dreamed of it. Planned it in his head for months. Gritting his teeth tightly, he squeezed the cold iron bars in front of him. He took a breath that fully inflated his broad chest just as Jezz rolled over and let out one of the loudest farts ever. Jezz's head appeared from under his duvet, and he was smiling. Hair stuck up all over the show. 'Call it a leaving present.'

They both chuckled as Charley came and sat on the edge of his bed. He was glad his pad mate was awake.

'It all starts now, Jezz. I need to get back on the horse and put my name back on the map. Sure, I've run this place, but it's different to running the streets on the outside. Archie Bennet will have been lying awake last night just like I was.' His tone sharpened, aggressive. 'I want what's mine and I'll do whatever it takes to get it back.'

Jezz sat up in his bed, alert now. 'All comes to those who wait, pal. Be careful and keep your head down for a bit, you know, to gather your thoughts together and all that? Don't be going in all guns blazing.'

Charley smirked. He knew the crack, he wasn't born yesterday. 'Nah, mate, I'm going to sit pretty for a few weeks and see what's what. I need some time to adjust. You're right.'

'Best way, Chaz. You don't want to end up back in the slammer. I wish I was getting out with you. I'd have your back, make sure no fucker gets a shot at you.'

Charley nodded. Jezz would be in this place for a few more weeks yet and Charley knew there was nothing he could do to help him until he was on the outside.

'I bet your Jen is excited today. She'll feel like a decorator's paste bucket when you get to her.' Jezz covered his mouth with his hand and cringed: he'd overstepped the mark. Charley never did see the funny side of anything when his wife's name was dropped into the mix. He smoothed it over before Charley started snapping. 'Sorry about that, you know what I mean. Your Jen is a top woman and I hope I meet someone like her when I get out.'

Charley smiled. The thought of his woman in his arms, her smell, her touch, sent a warm sensation down his body. 'She'll be outside waiting for me today. I can't wait to see her face.'

'Send her my love and tell her I'll come and see her when I'm out. Say hello to the lads, too.' Jezz dropped his head, sadness filling his eyes. 'You've been like my brother in this place. You've looked after me, kept me sane. You always look after me, Charley-boy. Honest, I'm forever thankful.'

'Yeah, relax. I'll sort something out for you when you're back out. Just keep your head down in here and keep out of trouble. The sooner you're home the quicker I can put you on the books.'

Keys jangled outside the door. Charley was alert, ears pinned back. 'Eh up, my taxi must be here.'

The cell door swung open, and a screw stood there with a clipboard in his hands. He casually flicked through his notes. This was the best part of this screw's job; he loved seeing the back of prisoners from his wing. Especially Charley Johnson.

'Come on, Big C, it's time to get you out of here.'

Jezz rolled onto his side; he hated goodbyes. He swallowed hard and tried to hold back his emotions. 'Yes, get him gone. I want to get some shut-eye.' He never meant it and Charley knew it was his way of saying he was going to miss him.

Charley bent down and gripped him, lifting him up slightly from the bed. 'Keep your head down and I'll see you soon.'

He hooked his black sports bag over his shoulder and stepped onto the landing. His chest expanded with every step he took. He smirked at anyone who crossed his path.

An inmate shouted from the other side of the landing, 'Good luck, Chaz. Hope we don't see you back in here.'

'No plans to come back, Mickey. I'm on the straight and narrow from now on.'

The screw rolled his eyes. If he had a pound for every convict who said they weren't coming back he would be a rich man.

Charley walked tall. A few of the screws were huddled together talking as he passed them. You could see the look of relief in their eyes as he left the wing.

He stood at the old wooden desk and waited until all his paperwork was completed. Even though he was leaving the jail, the officers would not take their eye off the ball for a single second. This man was dangerous, unpredictable. He sat down on the chair and sighed, fed up. 'How much longer, lads? I've got my woman sat outside waiting for me.'

The man behind the desk shot a look over at the clock, aware the man was agitated. 'We won't be long now. Last bit of paperwork and then you'll be a free man.'

Charley nodded slowly and his nostrils flared. This day had been a long time coming. He was ready for them, ready for them all.

———

Jenny sat back in the driver's seat and opened the window as she lit up another cigarette. She was chain-smoking again. A thick cloud of smoke circled her face as she exhaled. She watched the prison doors, waiting for them to open. In her own way, she knew what it was like to be imprisoned: a prisoner in her own home, her own life. But in her case she never had a release date, a time when all her suffering would be over. She knew she had to put a smile on her face and pretend everything was rosy in the garden. But it was far from that. Today, her sentence would begin again. She'd be watched around the clock, have to answer to her where-abouts, tell her husband who she'd been speaking to, even have sex with the man who made her stomach churn every time he put his hands on her. She focused on the large red-brick tower facing her. This was the landmark that was Strangeways Prison. It looked like a tower you would see in a fairy tale, the kind where princesses were held captive by wicked witches. The kind where a princess would wait every day for her knight in shining armour, her Prince Charming, to come and rescue her. But who would rescue Jenny?

She swallowed hard as she watched the large wooden gate open. A group of strangers walked out first. There was no sign of her husband. Maybe he'd kicked off, battered someone, and was being held for another few months. Her heartbeat doubled and her head was doing overtime. 'Please keep him. *Please,'* she whispered.

No such luck. There he was, standing outside the gates, looking up to the sky, his mouth moving but no words coming out. He spotted her. Jenny quickly flicked her cigarette butt out of the window and opened the car door. She knew how to play the happy wife, for sure. She'd done it a hundred times before. She stood in front of the car and watched her husband jog towards her. She had to smile, look excited, be the woman he wanted to see after his stretch inside. He dropped his bag on the ground and picked her up in the air, swinging her around and around.

'I've missed you so much,' he whispered into her ear. Sweet nothings; words she'd heard a thousand times, the same old bullshit. He placed her back down on the ground, gripped her face in his large hands and pressed his warm, wet lips to hers. She had to kiss him, show she'd missed him too. 'Come on, love, get me away from this place and take me home.'

Jenny got back into the car and Charley got into the passenger side, flinging his bags onto the back seat.

'I thought they were never going to let me out of that place. At one point I thought I'd be gate arrested. You know what these fuckers are like, they spring it on you at the last minute.'

'Arrest you for what?' she enquired, trying not to sound too keen.

'I don't know, the wankers always have someone up their sleeves when it comes to me. The bastards stitch you up for anything.'

'So, keep your neck clean. The last thing you want is to land back in the nick, isn't it?'

'Yeah, I know, but you know me, love, trouble has a habit of following me around,' he chuckled.

'You mean you attract it, Charley. If you had a normal job and kept out of trouble, you would have nothing to worry about.'

He glared at her, annoyed that she was lecturing him already. His eyes widened, and she gulped. She knew that look, knew when to keep her gob shut.

'You're not moaning when I'm filling your purse, are you? Running them brasses at Blossoms?'

She started the engine and pulled out from the side-street. She could have had a full-blown argument with him there and then and told the bastard what she really thought of him, but she kept schtum. Before she came to pick her other half up this morning, she'd visited her nana's grave. She always went to see her when things were going wrong. She didn't know exactly why she went – for someone to talk to, or maybe some beyond-the-grave advice, a sign from her grandparent that everything was going to be alright. Whatever, she never felt alone there. There were always people sat at the gravesides of someone they loved, talking to them, crying, hoping they could find the answers they were looking for. Death was such a horrible thing, so final. When Jenny's nana died it had broken her in two. She was close to her, and she'd spent a lot of time with her growing up. Charley never understood this, though. He had expected her to simply get on with it. Jenny had been spending more time with her own family lately and she knew that would change now Charley was home. He hated her going to see them and expected her to look after his own mother instead. Charley's mother Mona was a moaning old cow. She thought the sun shone out of Charley's arse and she would never have a bad word said against him. His sisters were like that, too. She'd never really got along with them. She only went to see them to keep the peace.

Charley turned the radio up and started singing. Today was a happy day for him and he was on a high. He was a free man. Jenny looked at him from the corner of her eye and her grip on the steering wheel tightened. Imagining it was his neck.

———

Rachel stood at the kitchen window peering outside, waiting for her old man to pull up. It was something she'd done many times before. She knew the script, knew what lay ahead. But this time, she'd be seeing her father with a secret in her heart. She hoped he wouldn't notice, but even she knew she looked different somehow. She was smiling from head to toe. Today she was a young woman in love. She'd kissed Niall Bennet, and made plans to see him again. But how she could do that now her dad was out? He'd have eyes and ears everywhere. Danny came up behind her and rested his head on her shoulder.

'Any sign of them yet?'

'Nope, any time soon though. Look at the time, it's nearly nine o'clock.'

Paul shuffled in but he kept his distance. Danny always hugged his sister, told her how beautiful she was. But not Paul, that wasn't for him. He sat down at the kitchen table and looked through his messages. He checked nobody was looking and zoomed in on a snap of an older woman. He typed quickly:

Any chance of seeing some more of u?

He sent the message and rammed his phone back into his pocket.

'Dad's here!' Rachel screamed at the top of her voice.

Danny pushed her out of the way and dragged the blinds back from the window. He could see him and he smiled. At last, his old man was home. 'Come on then, let's meet and greet him.'

The three of them made their way to the front door. This had been a long time coming and despite all the secrets and fears they carried at that moment, Charley's children were eager to get their father back home where he belonged. They were the Johnson family after all – they stood together.

Charley stopped at the end of the garden path, dropped his bags where he stood, his arms held out straight, and watched his children run towards him. The four of them enveloped one another in a family hug. Rachel was sobbing; from nowhere the tears flooded from her eyes. Charley clocked her crying and used the end of his finger to wipe away her tears.

'Oi, come on now, princess. Daddy's home, so dry them tears away.'

'I'm so happy you're home, Dad. We've all missed you so much.'

Danny and Paul each placed an arm around Charley and led him down the garden path to the house. They were soon laughing and joking. Rachel followed them, looking over her shoulder to see her mother left alone. Jenny was behind them all, picking up Charley's bag and trying her best to loop it over her shoulder.

Sweating, she mumbled, 'Yeah, leave me to carry your shit. I'll carry it like I've carried you for years, you wanker.'

Inside, Charley sat down in the armchair like it was a throne. He held his head back. His emotions were all over the place and his eyes looked like they had clouded over. His children were his world and his weak spot. He could be himself in front of them, let his guard down. When he was growing up, he often told them, he didn't have a great time. He was dragged up, he told his children when he was drunk. Charley's father was an alcoholic, not shy of showing his mother his fists. Even now when he spoke about his childhood, he cringed when he thought about his father and the way he treated his mother. Charley got a few slaps too from his old man, an arse-kicking, the belt. But, that all stopped when Charley got older and he realised what it was all about. He 'd been sick of lying in bed each night listening to his mother crying, hearing her pleading with her husband to stop the abuse. Enough was enough. One night, in the early hours, Charley ran into his parents' bedroom and gripped his dad by the scruff of the neck. It wasn't something he was proud of, but he let his dad have it. Punching, kicking, name-calling, he made sure this man never laid a finger on his mother, or him, again. Saxon Johnson left the family home not long after that and none of them had set eyes on him since. He simply upped and left. He was a womaniser and probably had another woman lined up somewhere. His mother never said a word to the other siblings about what had happened that night, she just told them her husband had found another woman and pissed off with her, and nobody questioned it. But Charley knew the truth, knew that his father would never darken their door again.

Jenny went into the kitchen and flicked the kettle on. Charley was a right tea belly and before he asked, she started to make him a brew. Tea, two sugars, plenty of milk, she knew the drill. But it was all she could do not to spit in his. She looked out of the kitchen window. She could hear them all talking in the front room. There was no rush for her to get back to see him. She was taking a few minutes to herself, she needed to plan.

Rachel sat on the arm of the chair with her arm stretched around the back of her father's neck. He was her protector, the one who kept the family safe. Although hadn't her mum done that, too? Jenny walked into the room and placed the drink of tea on the small table at the side of her husband. His spot, his table, everything in reach for him so he didn't have to move far. He nodded to her and watched her sit

down from the corner of his eye. Danny and Paul were waiting on instructions now, talks of taking back their empire
back and letting the world know they were back on the up.

Rachel sensed it was that time and went to join her mother
on the sofa. Why couldn't this family be normal? Why did it
always have to involve someone getting hurt, someone's
front door getting boomed in or someone being stabbed? She
sat smoothing her hair, waiting for the talk to begin.

Jenny could see she was getting anxious and patted her
knee. This wasn't the kind of talk she wanted her daughter
to be listening to, and plus, if the dibble ever came knocking
at the door, what she didn't know, she couldn't tell them.

'Why don't you go out and do a bit of shopping? It's
your day off so go and make the most of it. Dad will still be
here when you get back, don't worry.'

Charley heard the conversation, and he shot a look over
at Danny. 'Sort your sister out with a few quid for shopping
and I'll box you off later. You know how much our Rach
loves shopping and now I'm home I can spoil her again.'

Danny dug his hand in his pocket and counted out two
hundred quid. He smiled at his sister. 'Here you go, this
should get you a few outfits.'

Rachel reached over and took the cash from her brother's hand. It was dirty money, blood money, cash she knew
had come from somebody else's misery. Paul looked the
other way. He was a right tight git, wouldn't give a door a
bang. And there was no way he was parting with any of his
cash, he had plans for it.

Charley coughed to clear his throat, and this was Rachel's
signal to leave the room. They waited until she'd finished

kissing everybody. Once the living room door was closed, Charley sat forward in his seat with his hands cupped between his legs. Jenny dropped her head, wanting no part of this, but she knew it was too late for her. She was in up to her neck. If she could have been invisible, she would have been, hidden away from them all.

'So, what's the Bobby Moore then, Pops?' asked Danny.

'Nothing at the moment, Son. I want to chill for a bit and see what's going on before I make any decisions. The last thing I want is to not be prepared. I need to watch and listen to the word on the street before we make a move. I'm going to meet up with the lads soon and then I'll know more. I've heard a few whispers that the Bennets are bricking it, but I know Archie better than anyone, he's a cunning fucker and he'll have something up his sleeve. But let me get my head together first.' Charley shot a quick look over at his wife and she looked away.

Danny smashed his flat palm against the arm of the sofa, dust flying up into the air. 'Dad, we've waited a long time for you to come home and I'm not having them lot saying we've lost our nerve. The sooner we take it all back the better. Me and our kid are taxing any grows we come across. They belong to the Bennets, we know that already, so we need to be prepared and have our camp in order, sooner rather than later.'

Paul chirped in. 'Correct, Dad. We've had to watch them cheeky bastards for months raking in the cash and stepping on our turf. It's only these last few months that we have got back on our feet. Those robbing little shits had us over a few times and now it's payback time.'

Charley's voice was firm, and he stared his sons down. 'I said relax. Do you think I've built my empire over the years by rushing in? I'm older and wiser and, trust me, I know what I'm talking about. Ask your mother sat there.'

All eyes were on Jenny now, and her cheeks started to go bright red. 'Just do what he says,' she replied. Anything for a quiet life. If she agreed with her husband, he would let her off the hook. There was no way she was rattling his cage any more than she had to today.

Charley leered at his wife and licked his lips. Enough talk of business, he wanted some pleasure, to get his wife in the feather and ravish her body. 'Right, lads, give us a few hours and I'll have another chat with you. At the moment I only want to have a few hours in bed. I've been up early, and I'm knackered.'

Danny nudged Paul: they both knew what he meant. Paul chuckled as they got up to leave. 'Right, enjoy. Catch you later.'

The room was quiet, and Jenny looked over at Charley. Any second now he'd be on his feet and taking her upstairs to bed. She hadn't missed sex one little bit. She never had the urge to sleep with her husband. Any sex they'd had in the past was what he'd instigated; she never made the first move.

He yawned and stretched his arms over his head. 'Come on, love, let's go and have a lie down.'

Jenny stood up, thinking of any excuse not to go to bed with him. 'I'll make you some breakfast if you want. You must be starving?'

'I'm starved of love, Jen, nothing more. Get yourself up the stairs, you sexy woman,' he joked.

Jenny knew she was fighting a losing battle. She put a smile on her face, headed upstairs and obeyed his orders.

———

Charley's breath was ragged, his body covered in sweat. The deed was done. He wasn't as fit as he thought. Twenty minutes they'd been at it, his arse up and down like a fiddler's elbow. This wasn't love-making, it was a bang: hardly any kissing, hardly any foreplay. Jenny had tried everything to get it over as quick as she could, but he'd had trouble keeping his old man hard. Perhaps it was the shock of coming out of jail, the stress.

Jenny reached over and popped two fags from the packet. Once she'd sparked them up, she passed one to her husband. It was weird having a man in her bed again, sprawled all over her, creasing her white crisp Egyptian bedding. Charley was a big man and he took up most of the bed. He chugged hard on the cigarette and closed his eyes as he exhaled.

'That was just what the doctor ordered. A bit of slap-and-tickle is always a good way to de-stress.'

Jen lay next to him and spoke in a low voice. 'Is everything alright downstairs, love?' She shot a look down. 'I mean, I've never seen it go like that before?' She knew what she was doing, of course. He was a man who revelled in his power over people, his power over her. She had very few ways to turn the tables and make him feel small like he made her feel when he was being abusive to her.

He rolled about in the bed, fidgeting. 'There is fuck all wrong with my old fella. He's just a bit shell-shocked, that's all. Nothing to worry about.'

She was at him again. 'Sometimes it happens with age. Erectile disfunction is very common, you know. I watched a TV documentary about it last week.'

'Why are you watching programmes about men's toss-ers? Wow, is that how you've been getting your kicks while I've been away?'

Jenny laughed. 'I was flicking through the channels and came across it. If I was after getting kicks, love, I'm sure I could do better than watching it on the TV.' She cringed as soon as the words left her mouth.

He was right on her. 'What the fuck is that supposed to mean, eh? Are you saying you can get sex whenever you want?'

'Oh, Charley, relax, will you. It was a bleeding joke. Don't be so bloody uptight.'

'You know I hate the thought of you with someone else, Jen. Fucking hell, why do you have to open that big gob of yours and spoil things. You know how my head works.'

'I was joking, for crying out loud. Can't we have a laugh any more?'

Charley sucked hard on his fag, getting ready to put it out. 'Just saying, that's all. I'll have something to eat now if you want?'

And there it was. Her life back to normal at the blink of an eye. The skivvy, the servant, the woman who jumped to his every word when he shouted her name. Jenny finished her cigarette and put it in the ashtray, still burning.

Charley waited until his wife had left the room and reached over for her mobile phone, checking through her call log, her messages, her photos, studying each and every one of them, zooming in on every shot.

Downstairs, Jenny stood over the hot stove and watched as the bacon cooked in the frying pan. She'd promised herself things were going to be different in her life now that her husband was home. The second she got the chance, she was going to tell Charley she wanted things to change. It was about choosing when to tell him, picking the right time. If he didn't like the changes, she would tell him it was over, tell him how unhappy she was and that he was making her life a misery. She flicked the bacon over and watched it sizzle in the hot oil. It was bubbling just like her temper. She looked into her garden, stretching her neck slightly to look at the red roses in the corner. She wouldn't have time anymore to prune them, to make sure they were well fed. No, all her spare time now would be spent looking after her man.

She jumped when she felt arms around her waist and quickly turned around.

'I've missed all this, love, seeing you cooking, looking after us all.'

She tried to smile but it wasn't happening. Here was her chance, her moment to say how she felt. 'Charley,' she said in a soft voice. 'There is more to me than cooking and cleaning, you know. I want to try and make something of myself, maybe enrol on a course at college or something.'

Charley let go of her and stood back laughing. 'Are you having a laugh, love? Since when have you ever wanted to work? Don't I give you everything you need?'

'I want something for me, something I'm good at, that I like. I look after Blossoms, don't I? But that was always your thing. I want to make something of my own.'

'Like what? As far as I'm concerned, you've never showed an interest in fuck all except moaning.'

He was switching and she could see a familiar look in his eye that made her back off before she got a belt.

'Oh, forget I mentioned it. One thing I ask for, and you take the piss out of me.'

'Daft idea, that's why. You look after the family and that's a full-time job. Now I'm back, I'll run Blossoms again, give you more time to look after me. I give you money, so there's no need for you to be going out of the house looking for something new. Be happy with what you have, woman. Sometimes I just don't understand where your head is at. You want for fuck-all. Plenty of women would kill for what you've got.'

She turned away, her eyes filling, emotion rising in her throat. Nothing had changed, her life was the same as before. She stayed silent, clashing the pots and pans instead.

Charley sat down aware she was in a mood. She didn't have to say anything, he could feel it in the atmosphere. He sat scranning his meal. He loved his food and, even though he'd shed a few pounds in the chokey, he was still prone to put weight on. He patted his bare stomach.

'Smashing that, Jen. That food in jail has no bleeding taste, not like your cooking. I think that's why I decided to marry you. Do you remember that curry you made me after our first couple of dates? Nearly blew me apart it did. What was it, a madras or something?'

Jenny raised a smile. They were the good days, young and in love, when he'd never laid her finger on her, and promised her the world. She nodded, and she was right back in that moment. 'Yep, it was a hot curry. I found the recipe in some magazine and just followed the instructions. I must admit, it was hot though. I was sweating, too.'

'Come here and give me a kiss. I love you, Jenny.'

She was in his arms now, the arms that told her he would keep her safe, the arms that picked her back up when she was feeling low, but the same hands that slapped and punched her when he was drunk and feeling sorry for himself.

Charley kissed the top of her head and let her go. He seemed like he wanted to say something, but the words were glued to his tongue. 'Shall we go and see my mam later? You know she'll be sat waiting all day for me, don't you?'

'Bloody hell, Charley, can't we wait until tomorrow? She knows you've just got out of jail, surely she will understand?'

He was having none of it. 'Give it half an hour and let my food digest, then we'll go and see her.'

'That's fine. We can call to see my mam, too. I've not seen her for ages, and she will be happy to see that you're home.'

Charley let out a sarcastic laugh. 'Are you having a bleeding laugh? That woman has never liked me. She detests me. Come on, how many times has she banished me from her house? The woman has too much to say for herself. I don't know how your dad puts up with her. Bleeding nagging cow, she is.'

The gloves were off, and Jen fought her corner; there was no way he was slating her mother when his mother was twice as bad. 'How dare you speak about my mam like that? She's been good to us, Charley. You have a short memory, you do.'

'And she's had a good few quid from us, too. Who bailed her out when she couldn't pay the loan man, eh? Yeah, I thought you would be quiet on that front.'

'I'm not quiet, and for your information that loan man was having her over. She'd finished paying him and he was adding extra charges on, trying to get more money out of her. My dad had sorted it out, but you had to stick your nose in, didn't you.'

'I'm not arguing with you over it, Jen. I can't help it if I don't like sitting at your mam's house, can I?'

She was fuming and she should have zipped it, but the words came flying out. 'And I don't like sitting at your mother's house, either. All they do is gossip about other people's lives. They're like witches sat around a cauldron when they get going.'

Charley froze and stared at her.

She'd overstepped the mark, and she knew it. She sighed. 'Let's not fall out, Charley. Bloody hell, it's your first day home. We should be the best of friends, not fighting about our families.'

Charley chewed on his bottom lip, debating his next move. 'Get yourself ready and we'll go and see my mother. Not a big ask, is it?'

Family. It was meant to be everything, but sometimes Jenny felt it was more trouble than it was worth. Being a Johnson was a curse as much as a blessing these days.

Chapter Ten

In the upstairs room at The Wheatsheaf, Danny and Paul sat looking at the clock.

'For fuck's sake, I'm supposed to be meeting some bird tonight. Where the hell is he?' Paul muttered.

Danny nodded slowly. His brother was always in a rush and whoever he was meeting could wait: family came first. How many times did he have to tell this numpty?

Finally, Charley walked into the room, looking like he'd just got out of bed.

Paul sighed, restless. 'Come on, old man, we have places to go, people to meet.'

Charley slumped down in a seat next to him. 'Relax, will you? I was knackered and needed a bit of kip. Where's John?'

John Bucks was the landlord of the Wheatsheaf boozer and he always let Charley and his boys use a room when they needed a quiet space to talk. Of course, he got a bung, and as long as his pockets were filled, he never told a soul what he heard in these meetings. And he'd certainly heard things. He had lots of dark stories about each of these men.

'He's nipped downstairs. He said he'd let Barry and Sam up, and the rest of the boys,' Danny said.

Charley sparked a fag up and yawned. This would be the first time he'd seen his firm since he'd been out of jail. Maybe he should have made more of an effort and scrubbed up. His hair stuck up and he was dressed scruffy in black tracksuit bottoms and a black hoodie. But he often thought the younger generation put too much time into looking the part and not enough time actually earning respect. He looked over at his boys. They'd grown up so much, men they were now, and he knew he had to treat them like that.

'So, what's the crack with the grows? Who's selling what and who's raking the fucking cash in? Because it stops today, do you hear me? It's over. All these weasels who think they can sell drugs on our turf are getting carted. I want you two to sort that out. We supply shit around here, nobody else. We'll start at the bottom and build our way up to the big men.'

This was music to Danny's ears. His eyes danced with madness and narrowed as he thought of his chance for revenge. 'You mean the Bennets' dad?'

'Correct. We take things slow for now and chip away at the little stuff before we tackle Archie and his boys. I've not been around for a while, and I want to walk before I can run.'

Paul gritted his teeth. For years he'd sat here waiting for his old man to come home and now he was, he was doing nothing about the Bennets themselves, only planning to take out the foot soldiers. Had he lost his nerve?

He couldn't listen any longer, he had to say something. 'Dad, let's take it all back now – strike while they think we're still gathering the troops. Fuck waiting about. The Bennets have got too comfortable. We run shit around here, not them.'

Charley slammed his fist on the table, making it shake. 'Are you deaf? I said we will wait. I need to find out what's what first. Find out who's supplying them, who they have on their books. I've been in this game a lot longer than you two, so hang fire until I give the orders.'

Paul looked sour, words fighting to get out of his closed mouth.

The door opened and Barry and Sam smiled as they walked into the room.

'Oi, Oi, Charley boy. Looking good, lad,' Barry chuckled.

The men hugged each other and sat at either side of Charley. They were his wingmen, the ones who made sure no fucker got near him. Barry was built like a shit-house door. Tall, hairy, broad shoulders, arms full of tattoos. Sam was of similar build, and he had a look in his eye that suggested he wasn't the full shilling. The light was on, but nobody was home. He wasn't a man of many words; he was more of a listener. But that didn't make him a soft touch. Quite the opposite. Sam was a nutcase, sick in the head and he liked to torture his victims. He always carried a knife, and didn't think twice about sticking it in anyone who rubbed him up the wrong way.

Charley held his head back, clearing his thoughts, stopping his mind from racing. 'It's good to be home, lads. Barry,

Sam, I've worded the lads up about how I want things to roll. I want to start with the small suppliers on the estates and gradually hit the big-timers.'

Sam sat cracking his knuckles. 'You mean the Bennets themselves, Chaz?'

Charley nodded.

Barry took the stage now and he was raging as he spoke. 'You want to see that Archie, mate, he's driving around in a brand spanking new car and his wife thinks she's a fucking wag. On my life, he's bought her new tits and teeth,' he chuckled. 'Don't get me wrong, they're a nice set of titties and I wouldn't mind having a feel of them, but the fucker needs bringing down sooner rather than later. Word has it he's got the Malones eating out of his hand, too,' Barry added, knowing that if they didn't put the Bennets in their place, the other big families across Manchester would move in, too. 'Archie is not daft, you know. He's known you're due out of jail and he's getting his squad together. I think we should approach the Malones and see what the crack is.'

'I know who the Malones are. They mean fuck all to us lot, Barry. They're not on our patch. If we need heads, then I have plenty of guys I can call upon. For now, let's get the fucking foot soldiers out of the way, then we can tackle Archie. He's mine, anyway. Nobody touches Archie, only me.'

Barry clapped his hands together. 'Yep, I'm all over that. Like you said, let's clean our areas up. Monsall, Harpurhey, Collyhurst, Moston, are all ours, always have been.'

Danny chipped into the conversation. 'Right, we can start that tonight. We will get our boys together and make sure we're seen to be back. Even if we don't touch the big fish yet, we can show the small fry what's what.'

Paul squirmed, no eye contact. 'Nah, can't tonight, I've made plans. You can go, Danny, and take some of the boys with you. You're not going to miss me for one night, or do you need your baby brother to hold your hand?' he sniggered. He knew Danny would never admit to needing him.

'Do I hell need you to take down a few muppets. Dad, leave it to me, it will be sorted.'

'Barry, I want you to get all the boys together over the next few days and we can talk about the bigger stuff.' Charley shot a look over at his boys to let Barry know he wasn't going to speak about serious business in front of his lads. He'd always tried to keep his own lads away from the really messy stuff.

Danny raised his eyebrows when he saw that look. For crying out loud, he'd been manning the ship whilst his old man was in jail and, now that he was a free man, he was hiding shit away from him already. What the hell was all that about?

Paul bolted up from his seat. 'Right, I'm out of here. Danny, if them kids on the estate give you any shit, bell me.'

Danny stood tall and didn't even bother replying to him. He turned on his heel and followed his younger brother out.

Charley surveyed Barry, then Sam, with an expression they'd come to know, oh so well. 'Right, first order of business: if you know anything about Jenny tell me now before

I find out myself. Don't have me looking like a daft bastard, lads.'

Sam shook his head. Jail had not changed his boss. 'For fuck's sake, how many times do you need telling that she's been as good as gold? We've followed her like you said and she does nothing out of the ordinary.'

Charley scratched his chin and chewed on his lip. 'These women are crafty fuckers, you have to watch them like a hawk. In a blink of an eye they will have their knickers down and no one is any the wiser.'

'Well, not Jenny, Chaz. Home, Blossoms, a wine or two with that Gina bird – she barely goes anywhere else.' Barry backed Sam. 'Mate, I'm here to earn some money not sit talking about domestics. If you think she's given us the slip and been unfaithful, cart her. End of. But you won't get any proof from us.'

Charley was on the spot, aware his boys were looking at him like he'd lost the plot. He was the main man and here he was stressing about a woman. He had to get a grip. 'Enough said on the subject. You're right, we need to get our ship in order and make sure Archie Bennet never rises again. This time there's no sharing: I want to take the fucking lot from him.'

Sam let out a menacing laugh. This was more like it.

Charley sat cracking his knuckles. 'Firstly, let's show our faces in the boozer. I want to look him in the eye. He knows he stitched me up, and for that he will pay.'

Sam nodded. 'Let's go down the Mitre and get a few scoops down our necks. Our Charley Johnson is back in the game and we need to celebrate.'

Chapter Eleven

Jenny sat at the kitchen table gazing over at Gina, but lost in thought.

Gina tried to snap her out of her trance. 'So, what's it like having that hairy bastard back home?'

Jenny sucked on her cigarette and blew out a thick cloud of smoke. 'It is what it is, Gina. He's still a control freak. Honest, I had to stop myself telling him a few home truths when he walked in through that door. I can't believe I kept my gob shut. I swear, it was on the tip of my tongue. He sat in his chair like the bleeding King of the Castle, like he'd never been away.'

Gina sniggered. 'I bet the sex was good, though? Come on, you must've had cobwebs down there, it's been that long?'

Jenny smirked. 'I've had better thrills on the roller coasters at Blackpool, if I'm honest.'

Gina's eyes widened and her jaw dropped. It was usually her telling all about her love life. This time she was the audience. 'I thought Charley was alright in the bedroom. I mean he acts like he's a bit of a porn star. Is that all lies?'

Jenny squirmed. 'He might have been good years ago.' She paused. 'His – you know – isn't working properly.' She held her little finger out and wiggled it about.

Gina covered her mouth with both hands and tried not to laugh, but Jenny burst out laughing and they giggled like schoolgirls.

'It was like a wet slug. I should be able to be honest with him, shouldn't I? I think he's got that erectile thingy, you know, when they can't get a boner?'

Gina tapped her fingers on the table. 'This could be serious, Jen. Imagine if he can't satisfy you anymore? What will you do then?'

'I'm not bothered about sex. I would rather watch a good film and eat some chocolate.'

The two of them laughed their heads off and Gina thought it was nice to see Jenny relaxing.

'I'm thinking of taking up something new, Gina, something I'll enjoy.'

'You've never mentioned anything before. What's brought this on?' Gina looked puzzled.

'I feel like I haven't achieved anything in my life. I want to have a go at something and see if I can do it. I've always just been Charley's wife, a mother. I want something for me that doesn't have anything to do with him.'

Gina changed the subject. 'Are we going to town, or what?'

Jenny stood up. 'It's you who hasn't shut up talking. I've been waiting on you.'

Rachel rushed into the kitchen. 'Mam, where are my black boots?'

Jenny looked under the table. 'You mean these? You put them here last night, don't you remember?'

'Oh yes, so I did.' Rachel grabbed her boots from under the table. 'See you later, got to rush.' She pecked Jenny on the cheek. 'Bye, ladies, see you later.' And, as fast as she'd arrived, Rachel was gone.

'Gina, is it me or is our Rachel acting a bit strange lately? You've just seen her then. Usually she would have sat down and had a chat with us both, but she always seems like she's in a rush these days.'

'You're overthinking things like you always do. Hurry up and let's get going. Now that Charley's home, I'm sure you're not short of money. So, moneybags, get a smile on your face and let's hit the high street. You can even get some sexy underwear for Charley and see if you can put some life in his old man again.'

Jenny playfully pushed Gina and chuckled. 'This stays between us. Don't you go blabbing my business to the world and his wife like you usually do.'

'I've never said a word to anyone about anything. That hurts, Jen, take it back. I'm a loyal friend. I would never discuss your business with anyone else. I know what it's like around here for gossiping.'

Jenny put her coat on. 'More than once, Charley has got wind of things I've only ever told you. How can you explain that?'

Gina reddened and made her way to the door. 'You're barking up the wrong tree with me, love. My lips are sealed, I never breathe a word.'

By the time they reached the shops, the accusations were forgotten. They were window-shopping, deciding where to go next, when Gina stopped in her tracks. 'Fuck me, look, that's Andria Bennet over there.'

Jenny followed Gina's eyes and there she was in her full glory, Miss Tits and Teeth herself. Andria Bennet stared back at Jenny, and anyone could see there was no love lost between them.

Gina rolled her shoulders back and sneered. 'All fur coat and no knickers. Look at her, Jen, who the hell does she think she is? If she says so much as a word out of line, I'll go over there and kick every one of them pearly white teeth out.'

But Jenny was in the zone. She never blinked, only locked eyes with Andria Bennet. In the past, they'd had their confrontations. Jenny had told her straight that if she ever disrespected her again, she would scratch her eyes out and rip every hair out of her scalp. But Andria was a big mouth and she wasn't scared of Jenny's threats. She gave as good as she got.

She was dressed in tight skinny jeans, a bright-pink vest top and candy-pink blazer. She did look good, Jenny could never take that away from her. Andria stood tall, flicked her long hair over her shoulder casually. Jenny approached her with caution, determined not to give ground, yet aware that this woman was a preying lioness and wouldn't think twice about jumping on her. Jenny inhaled, close enough to smell the sweet floral scent coming from her. Gina was close behind her and she eyeballed Andria as she walked past.

Andria couldn't keep her mouth shut. 'What the hell are you looking at?' Her voice dripped with contempt.

Jenny froze as she heard Gina stop behind her. Slowly, she turned. Gina didn't need anyone to back her up, she could hold her own, but Jenny moved closer to her side.

Gina replied to Andria. 'I'm looking at you, shag-bag.'

Andria's eyes opened wide. No one spoke to her like that. 'Piss off, Gina. We all know about you and what you get up to. So, move along before I let everyone know what a dirty slag you are.'

Gina was ready to pounce on her, but Jenny gripped her arm. 'Leave her to it, Gina. What goes around, comes around, and it'll only be a matter of time before she's back on universal credit and scrounging from anyone who will have her.'

'Oh, I knew it wouldn't be long before Mouth Almighty chirped in. So she has a voice now her husband is back home, does she? Nobody heard nothing from you for years, so climb back under whichever rock you crawled out from.'

Now it was Gina holding Jenny back. 'Leave her, Jen, she's just a gold-digging bitch. I can't wait for her to fall flat on her face.'

But Jenny couldn't leave it like this. No way was she letting a Bennet have the last word. 'Watch your back, love, because one of these days when you least expect it, I will be there waiting for you.'

'Do it now, come on, whatever you're going to do – don't let me stop you. Stop making threats unless you're ready to act on them.'

Jenny approached Andria with evil in her heart. She whispered hot breath into her ear. 'I could break you anytime I want to, remember that.'

Jenny stalked on with Gina behind her. Andria was clearly searching for a come-back, but it was too late. One–nil to Team Jenny. They walked into the store and ignored the few shoppers who were stood whispering around the front of the shop.

'What did you say to her, Jen? Her face dropped, whatever you whispered in her ear.' Gina knew Jenny wasn't easily riled – but when she was, she meant every word.

'Nothing much, just something for her to think about.' Jenny started looking at new outfits. There was no way she was letting that bitch mess her day up. She pulled out a slimline red dress and held it out in front of her. 'That's it, Gina. I'm starting to look after myself from now on. I'm sick of looking like a mourning widow. What has happened to me? I used to buy such bright clothes and be in the hairdresser's every bleeding week for a nice curly blow. Sack that. Today is the day when I'm back on top.'

Gina gawped at Jenny. 'I think you look fine as you are, love. Don't let that bleeding Andria Bennet get under your skin.'

'I'm not, it's just given me the wake-up call I needed. Right, let me start off with some new outfits and then I can buy new underwear. I'm going to feel new, inside and out.'

Gina smiled and, looking at tops near her, didn't reply. Jenny was a woman on a mission and maybe today she'd found her new hobby, her interest in life again. Project Jenny was launched.

Chapter Twelve

Rachel was busy at work, cleaning the front window while watching the rain drops trickle down the glass. It was therapeutic, and she loved listening to the rain on the windows, too. When she lay in bed at night, she would turn her TV down if there was a storm and close her eyes to listen to the rain smashing against her bedroom window. It was really pissing down now, shoppers running to get out of the wet.

The café door opened, and she turned to see who it was.

'Hiya, gorgeous, do you not answer your phone, or what?' Niall asked.

She smiled softly at him. 'It's in my coat pocket on silent. I don't have it on when I'm at work.'

'I popped in to see if you're still up for tonight. Date night?'

Rachel blushed and twiddled with her hair. 'Niall,' she whispered. 'I'm not sure we should be meeting up. If my brothers found out, my life would not be worth living. Honest, it's stressing me out and giving me bad anxiety.'

'I thought we agreed this, Rach? If you're bothered, we'll go somewhere out of the way, but I've told you before, I'm not arsed about your brothers finding out. It is what it is.'

'It's not only my brothers though, is it? My dad is home now, and that means it's not a cold war anymore – they'll be out for blood.'

Niall stared at her. There were plenty of girls begging for his attention and he could have slept with them all. But, as he looked deeper into her eyes, he realised he was smitten with her. She wasn't the same as other girls. Rachel had chosen him despite who he was – not because of it. She made him graft for her attention, gave him flutters in his heart, kept jumping into his thoughts every day.

'Be ready for half eight. I'm not ringing you again. I'll pick you up at the side of the Shiredale pub. Wear something nice and we'll go anywhere you want.'

Niall left and Rachel had to sit down before she fell down: she'd gone weak at the knees. She made sure nobody could see her. Was this love she was feeling?

The door went again and Dot hobbled into the café and just about made it to her seat. She didn't look well: her skin was grey and her eyes looked tired.

Rachel called from behind the counter. 'Dot, don't you move. I'll bring you a cup of tea over and your toast.'

Rachel made up the order and sat down next to Dot. Something wasn't right: the old dear looked worried to death. Rachel looked at her more closely and noticed she had a thick lip and bruises on her arm, deep-purple marks.

'Dot, what's happened to your mouth, it looks sore?'

The pensioner lifted her hand slowly and touched her lip with the tip of her finger. Her eyes clouded over as she spoke. 'I'm such a walking wreck these days, Rach, love. I walked into the door, blind as a bat I am sometimes, especially when I'm tired.'

Rachel examined the marks on her arms. 'And these, Dot? These look new.'

The older woman pulled her arm away and quickly yanked her brown cardigan down over her arm. 'I bruise so easily, love. Honest, I only have to nudge something, and I get a bruise. I'm old now and I suppose it won't get any better, will it?'

Rachel kept her voice low. 'I thought you had help at home. Did you say your son helps you?'

'Yes, he does. When he's free. But I like to do things for myself. I hate to be a burden on anyone.'

'Maybe you should let your son do more for you, Dot, especially if you're bumping into things and falling all the time. You might want to think about getting a carer in.'

'Oh, don't you worry about me, I'll be fine. Never mind anything else, give me an update on that handsome young man who you've had your eye on. I've just seen him leave.'

Rachel felt herself blush and couldn't help but smile. 'Dot, he's lovely. He's so kind and caring. But it's our families. My family would go mad if they knew I was dating a Bennet. My life would not be worth living.'

Dot smiled and whispered. 'So, don't tell them. You do what makes you happy, lovely. And if they find out, you can deal with that when it happens. But, for now, enjoy all the good times you're having.'

Rachel sighed. 'You always make it seem so easy, Dot. I wish I had your outlook on life, but I'm a worrier. Niall told me we're going out tonight for a meal and my stomach is churning knowing that I'll have to lie to my family and sneak about.'

Dot reached over and patted Rachel's hand. 'Let love guide you. Let your heart show you the way. If you follow your heart, you can't go far wrong.'

Rachel noticed Dot was trembling, colour draining from her face. She quickly reached over in time to stop her keeling over off her chair. 'Dot, Dot, come on, love, what's up?'

Her friend seemed to be having a funny turn. Rachel shouted to Katie to bring over a glass of cold water and tried to help Dot upright. They both sat with her until she got a bit of colour back in her skin. Rachel looked at Katie and then at Dot. 'Dot, I'm not letting you go home alone today. We can get a taxi and I'll make sure you get home safely. What's your address? Can you remember it?'

Dot got all flustered. 'Of course I bloody can. I'm not senile.' She sat thinking for a few seconds. '109 Crescent Road,' she said finally.

Katie agreed with Rachel. 'Yeah, you take her home. I'll be fine.'

The taxi was ordered, and Rachel sat with Dot until it arrived.

Dot sat in the taxi looking out of the window. She'd not spoken a single word. Her health wasn't good, and this funny turn had definitely left her shaken. Rachel paid the taxi as they reached their destination and helped Dorothy out of the car. She had to support her all the way up the garden path, as her legs seemed to be giving way. The garden was overgrown, and big weeds poked their ugly heads up through the grey flags leading up to the house.

'Where are your keys, Dot?'

The old woman sank her hand into her coat pocket, still shaking. 'Oh, they're here somewhere. Bloody hell, why can't I find them?' She was getting worked up.

'Shall I have a quick look, Dot? They've probably gone into the corner of your pocket. My keys do that all the time.' Rachel opened the pocket wider, and sank her hand in. 'Got them,' she said.

She walked a few paces towards the door with Dot at her side.

'It's the gold key, love, but be quiet when you go in. John might be asleep and he'll be annoyed if I wake him up.'

Rachel slid the long gold key into the lock and pushed the front door open. Dot hesitated, and it took a few seconds before she stepped into the house. Rachel tried to fix her face as she smelled the house for the first time. It was vile. As she walked into the living room, she was alarmed at the state of the place. There were clothes piled high, rubbish all over the floor. It was fair to say the house was a tip. This poor old woman had to live here every single day; it was a crying shame her son had let it get this way. Rachel moved some old newspapers from the armchair and helped Dot to sit down. She knelt in front of her and looked her deep in the eyes. 'Dot, I'm going to stay for a while and give it a quick clean around. No bloody wonder you keep falling with all this in your way.'

Dot's head drooped and a single fat tear ran down her cheek. She seemed ashamed of her living conditions.

'I'm not as fit as I used to be. I loved cleaning when I was younger. Everything was polished and in its place. Ask anyone, they always commented on how fresh my house smelled. And my brass always sparkled, you could see your face in it.'

Rachel realised how proud this woman was and she could see she was upset about how she'd been living. 'And, it will be again. Just let me take my coat off and I'll get cracking. It won't take me long. I'll put the TV on for you, should I?'

Dot shook her head. She was looking around the room anxiously. 'There is no electric or gas. John said he would go and get some when he woke up, but he must have forgotten.'

All was not what it seemed here, and Rachel had a gut feeling that this old lady was not only being neglected, but taken advantage of. How could she help without offending her? 'Alright, the corner shop is just down the road. If you give me your gas card and electric card I will nip down and get some.'

Dot's bottom lip started trembling. 'I have the cards, but I don't have any money. John cashes my pension, and he deals with all the bills and shopping. He told me I'm using too much gas putting the heating on all the time, but it's cold. What am I supposed to do, freeze?'

Rachel smelled a rat. She walked into the kitchen and her jaw nearly fell to the floor when she saw the state of the place. Pots piled up high, rubbish pouring out of the bin, and you couldn't even see the stove with all the grease spread across it. It was a wonder there weren't mice scavenging everywhere. She walked over to the fridge and opened the door. Exactly what she expected: empty. She checked the cupboards, and they were bare, too. She thought for a few seconds and went back into the living room. Dot cringed as she stepped back into the room. She clearly knew what Rachel had seen and she hung her head.

Rachel sucked in a large breath. She had to say something. 'Dot, John is not looking after you properly, is he? There is not a scrap of food in the kitchen.' Dot tried to stand up, but Rachel stopped her. 'Please don't feel embarrassed, Dot, this is not your fault. I'm going to the shop and when I come back, I will sort all this out.'

Dot choked up. 'You're such a kind soul, love. Thank you so much. Thank you from the bottom of my heart. But this is my problem, not yours.'

Rachel would hear none of it. She couldn't walk away and leave her like this. She wasted no time; she picked the house keys up and rammed them into her pocket. 'I will be back soon. I'll get some shopping too, and some teabags so you can have a nice cup of tea.'

And with that, Rachel was gone. Dot sat back in her armchair; she heard the floorboards creaking upstairs. Her hands gripped the sides of the armchair, fingers turning white. She looked up at the ceiling. More noises. After a few minutes, a man appeared at the living room door, hair stuck up, unshaven, and stinking of stale tobacco.

'Have you been talking to yourself again, old woman? How many times have I told you to be quiet when I'm sleeping? ' He walked into the room and flung the clothes from the sofa as he plonked down.

'John, we don't have any gas or electric, and you haven't been shopping, either.'

He bolted up from the sofa and grabbed her by the scruff of the neck, dragging her up. 'We don't have any bleeding money, do we?' His face was inches from hers. 'I've told you before about having the heating on all the fucking time. That's why we have no money, woman. And eat a bit less. How many times do I need to tell you?'

'John, I hardly eat anything. I go to the café every day for a piece of toast and a cuppa and the sweet girl who works there gives it me for nothing. So I don't spend any money.'

He was fuming, steam almost coming out of his ears. 'You're telling people I don't fucking feed you?' He never gave her time to reply, but slapped her on the cheek. 'Always looking for sympathy, aren't you?'

Dot was struggling to breathe. Bright-red claret trickled from her wrinkled nose. John stormed back over to the sofa.

He sat with his head in his hands and screamed at the top of his voice. 'I need a drink! Go next door and borrow a tenner from Norma. Tell her you've had a fall and need the cash to get some plasters or something. Go on, it's your fault I'm stressed out, so you can sort me out, you old bat.'

The poor old woman could hardly move, and her son sat watching her struggle. She had made it to the hallway, using the wall to steady herself, when the front door opened and Rachel walked in with two big bags of shopping.

'Bloody hell, Dot, what've you done? You're bleeding!' Rachel dropped the bags and ran to her side. 'What are you doing up? Go and sit down. Have you fallen again?'

The shadow of a man appeared at the living room door and growled at Rachel, 'Who the fuck are you? Get out of my house. How dare you come in here when you've not been invited.'

Rachel wasn't daft and it didn't take a rocket scientist to work out what had been going on. She marched to the kitchen and placed the bags on the floor, taking out her phone she sent a short text to Danny.

Need you. 106 Crescent Road. Please hurry!

Putting the phone in her pocket, she returned quickly to Dot and locked eyes with her son. He was a big, strapping bloke, and she knew she could never tackle him. She had to stall him, get Dot back into her armchair before she collapsed. 'I was invited – I'm a friend of your mam. Can you help me get her back into the chair, please? I know your mother from the café. She's had a funny turn today and I brought her home to make sure she got here safely. I'll be gone once she's settled.' She knew now wasn't the moment to call him out. She'd need Danny here for that.

He grunted, hands down the front of his pants, scratching his nuts. 'Meddling do-gooder bitch. Get her in the chair and piss off out of here.'

Rachel carried on gently steering Dot. It bought her the time she needed. 'Dot, come on, love, let's get you back in the living room.'

Dot never said a word. She staggered back to her seat with Rachel's help. John sneered. 'What are you waiting for now?'

Something snapped inside Rachel, and she faced him. Why should she walk away and pretend this was not happening? No, she wasn't going to leave it to Danny to sort. No way. She had morals. She had a conscience.

Her voice was shaky. 'I know exactly what is going on here, you idiot. You have neglected your mother. There is no gas or electric and there is no food in the house, yet you seem to have enough money to spend on beer. That pension is for your mam – not for you to piss away at the boozer. And look at the state of it in here. How can you let her live like this? You should be ashamed of yourself.' She went closer to him. What the hell was she doing? He could grab her, hurt her. 'You've been hitting her, I know it. Look at her, she's covered in bruises. I'm reporting you, you horrible bastard.'

Dot covered her eyes, the truth too much for her to bear. This was her own flesh and blood. John bolted up from the sofa and launched his fist at Rachel. But she was a tougher target than he was used to in Dot. Rachel didn't like to show it, but she could handle herself. She'd had many a playful fight with her brothers and they taught her from an early age how to kick arse, grapple, find someone's weak spot. She twisted his hand back and kicked him in the nuts with an almighty swing of her leg. John folded in two, eyes watering. And she didn't stop there, but launched her clenched fist into his head and his body. This big, dozy lump was getting his arse handed to him.

The front door swung open, and she could hear her brother's desperate voice. 'Rach, where are you? Rach, it's me, Danny, where are you?' He stormed into the front room and clocked his sister. He asked no questions, but skull-dragged the man into the front garden, away from the ladies. John was screaming and shouting the odds out, but Danny didn't stop to listen to a word. Rachel called the police and told them what had happened. Her breathing was rapid and her heart beating like a speeding train. Dot, meanwhile, couldn't stop sobbing her heart out.

'Rachel, please don't let anyone hurt John. He's got problems with the beer. He's a nice person when he's sober.'

Rachel sat by her side and consoled her. 'Everything is going to be fine now, Dot. I'm not leaving you. I'm staying here with you until all this is sorted out. You can go into a little flat and be looked after properly; you can't stay here. I promise you everything will be alright. John needs help, serious help.' Rachel was sobbing too now. What a cruel world where a man could treat his mother like this. She'd never dream of telling Dot but, as far as she was concerned, they should throw him in jail and let him rot there for ever for what he had put his poor mother through.

The police were prompt to respond to the call – although Danny made sure to clear off before they arrived. He was never keen to be around the Old Bill a moment longer than he had to be. But Rachel felt a surge of confidence when the patrol car arrived. For once, they weren't looking at her as a suspect but as a good citizen. As soon as she'd confirmed what she'd told them over the phone, it didn't take them long to look at Dot and her meagre home and see what had been going on. They phoned social services on the spot and it was agreed that Dot would go into a care home, temporarily at least. She refused to tell the police where her bruises had come from, so John likely wouldn't be charged with any offences but Rachel was glad they were at least taking him in for what they called 'some questions'. She hoped it would scare him off thinking he could ever take advantage of the poor woman again. As he watched his mother leaving the house with the police by her side, he screamed from the police car. 'Mam! Please, Mam, I'm so sorry, please don't leave me.'

Dot only looked at him once, then got into the back of another police car and bent her head. Rachel stayed with her and sat in the back of the car with her holding her hand.

Dot choked up, her words hard to get out. 'I'll never forget what you have done for me, sweetheart. One day I will pay you back for all your kindness.'

Rachel lifted a gentle smile at the pensioner. 'You don't have to do anything, Dot. I'm just glad you're safe now.'

Dot looked into Rachel's eyes. 'You truly are an angel in disguise. I'm so thankful for what you have done for me. I know it was only a piece of toast each day and a cup of tea, but it meant so much more to me. You kept me alive, love, and for that I will always be truly thankful.'

'Aw, stop it, Dot, you'll have me crying my eyes out again. I'm happy to help. There's too much trouble that goes on behind closed doors, too many people who never ask for help.'

Dorothy was welcomed into the care home by friendly staff members and, once they had sorted her medication out and bathed her wounds, she was shown to her room. Her eyes twinkled as she surveyed it – small, but neat and clean as a pin.

As she left, Rachel knew Dorothy would be happy there.

Her phone had been ringing endlessly and now she had time to look at her screen she could see over twenty missed calls from Niall. She made sure nobody was about, then sat on a wall outside the care home and returned the call. Niall answered quickly, clearly annoyed she hadn't answered earlier. He was not the kind of man people stood up.

Rachel said, 'See, I told you I was going to be hard work. You won't even believe what has happened today. Honest, it's been a nightmare.'

Niall listened to every detail of the day's events, amazed. 'Where are you now? Is it too late to see you? I can pick you up?'

Rachel glanced at her wristwatch. It was nine thirty. She'd not even been home yet and if it got any later her family would have the search party out for her, so she declined his offer. 'Can we rearrange, Niall? Today has knocked me for six. I feel sick in the pit of my stomach how somebody can treat their parent like that.'

Niall's disappointment was clear in his voice. 'What about tomorrow, then? Can we meet at seven o'clock tomorrow and I'll take you out on a proper romantic date? I know a lovely place up in the hills that does nice food, if you fancy it?'

Rachel agreed and after a few more minutes she ended the call. It sounded perfect – an evening out in the country-side where she could forget not only everything she'd seen today, but all the reasons why she and Niall shouldn't be seeing each other. Right now, though, all she wanted was to be at home in her bed. Rachel phoned Danny and told him she was ready to be picked up. Today had been a long day, a very long one indeed.

The minute Rachel was home she had to tell the whole family every single detail about her and Dot's ordeal. Charley sat up straight and was on the edge of his seat when his daughter told him how she tackled Dot's son.

'That's my girl,' he cheered as she described how she kicked her attacker in the nuts.

Jenny stroked her daughter's long hair. She was so proud of her that she had saved a woman from such abuse. Maybe she should have taken a leaf out of her book and done the same, kicked her husband right in the gonads when he first slapped her about. She looked over at Charley. 'Maybe she gets her strength from me?'

'My mam: the strongest woman I know,' Rachel said, backing Jenny even though she could see her brothers scoffing.

Jenny squeezed her daughter a little tighter and kissed the top of her head. These were lovely words and they made her feel warm inside. And, yes, the more she thought about it, she had tackled a lot in her life and here she was, still standing.

Charley's mobile rang. He checked the name on the screen and answered the call eagerly. 'Hello, Larry, what's up?'

They all watched Charley's expression as he listened to the call.

'Bastards, fucking bastards!' he yelled.

The call ended and he sat there, fists curling, jaw tensing. 'Some men have just been into Blossoms, nicked all the takings, and they've given the girls a few slaps, too. Mark my words, this is war, fucking war.' He jumped up from the armchair and paced around the front room, raking his fingers through his hair. 'I'll show them who they're messing with. Fuck me, why wasn't any of the boys there?'

Jenny looked over at Danny and she knew what was coming next.

'Dad, let's get over there. See what I mean? We should have sorted Archie out the moment you got out of pen. Now look what's happening. He's taking the piss, he thinks he's the main man.'

Charley's eyes bulged from their sockets. 'I'm only going to say this once, Son.' Danny held his ground as his old man stepped towards him. '*I* say when and where shit happens. Don't ever fucking question me again. Get back in your box and chill the fuck out before I put you back in it.'

Jenny moved Rachel from her side, ready to drag Charley from her son if he struck a blow. The red mist had come down, and he wouldn't have thought twice about giving his son a dig.

Paul looked away; this wasn't his beef and there was no way he wanted his dad screaming in *his* face, too.

Jenny mumbled, 'Don't do it, Son. Sit down, for crying out loud.'

Charley went nose to nose with Danny. 'You think you've got it in you, lad? You're eyeing up my seat, I know it. Now sit down before I knock you down.'

This was getting out of control; someone was going to get hurt.

'Christ!' Jenny roared. 'Like I need you lot fighting, you're bleeding *family*. Stop arguing. Get down to Blossoms and make sure those girls are alright. I bet they're trauma-tized. Everything else can bloody wait.' Part of her wanted to rush down there herself – she thought of the girls as her team, after all the years looking after the place. But she knew Charley didn't think of her as the boss, only the care-taker. She'd go and see the girls once it all died down to check they really were OK.

Danny backed away, but his eyes never left his old man. No, he was ready for him. The day was coming. The day when Charley could no longer dictate to his boys. They were men now, strong, ruthless men who could put Charley on his arse if they really meant it. He was older now, not as fit as he used to be. He grabbed his car-keys from the coffee table and shouted behind him, 'Come on then, what are you waiting for?'

Jenny breathed out as she heard the front door slamming shut.

Rachel shook her head. 'Mam, will they be alright? Dad's only just got out of jail. I don't want him getting into more trouble. Ever since I can remember, this family has had police knocking at our door. Don't tell me you're not sick of it, too?'

Jenny stuttered, 'I know, baby, it will get better, trust me. Your dad's getting older now and he can't keep living the life he does, can he? He'll end up six foot under if he carries on like he has been doing.'

Rachel sat down and Jenny plonked down next to her. 'Why does my dad hate the Bennets so much? It can't all be about that boxing match Dad always goes on about. Come on, you must know something more?'

Jenny sighed. She sat back in her seat and folded her arms tightly around her body. This question was always going to come, and now she was ready to answer it. Really ready: the truth had to come out. She played with her fingers. Her mouth was dry, and she reached over to the table to get a swig of her drink, wishing there was a double vodka in her coke. Taking a deep breath, she began. 'It's gone on for years. Pathetic, really. Archie was one of your dad's best friends when they were growing up. They were always jealous of each other, always in competition to be the best. You've heard about the trophies they fought for. But it wasn't only the boxing they were trying to win.'

Rachel had never heard this story before. She pulled her legs up to her chest. She was engrossed already and urged Jenny to continue.

'I met Archie when I was eighteen and we always got on. He made me laugh and that. We had some good times.'

Jenny closed her eyes slightly, the corners of her mouth rising as she reminisced about the days gone by. 'But then I met your dad. They were both good-looking men and, I'm not going to lie, I was attracted to both of them.'

Rachel winced. A love triangle, her mother the woman both men wanted. It was like a film, the kind that didn't usually have a happy ending.

'I kissed Archie one night after we'd all been out in the pub, but I was still single, we were never an item. To cut a long story short, soon after that kiss I got with your dad and Archie went nuts. You know what men are like. They had a bit of a fight. Well, a big fight. Honest, I've never seen anything like it. They were like two gladiators, neither of them giving up. It took eight men to split them up.' Jenny shuddered, remembering it. 'They were never the same after that. You couldn't put them in the same room together. One of them always had something to say to the other. And as they grew up, instead of fighting over me, it turned into a turf war. Petty stuff at first – trying to run the dealers on this street or that. But over the years, it grew from tit-for-tat to all-out war. I sometimes think I should have walked away from both of them that first night, saved everyone the heart-ache. Anyway, I've said enough. Past is past, and I shouldn't be telling you about stuff that happened years ago.'

'But why have you never told me this before?'

'What's done is done. What you can't change, you've got to live with,' Jenny said sternly.

Rachel was still eager to keep her mother talking. 'So, my dad hates the Bennets because of you?'

'Oh, your dad has collected plenty of reasons to hate Archie since then. But yes, he's still got a particular thing about me and Archie over the years. He accused me of having an affair with him when he was in jail. He needs to get over it. I married him, didn't I?'

Rachel looked at her mother more closely. She was still a pretty woman. She tried to imagine her back in the day and smiled. 'What did it feel like having two men fighting over you?'

Jenny chuckled and turned to face her. 'It was a lot of years ago, Rach, and it's caused a lot of trouble since. I wouldn't recommend it.'

'Do you think you made the right choice? Like, do you think Archie would have been the better choice? Any regrets?'

Jenny swallowed hard and fidgeted. 'I've never thought about it. I married your dad. That was that. No point in going over coulda woulda shoulda, is there?'

Rachel loved a love story, and this was one she would never forget. But the look on her mother's face told her not to keep digging.

Jenny said, 'This stays between us, OK? I don't need the aggro of your dad going on about it again. Like I said, it was a lot of years ago.'

'My lips are sealed, Mam. I'll never say a word, cross my heart and hope to die if I do.'

Jenny walked over to the living room window and pulled the blind back slightly. 'It's going to get worse before it gets any better, this grudge.' She rubbed her arms. 'And I can't take much more of this. This life, always waiting for the knock on the door to tell me someone has died or been injured. It's a wonder I'm not in a wooden box myself. My nerves can't take it any longer.'

Rachel was behind her now, hugging her, her chin dug into her shoulder. 'Everything will be alright, Mam. Don't worry.'

But worrying seemed to run in the family – for the women, at least. It kept Jenny awake at night, restless, always up at the window if she heard a noise. Wondering if someone was going to rush her house, tie them up, hurt her family. And, for what? Money, power, greed. Three things certain people could never get enough of. Where would it end? It did her head in.

She changed the subject. 'You've been going out a lot more than you usually do, and I reckon there's a boy involved. Don't even try and lie to me. I can see love written all over your face,' she giggled. 'Come on, let's grab a brew and you can tell me all about it. The lads will be gone for ages now, so we may as well have a bit of a girlie night instead of sat here worrying. I know it's late but what's the point in going to bed to lie there staring into space?'

Rachel checked the clock on the wall. It was nearly half past twelve. She would usually be tucked up in bed at this time, but her mother was stressed out and she couldn't leave her on her jacks, could she? She'd forgotten what life was like with her dad at home. Something was always kicking off. Her mum had tried to protect her from it when she was younger, but she was a grown woman now and would rather wait up to find out what had happened when the men got home. The trouble was, if her mam wanted to know who she was seeing, telling the truth would be adding fuel to the fire. She didn't want to make things worse. She'd have to tread carefully.

She said, 'Right, let me go and shove my pyjamas on then. You brew up and I'll be down in five.'

Rachel left the room and Jenny went into the kitchen. A cup of tea was like a miracle cure sometimes and, god knows, this was a family in need of a miracle right now.

Back downstairs, Rachel sipped her mug of tea. It was only a matter of time before her mother started to quiz her again about her love life. So, before she asked, Rachel grabbed the bull by the horns and began the conversation. 'You're right, Mam. I've met someone, he's really nice.'

Jenny pulled her feet underneath her bum and snuggled into the sofa. They'd not had a mother-daughter chat like this for what seemed like forever. What with Charley coming home, and all the stress she was under, she never found the time. But they were here now and that was all that mattered.

'So, does this guy have name?'

Rachel nibbled the side of her fingernail and, although she hated lying to her mother, she had to. 'He's called Jack. He comes into the café and I've fancied him for ages.'

'Have you been on dates with him?'

Rachel fluttered her eyelashes. 'Yes, we've been out on a few dates. He's so easy to talk to. I lose track of time when I'm with him.'

'Is it serious? Are you having sex?'

This was not the question Rachel was expecting. She felt herself blush. 'Wow, Mam, you can't be asking me things like that. I've only just met him. When I have sex, I want it to be special, not in some back alley or on the back seat of a car.'

Jenny raised her eyebrows and smirked. 'So does he give you butterflies when you see him? And when you kiss him do your knees feel like they're going to give way?'

'Yes! How do you know that?'

Jenny burst out laughing. 'You've got it bad, girl. Trust me, when that happens, you're on your way to falling for this lad, hook line and sinker.'

'Do you mean I'm falling in love?'

'Yep, darling, that's what it sounds like to me.'

'Is that how you feel when you kiss Dad?'

Now it was Jenny's turn to be lost for words. She reached over and grabbed her fags. 'We've been together for years, me and your dad, love, and things like that fade. The years he's been in jail, and the life he chose to lead, play a big part, too. That's why when you're younger you should relish all the kisses you have, because once you're married that all goes downhill. They forget how to appreciate you, tell you they love you, show they care.'

Rachel sensed her mother wasn't having the best time right now. 'But, you still love each other, don't you?'

And there it was again, that pause, that moment when Jenny wasn't sure how to answer the question. 'Me and your dad have been through the mill lately, love. He's hard work and you know what he's like when anything is not going to plan. I'm a bleeding skivvy in his eyes, someone to pick up after him, wash his clothes, and cook his meals.'

'You should tell him how you feel, give him chance to make it right. Mam, you do still love him though, don't you?'

Jenny could hear the desperation in her daughter's voice. 'Stop bloody worrying about me and your dad, we're fine. I'm asking you about your relationship. How have we got talking about mine?' Jenny held her emotions back. 'When can I meet this lad, then?'

Rachel panicked. 'Not yet. It's early days. Give it a few more weeks and then I'll think about it. Imagine Danny and Paul's faces if I brought a lad back here. No, I'm not ready for that yet. He'd go under, meeting those two idiots.'

Jenny agreed. She knew her sons of old. Given the chance, they would interrogate Rachel's new boyfriend for hours before they let him go anywhere near her. For now, this boy would have to stay under the radar: another secret in a family full of them.

Chapter Thirteen

Charley stormed up the stairs at Blossoms, his boys close behind him, taking two stairs at a time, red in the face, burning up with rage. He booted the door open and looked about, ready for action.

'Where the hell is everyone?' he hollered.

Paige came out from a room to the right of him, hysterical. It took her several minutes to calm down enough to spit some words out. 'This is not good. We pay you lot good money to look after us, and look at the state of me now. I'll be gone from here if this carries on. The job's not worth dying for.' She pulled her silken dressing gown up her arm to reveal big bruises, purple and black. 'He was a right cheeky prick, too. Cocky, he was, full of himself. Look at my neck where he fucking bit me. The guy wants chopping up for what he's done to me and the others. Let alone nicking the take.'

Charley was listening, digesting everything she said. Danny and Paul sat down on the sofa behind him.

Paige continued. 'The other girls are covered in marks, too. There was about six of them. He went straight for me. He didn't give me chance to say a word. 'Give me the fucking money before I smash those lovely white teeth out,' he screamed at me. A big bastard he was, otherwise I'd have taken him out myself. He's lucky I never scratched his eyes out.'

Larry came sprinting into the room. He clocked Charley and hung his head. He should have been here, should have been protecting these girls.

Charley growled, 'Where the fuck was you, Larry? You know the score. I thought I could trust you?'

Larry knew he was up shit street and cringed as he spoke. 'The mrs had her family around for something to eat and I got carried away. I'm not gonna lie, I had a few scoops and lost track of time. You know me, mate, I'm always here on time, usually. I let things slip tonight, I hold my hands up, I should have been here.'

Charley walked over to a chair and sat down. 'Paige, go and get the girls. I want to speak with each of them.'

She rushed out of the room to follow his orders.

'Charley, it must have been somebody close, because who knew that I wasn't here?' said Larry. 'They must have been watching me. Someone has bubbled on me, I know it.'

'No use crying over spilt milk, is there? You fucked up, so own your shit and we can move on. I can't believe it, on my life. Who the fuck do these arseholes think they are playing with? Let's talk to the girls, find out more details, and then we'll be booming some doors in. Nobody has Charley Johnson over, fucking nobody.' He gave a roar from the pit of his stomach and smashed his clenched fist into the middle of his chest.

Danny wasn't impressed. These were just words again. Where were the actions everybody was waiting for? Had the old man lost his bottle?

Charley talked to the girls and apologised for letting them down. There were some new girls here who he'd never met before, and he took a shine to one of them. Jackie. In her early thirties, she had a plump figure complete with the big rack he liked on his women. He watched her leave the room and followed her. The corridor was dimly lit and there were six doors along the hallway. He opened the door at the end and looked around the room. Jenny had done well giving this place a makeover. Everything looked tip-top, he had to say. In the middle of the room was a king-sized bed and lots of candles were placed on shelves around it. They must be scented because you could smell flowers as soon as you walked into the room.

Charley eyed up Jackie. 'So, tell me a bit more about yourself. I've not met you before, but I bet you know plenty about me, even if my wife has been managing things for a bit.'

Jackie sat on the edge of the bed and patted the spot next to her, inviting Charley to join her. 'I've been here over six months now. Things have been great until tonight. Apart from the odd dodgy punter, I've enjoyed working here. Jenny's done a good job of looking after us.'

Charley moved towards the bed and sat down, never taking his eyes from her. As attractive as she was, he never trusted people he'd just met. Was she a double-agent, or what? He wasn't sure. 'So, who told you about our little set-up here?'

Jackie reached over to a bottle of vodka and poured two glasses. That's what she did when clients were nervous, she gave them something to calm them down. She passed one to Charley. 'If you think I set this up, then I'll pack my shit up now and I'll be gone in a jiffy. I've been in this game for a long time and know not to shit on my own doorstep. The men who came here were after the money. They knew what they were looking for and I think, because a few of us girls got gobby, that's why they manhandled us. Proper lowlifes to hit a woman, don't you think?'

Charley took a large gulp from his drink and held it in a tight grip. 'Where you from, Jackie?'

'Oldham originally, but I moved down to Moston about a year ago.'

'And what's your story? Why have you ended up doing what you're doing?'

Jackie frowned. Who did this guy think he was, bleeding Jeremy Kyle? There was no way she was going into her private life. She was here to do a job – nothing more, nothing less – and if this guy didn't like it, he could kiss my arse, she'd be gone. 'Listen, I do my job and I go home. You don't need to know anything more about me. What are you, a bleeding therapist?'

Charley cracked a smile. This woman had nerve, and a big gob she wasn't shy of opening. 'I was only asking, no need to bite my head off. I think it's nice sometimes to find out a bit about the girls who work for me, that's all.'

Jackie folded her arms across her chest. 'I work for myself, love; nobody owns me. I pay my fees, the same as the other girls, so don't think you're doing me any favours.'

Charley chuckled and swigged his drink. 'You've got some attitude on you. Have you got a fella at home waiting for you? Or is that something I'm not supposed to ask, either?' He rolled his eyes.

Jackie smirked and started to let her guard down. 'Nope. Single and free, so to speak. Having a boyfriend is hard work when you do what I do. They get jealous, or they think they can sponge from you and spend your hard-earned cash. Let's say I've been there, done that and worn the t-shirt.'

'You don't look like the type of woman who would let any man walk all over you?'

'I never said I gave them any money or listened to them, did I? I said that's what they wanted. Men are too much hard work. Plus, I'm out all night, so what man is going to wait at home for me, knowing I'm doing what I'm doing?'

'Well this is your chance to get revenge. Tell me more about these men who came here. Old, young? Anything about them that might be of use to me – tattoos, accents, something identifiable?'

Jackie sat thinking and shook her head, cool as a cucumber. 'No, I told you everything before. I just want a safe place to work, Charley. No grief, no dibble, you know the script.'

'And that's what you will get from now on. Like I said, I've been off the scene for a while, but now I'm back you can rest assured this won't be happening again.'

'And what about the money they took? Surely you're not expecting us girls to go without, are you? I think it's only right we should get the money we earned.'

Charley smiled. She was ballsy, he had to say. 'Yes, Jackie, I'll throw some money into the pot for the girls.'

She purred, looking at her long red nails, 'You're not as bad as they make out, are you, Charley Johnson?'

He drank in the compliment. 'Whatever you have heard is probably a load of crap. I don't take shit, but I do look after the people who look after me, so bear that in mind for the future.'

She moved in closer, and he could feel the warmth of her before she planted a soft, wet kiss on his cheek. 'And I look after the men who look after me.'

Charley was taken aback and stood up quickly. He never usually said no to a freebie, but he had bigger things to sort out. He left without saying goodbye.

He walked back into the reception, feeling flustered, still finding it hard to accept that his gaff had been rinsed. 'Come on, we're out of here. Paige!' he shouted. 'Larry will sort out the money that was taken, for the girls. He'll be here every night from now on. On time, won't you, Larry. And the money will come out of his pocket, so you all know how sorry he is. His mistake, so he can fix it. That's right, isn't it, big man?'

Larry walked over to Charley with his hand held out, clearly relieved he was going to be paying for his mistake in cash rather than blood. 'Yeah, I'll sort it, pal. This won't happen again, trust me.'

'It won't happen again, Larry, because if it does I'll be knocking on your front door and it won't be to join the fucking family for something to eat, you get me?'

The message was loud and clear and understood. Charley left with his sons, one job done.

The three of them sat in the car and not a word was spoken until they hit the main road. Paul was in the back. He leaned in between the front seats looking at Danny, who was driving, in the rear-view mirror. 'So, what's the score, Pops? Are we sitting pretty or are we going to do something about it?'

Charley didn't turn around to face him, he just stared out of the window. 'For fuck's sake. Like I need you two pressurising me. Get off my back and wait.'

Danny kept driving, saying nothing.

When they pulled up outside their house, Charley didn't have much to say, either. He opened the car door. 'See you two later. And remember, I run the show around here. Nothing happens until I say so.'

Paul jumped out from the back of the car and into the passenger seat. He shot a look at his old man walking away and turned to Danny. 'What's up with your kite, then? You've hardly said a word.'

Danny sneered over at his brother and his grip on the steering wheel tightened. 'Does he think we're still kids? The guy is past it. He has no balls anymore. I remember the day when he would have been round at the Bennets', dragging the fuckers out of bed. Go on, tell me you don't think the same?'

Paul had always been a people-pleaser and so he nodded. He never voiced his opinion because, if he did, Danny would drag his name into the mix when he was discussing it with anyone.

Danny pulled off with speed. 'It's time I started to make my own name around here and stopped living in the shadow of his. I can do what the fuck I want. The man has been in jail for like forever and it's us two who have been keeping things ticking over, not him. I think we should get the lads together and do our own thing. If we don't do it now, we'll always only be Charley Johnson's sons, won't we?'

Paul was happy to take whichever option sounded like the least work. 'Dad's still finding his feet, Dan. Give him some time to get his head around things, then he'll be back in the game.'

'Time! Do you think we have time to sit about letting the Bennets take the piss out of us? We are up and coming, mate, and we don't need some fucking pensioner, some has-been, calling the shots for us.'

Rachel and Jenny were sitting on the sofa when Charley walked into the front room. It was late and they were watching the end of *The Greatest Showman*. It was Rachel's favourite film and whenever she got the chance she would put it on.

Jenny was singing along and Charley sneered at her as he sat down. Here she was, singing her head off, whilst his world was falling apart around him, no respect.

Her dad wasn't happy. Rachel picked up on the mood, stood up and stretched her arms over her head. 'Right, I'm off. It's well past my bedtime.' She walked over to her dad and pecked him on the cheek. 'Night, Dad.' There was no way she was asking what had gone on at Blossoms: her head couldn't deal with any more stress. Her mum would tell her once things had calmed down. She said goodnight to her mam and went upstairs.

Jenny was tired. She straightened the cushions behind her as she stood up. Every night she would plump up the cushions and put them neatly back on the sofa. God knows why: nobody would see them. She could feel his eyes burning into her. He coughed and she turned to him.

'What's with all the fucking singing, when you know the trouble that's been happening tonight?'

'Oh, Charley, shut up, will you. I watched a film with Rachel and sang a bloody song, it's not the end of the world, is it?'

She turned away and was instantly dragged to the floor. It all happened so fast. He stood over her and pounded his fist into her stomach. Then he booted her.

'How dare you be happy and take the piss out of me when I'm feeling like this? You're my wife and you should stand by me. It's like you get a kick out of seeing me fall flat on my face. Do you? Do you get some kind of a thrill seeing me fail?' He dragged her up from the floor and held her by her face.

She wriggled free. 'Take your hands off me. You prom-ised me, Charley, you'd not lay a finger on me again. You was the one who said it, not me. All lies. Look at you. Nothing's changed, has it?' Normally she tried to calm him down, stroke his ego. But she was through with that.

He pushed her back up against the wall, nose to nose with her. 'Keep that voice down. If I have to tell you again, I'll make sure you don't fucking speak again. Quiet.' Then he whispered into her ear cold, chilling words that made the hairs on the back of her neck stand on end. 'Get upstairs and wait for me on the bed. If you try any funny business, you know what will happen.' He bit her cheek, just enough to make her squeal.

Her chest was rising and falling frantically, and her heartbeat had doubled. But years of frustration came bubbling to the surface. A woman can only take so much, and she'd reached her limits. She looked him straight in the eye. 'I'll go upstairs, Charley, but if you come within an inch of me, I'll stick a knife so deep inside you it will take the paramedics two weeks to find it.'

Charley swallowed hard and brushed her comment off. She'd never have the guts to do something like that to him. Or would she? 'Fuck off to bed. If I want to come and get in with you, I will. Have you been sleeping with some other cunt while I've been locked up? Is that it – you want rid of me because you've already got the next bloke lined up?'

'Always the same story with you, Charley. Paranoid. You need to go and see a doctor, because you're not right in the bleeding head. Are you sure it's not you who's been fooling around? The best form of defence is attack. Yeah, that wouldn't surprise me one little bit.' She made her way to the door, but couldn't resist one last pop. 'Maybe that's why you're having trouble down there.' She shot her eyes to his crotch. 'Guilty conscience.' After that, she scarpered upstairs.

Jenny was in pain, marks already appearing on her lower stomach, but she held herself together until the bedroom door was shut. Tears streamed down her face as she started to get undressed. Every movement caused her to wince. She sat on the edge of the bed, listening. Nothing. Not a sound from downstairs. Tonight, she would lie awake, ready for him, ready to end her misery if he came for her again. There was a baseball bat under her side of the bed and, finally, she wasn't afraid to use it if she needed to. She looked outside at the full moon, so still and pure.

'No more,' she sobbed. 'No fucking more.'

Chapter Fourteen

Danny sat with Tomo and Marzy, and the rest of his boys, in their dingy lock-up. He'd known most of them since school, and he would have trusted them with his life. Brothers in arms and all that. Tomo was a bit over-weight but had the biggest chocolate-brown eyes that always got the girls. He was built, though you couldn't tell if he worked out in the gym or had been on the steroids, with his big shoulders and bulging biceps. A lot of guys took that road nowadays. They popped pills or injected steroids into their bodies to save hours pumping iron. They didn't realise the side-effects of what they were pumping into their bodies. Marzy, on the other hand, looked like he could have done with a few pans of potato hash shoved down his neck. If he turned sideways, he'd be reported missing. He was scrawny and thin, cheekbones visible. He wasn't as well dressed as Tomo either. He was more the rough-and-ready type, but attractive in his own way. Not every woman wanted a man who took longer getting ready than they did. Both Tomo and Marzy had been to jail in the past, served a few years each. Water off a duck's back, it was pretty standard for where they'd grown up. They thought they knew it all, but they'd come unstuck a right few times, wet behind the ears. They'd come out of jail with even more criminal knowledge than they went in with and a far bigger circle of underworld friends. That was the way it worked round here: you went in the chokey not knowing inmates from other areas and, by the time you left, your network had doubled. Even if they'd wanted to go straight, they had precious little chance when there was always someone offering them some dodgy deal to get involved in.

Danny started to build a spliff. He'd smoked weed since he was a teenager, showing off at first, proving to all the other kids he could get the stuff to get them stoned.

'I'm ready to take it all, lads,' Danny told the little gang now. 'No more waiting around for orders from my old man. Come on, let's put our cards on the table here and be honest. Archie is an old-timer, just like my old man is. No disrespect to my dad, but I say what I see: he's past it. He should take up fishing or something, chill out and let the big boys run shit around here now.' He paused to think. 'Yeah, listen. The only thing that's stopping us running things around here are Archie's muppet sons and a few heavies. We can sort that, can't we?'

Tomo smirked and lit up the spliff he'd taken from Danny. 'I'm ready, mate. We have pure heads that back us around here and, if we do a head count, we'll take the Bennets down in one rush. We pick the family off and it's easy. There's five brothers. We can start with the youngest one, Niall. One by one, we take them down. I've seen that Niall knocking about loads of times and he is an easy target. It will be like taking candy from a baby.'

Marzy nodded and twisted his fingers like he was wringing a chicken's neck. 'Leave that runt to me. We'll bang him up here in the lock-up for a few days and kick the fucking living daylights out of him. Let's see how big his brothers are when their baby brother is being fed through a fucking tube.'

Danny took the zoot back from Tomo and sucked hard on it. 'Yeah, I knew you'd see the sense in backing me. Let's get our boys in order and we'll start by taking Niall Bennet down as a warning to the rest of them. I don't want our Paul knowing anything about this, either. We all know he's a gobshite, and he'll spill the beans to my dad, given half the chance.' He clapped his hands together. 'This is our graft. Together we'll put our name on the map and show these chancers around here who we really are. I've stayed in my old man's shadow for long enough, and now it's time to make my own name. I want everyone to know who Danny Johnson is, fucking everyone.'

'Nice one,' Marzy punched his clenched fist into the air. Tomo sat thinking, looking around the lock-up, planning already. They'd had this place for a few years now and only a handful of people knew where it was. They always kept it on the low. They hid things here, brought people here for secret meetings and, every now and then, beat the living daylight out of some poor soul who had crossed them. If you looked close enough you could still see splashes of red, now turned a rusty brown, sprayed up the grey walls.

Tomo said, 'Let's take the warehouse at the bottom of Factory Lane, too. We know they've got a grow going on in there. A right few quid to be earned. Then they'll know we're serious. Hit them in the wallet *and* hit them where it hurts with their little brother. He's a cocky wanker, that Niall is. I've seen him in clubs thinking he's the main man with the ladies. I'll show that pretty boy.'

The group sat laughing and started getting stoned. Today was a chill day, and all Danny wanted to do was sit back and put his feet up while he could. The shit was going to hit the fan soon and he needed to be ready. At last, he would sit on the throne and rule the area. Danny Johnson was the main man now.

Jenny sat at the kitchen table the following morning, drinking a cup of coffee, biding her time. Charley was in the living room, and she could hear him stirring. She knew what was coming next, knew he would be at her side, telling her how sorry he was. She knew the ropes well, knew how he worked. It would be the same as it had always been. He'd be pathetic, grovelling, making her think he was upset, that he was the victim yet again.

The kitchen door slowly opened, and it seemed like his body blocked out all the sunlight. She kept her head down, determined not to look at him. Her stomach churned. She heard the chair scraping on the white marble floor. He was by her side now. She could smell his stale tobacco breath. She reached over and popped a single cigarette from the packet. Her eyes were still down as she lit her fag. She put the lighter back next to the packet and took a long, deep drag of her cigarette.

His voice was low. 'I remember when you used to light mine up, too. You used to do a lot of things for me, Jenny, that you don't do anymore. Do you hate me that much? Go on, tell me. If you don't love me anymore, put me out of my misery and stop all this torment you're putting me through. My head can't take much more. Do you know how it feels to not know if your wife is cheating on you?'

There he was again, making himself out as the victim. He had no remorse for the beating he'd given her the night before, wasn't bothered that her body was covered in bruises. He was always telling her it was her fault. She refused to reply to him, not a word. She tried to pretend he wasn't there sat next to her. Rachel came into the kitchen, rushing about like she did every morning.

'Mam, have you seen my white top? The one from River Island with the gold writing on?'

Jenny shook her head. Even talking was causing her pain. She held her palm on the side of her stomach as she answered. 'No, love. Try the washing pile in the box-room.' The box-room was what Jenny liked to think of as her room. She liked to iron in there with her music on. She loved listening to music and almost every day she would have the radio on, listening to her local station, Key 103. The presenters made her smile, made her feel like they were in the room with her. Sometimes she would answer them back when they were talking, tell them how she felt.

But right now, she wasn't going to breathe a word about the pain she was in. She could see Rachel was concerned, though. She must be slacking: she never normally let her kids see she was injured. Over the years, she'd become a dab-hand at hiding her injuries.

'Mam, what's up? Are you alright?'

Jenny moved her hand away from her waist and tried to sit up straight, bring a smile to her face, show her daughter she was fine. She knew Charley was watching her, making sure she never told Rachel the truth and exposed him as a wife-beater and bully. 'Yes, I had a sharp pain in my side, that's all. It's gone now.'

That was enough for her daughter to go about her business. Rachel smiled at her father and rushed out of the room. Charley moved in closer and licked his lips. She knew what was coming; it always happened this way.

'I'm sorry, Jen, but you know how I get when I think you don't care about me anymore. I see red, I can't help it. I'm sorry, OK? Let's move on from it. Don't be kicking the arse out of this for days like you always do. Let's put it to bed and move on. I can't be doing with any more drama. Fuck me, don't you think I deserve a quiet life after getting out of bleeding jail? Come on, woman, think about it.'

Like he always did, he thought he could sweep it under the carpet and pretend it never happened. But Jenny didn't challenge him, she only sat there smoking, like he wasn't there. She had decisions to make.

'So, are you not saying anything back? I've put my heart on the table here and you're fucking with my head again, leaving me in the lurch. Are you playing head games, Jen? Because, trust me, it won't end well for you if you are.'

A chill passed through her body like somebody had walked over her grave. She swallowed hard. She had two options here today: one, to keep silent, or two, to speak to him and simply crack on with her life. He was waiting, tapping his fingers rapidly on the table. She stubbed her fag out in the ashtray and lifted her eyes to the ceiling. 'Like I said, keep away from me. I don't know who you think you are, hitting me like that. Maybe I should go down the boozer and tell all your boys how Charley Johnson treats his wife. What would they think then, eh? You're just like your father was, Charley, a bloody wife-beater.'

Her words hit him hard. She knew he hated being compared to his old man. He dragged her closer to him, desperately making sure she looked into his eyes. 'Carry on, Jenny, and I'll end you. I'm nothing like my dad was. You're only saying that to hurt me, aren't you?'

She could see the large vein at the side of his neck bulging through his skin. She pulled away and stood up, looking at him for a few seconds longer than she needed to.

He knew she meant every word she'd said, and he dropped his head into his hands. 'Look what you're doing to me, Jen. You're going to walk away from me and say nothing more? Do you wonder why I snap, woman?'

She was treading on eggshells and, normally, she kept her mouth shut to save any further abuse, but today she stood up to him. Strength grew from within, and she was no longer scared of what he could do to her. 'It's always about you, isn't it? All of my life I've jumped to your tune and done whatever you told me to. But, let me tell you something for nothing.' She placed her hands on her hips and bent slightly towards him. 'You can't hurt me anymore. I'm immune to it, Charley. I died years ago, if the truth is being told here today, so your threats of putting me six foot under don't wash with me now. Death would be a treat to me instead of having to endure this fucked-up life I lead with you. You do you, Charley, and I'll do me. Keep your hands off me and everything will be fine. But if you ever, *ever*, lay one finger on me again, I'll ring the police and I'll tell them what a low-life bastard you really are.'

She was gone before Charley could say anything back at her. He slammed his clenched fist into the kitchen table and screamed like a wounded animal. 'Jenny, get your arse back here now! Don't make me come and get you, woman!'

Rachel came running into the kitchen. 'Dad, what on earth is going on? Why are you shouting like that?'

He fixed his face, forcing a small smile. 'Nothing, princess. It's just your mother moaning at me again. She must be due on her monthlies.'

Rachel studied her father, then went to the sink to get a drink of water. She reached for a glass from the draining board. 'Dad, is everything alright with you and my mam? Since you've been home, she's been really quiet.'

There was no way he was telling her the truth. He walked up behind her, needing to hide the ugly truth. 'It's been hard for your mam whilst I've been away. Sometimes I don't realise that. Don't you worry, my girl. I'll go out today and get her some flowers and chocolates to cheer her up. She'll be fine in a bit, don't you worry about it.'

Rachel filled her glass and turned to face her dad. 'I'm going to call at the care home to see Dot today. I worry about her. How a man can raise his hand to a woman is something I can't get my head around.'

Did his daughter know he'd given her mother a few backhanders? 'You be careful, love. It was great what you did for that old lady, but it could have been a different story if that bloody idiot had got his hands on you.'

Rachel washed her glass out and headed to the door. 'It's a good job I've got your genes, then,' she chuckled.

Chapter Fifteen

Niall Bennet sat in his car waiting for Rachel. She was late. He flicked through his playlist and found a tune he liked. He loved the artist Dave and put on 'Professor', one of his favourite tracks. He turned it up to get the bass line pumping through the speakers. His was a nice motor, a snazzy whip. A black Golf GTI was the car most lads on the estate would have given a kidney to own. The interior was tip-top, too. It smelt like vanilla, sweet and clean. Niall admired himself in the rear-view mirror. He pushed his hair to the side with a quick flick of his wrist. The passenger door opened unexpectedly and made him jump. And there she was, flushed and out of breath and absolutely stunning.

'I'm so sorry I'm late. I went to see Dot and she kept me talking. I couldn't get away. I felt so bad leaving her. The poor woman only has me visiting her. Her son is not allowed near her after what he's done to her. And she didn't look that good. You know when you can just tell someone is ill? Her eyes looked cloudy and she was coughing all the time.'

She got in and clicked her seatbelt into the socket.

'It's a good job I've not booked anywhere yet. I thought you'd carted me. I was going to get off,' Niall smiled.

She playfully punched him in the arm. 'Shurrup. I'm here now. Where are we going?'

Niall flicked the engine over and grinned as he pulled out from the quiet side-street. Rachel insisted they met in quiet places, away from prying eyes, and a part of him loved the mystery. He was her secret and she seemed to want to keep it like that. He wasn't afraid of her family, but he didn't want to rush into telling anyone about them. 'I've booked us a surprise. Can you stay out for the night?'

Rachel gulped. 'What do you mean?'

'I'm taking us to a posh hotel in Cheshire for the night. We're out of the way there and we can have a proper date night without you looking over your shoulder all the time.'

They'd been seeing each other for a while now, and she'd known this day would come. They'd played around but, up to now, she'd not had sex with him. But she found herself grinning back at him. She knew she shouldn't be *talking* to a Bennet, let alone contemplating spending the night with him, but this was what she'd always wanted – the big romance.

Niall pulled onto the main road and asked her again. 'So, are we going to the hotel?'

'Yeah, erm, yes,' she replied, trying to be confident. She pulled out her mobile phone and texted Hannah:

> I'm staying at yours tonight if anyone asks. Thx a million.

She pressed the send button and wrote another message, this time to her mother:

> I'm going to stay over at Hannah's tonight mam, we're having a girly night. Love u see u tomorrow

The messages were sent. A message alert came back almost straight away from Hannah:

> Where are you staying really?

Rachel's fingers moved with speed, replying, making sure Niall couldn't see her screen:

> Hotel with Niall. Cheshire. Posh place.

Another reply from her friend with several aubergine emojis in a line and a laughing face emoji. Rachel sent a red love-heart emoji back to her and rammed her mobile phone in her jacket pocket. Niall was singing his head off, really into the tune. Rachel smiled as she watched him. This guy was more than a pretty face: he had talent.

Rachel whistled as they reached the hotel. This was no budget chain joint. It was not like anywhere she'd stayed before. Bright-yellow lights lit up the frontage as they walked inside the double doors. She twiddled her hair nervously and followed Niall to the reception desk.

'Can I book your best room for the night, please, for myself and my beautiful girlfriend?' He grinned.

The receptionist smiled as she checked the computer for vacant rooms. 'We have the Presidential Suite available?'

Niall winked at Rachel and pulled out his credit card. 'Smashing, bang it on that for me. Can I have a bottle of champers sent up, too?'

'I will organise that for you now, sir. Would you like to order any room service?'

Rachel didn't know what to say. Her bank balance would never have covered anything in this place. But Niall looked at ease here. He bent over the wooden desk, umming and ahhing at the menu. 'We'll phone down later, if that's alright.'

'Of course. Here is your door card. If you need anything else, just call me.'

Rachel clocked the receptionist's envious glance as they left the lobby. She walked behind Niall, apprehensive of stepping into the lift. This was it, there were no excuses tonight. She was going to spend the night with Niall Bennet.

Niall jumped onto the bed and rolled about. 'Come on, Rach, get on here with me. This bed is epic.'

She kicked her shoes off and sat on the edge of the bed, nervous. She slowly pulled her legs on and sat up straight like she had a board up her back. The room was top-notch and the bed was the biggest she'd ever seen. It could have fitted six people in it.

Niall looked into her eyes. 'You can relax, I'm not going to hurt you.'

'I'm not nervous, I'm just digesting this place. It's beautiful.'

'Yeah, you are. You're melting. Come on, admit it: I make you nervous.'

What would have sounded arrogant from someone else sounded sweet from Niall. She laughed and pushed him playfully. This guy was quick. He saw his opportunity and rolled onto her. He looked deep into her eyes, no words, just staring deep into her eyes. The two of them started to kiss, a long, passionate kiss. This was the moment she'd been waiting for. But she needed to go into the bathroom, check she was ready, make sure she was fresh.

She wriggled free. 'Just let me nip for a wee.' She was gone before he had chance to say anything. She locked the door and stared into the mirror facing her, trying to take on board what was happening. She was here now and she needed to calm down. She ran her fingers through her hair and scanned the bathroom. There were lots of complimentary products at the side of the sink. Rose petals they smelled like, fresh and inviting. She wasted no time freshening up. One, two, three, she was ready.

She unlocked the door and stepped back into the bedroom. Her eyes met his as she made her way back to the bed. This time she made the first move and kissed him. His fingers ran through her hair, and she was lost in the moment. Slowly, Niall slid his hand up her top, touching her cold flesh. This was getting intense. Their two bodies connected, and she was ready for more.

He looked deep into her eyes, then his head disappeared between her legs and whatever he was doing with his tongue made her toes curl in pleasure. She threw her head back and arched her back. He was inside her now. Niall held her hands over her head and kissed every inch of her breasts. It was all about her now. She was in heaven, nothing mattered any more, any inhibitions had gone through the window. He was nearly reaching orgasm, his rhythm doubled, and Rachel was on the verge of climaxing too. This was a night she would remember forever.

Niall remained on top of her, stroking her face, kissing her neck. 'I love you, Rachel. I know you might think I'm saying this because we've just had sex, but no, I've felt it for weeks.'

She softly smiled. 'I feel it, too.' And right then, on the crumpled sheets, the smell of mint and roses in the air and his smooth strong hand on her bare skin, she meant it.

He kissed her lips; a more meaningful kiss, one that meant something to them both. This had all happened so fast – no chance to think about their families tonight. There would be war if anybody ever found out about this; heads would roll. But they said love conquers all, didn't they? Surely, if two people love each other, nothing else should matter? Rachel lay in her lover's arms, and felt in that moment her world was complete. He was her protector, her Prince Charming, the man who made her happy, and nothing would ever make her change her mind. Not even her family.

Chapter Sixteen

Charley Johnson sat with his boys in the boozer. He'd been out of jail now for what seemed like forever and still he'd not made his move. Archie Bennet was still running the streets, and everybody knew that.

Charley was loud and you could see he'd had a fair few pints. Larry was sat next to him, and Charley turned to him. 'Do you think I'm too old for the game, mate? Go on, tell me what you think, because I know that's what people are saying behind my back.'

Larry took a deep breath and knew this was going to be a long night. He placed his arm around Charley and kept his voice low. 'Mate, you're fresh from the big house. I think you're still finding your feet. Jail changes a man and maybe you've mellowed since you've come out.'

'Are you having a fucking laugh? I'm still the man around here, still the one people should be scared of.' Charley stood up and flicked the table over, smashing

154

glasses all over the floor. Larry bolted up from his seat, not sure if he was trying to calm Charley down or back him up.

'Fuck me, mate, what the hell have you gone and done that for?'

Charley's eyes changed, a vacant look appearing. He stepped closer to Larry. 'Should I start with you, eh? Knock ten tons of shit out of you and show these cunts that nobody matters to me, friend or no friend?'

The pub went silent, other men edging to the corner of the room. The barmaid behind the bar moved from her spot, keeping the exit in her sight. There was no way she was staying here if it was kicking off. They didn't pay her enough to get bottled or something flung at her head.

Larry tried again to quieten his pal down. All eyes were on him, and he knew this could end up with him flat on the floor when Charley was in this kind of mood.

'Charley, sort it out, mate. Everyone here knows what you can do. We don't need any hassle, do we? The dibble will get rung if you carry on ballooning. You'll be slung back in jail, and for what, mate? Fuck all. Come on, help me pick this table up and we can go back to having a few beers and a laugh.'

Charley's chest expanded and he beat his two clenched fist into it like a gorilla. 'Nobody fucks with Charley Johnson, fucking nobody. Do you hear me, you lot?' His finger pointed around the pub. 'I'll be back to where I was and none of you will be laughing at me then, will you?'

Larry picked the table up, making no eye contact with Charley. Charley booted a chair out of his way and sat back down.

The room was still quiet when the door opened and in walked Andria Bennet with a friend. Larry quickly moved in front of Charley and started to talk to him in hope that he'd not clocked her. Someone was going to get hurt with Charley in this frame of mind. It was too late, Andria was not the kind of woman you could fail to notice.

Charley's voice rang out, louder than before, full of attitude. 'Oi, Mrs Bennet, where's your so-called husband tonight? I bet he's stuck up some brass like he always is.'

Andria turned her head slowly. She flicked her hair back and angled her head as she spoke. 'Oh, look what the cat dragged in, Donna.' She smiled at her friend as she continued. 'Look at you, Charley, you're just like everyone said you are. Old, drunk, and no backbone. Might I suggest you get yourself another drink, old man, and keep that big mouth shut before I get on the blower and get my Archie in here.'

Charley roared from the pit of his stomach and stumbled to her side. Andria didn't flinch. She stood her ground and barely moved a muscle.

'Get your old man down here. Go on, ring him and see what happens.' Charley lay down the challenge.

Across the room, stood in the corner so nobody could hear him, Larry was already on the phone. 'Hello, Dan, you need to get down here and sort your dad out. He's had a skinful and he's kicking off. Andria Bennet's just walked in and he's telling her to call Archie down.'

Larry ended the call and made his way to the bar to back Charley up. Andria was square on to the big man, looking him up and down.

She turned to Larry. 'Take this chimp home, will you, before I call my husband and get him to take him out cold. I'm out for a few drinks with the girls and I don't need a pissed-up has-been ruining my night.'

Larry shook his head, gripped Charley by his arm and pulled him away. 'Come on, Charley. Let's get you home, you're steaming, mate. You don't want to meet Archie when you're like this. This is not the time or the place, is it?'

Swaying about, Charley's legs seemed to be giving way, his words slurred. 'I'm not washed up. I'll show these fuckers, just you watch. I'll show them all.' He staggered out through the door, booting tables as he went.

Andria laughed out loud and waved to order her drink. 'I thought so, Donna. Like I said, he's just a mouthy prick. No threat to anyone, anymore.'

Charley swayed down Rochdale Road. At times he nearly fell into the road. Cars honked their horns at him, motorists yelled at him. He shouted abuse at anyone who passed him, anyone who would listen. Eventually he found a small wooden bench and collapsed on it. He was crying now, feeling sorry for himself. The beer had got to him, unleashed his emotions.

'It's all going fucking wrong. My family, my wife, my reputation. What the fuck is happening to me?' His head tilted to the night sky and tears fell from his eyes. 'I'll get it all back. I'll take everything back, you watch, just you watch.' He fell back on the bench and his head dropped to one side. He hadn't even realised Larry was no longer there. No one was there to hear him. Words fell stuttering from his mouth, he was talking broken biscuits now. Charley Johnson was a shadow of his former self, a drunken mess.

Danny stormed into the pub and looked about. Something was bulging from his pocket; he was carrying for sure. Larry ran to meet him and shook his head. 'He's done one, mate, about five minutes ago. Off his fucking rocker. What the hell is up with him, Dan? Something is not right. I mean, he turned on me, too. He needs to sort his napper out and either tap out or get back in the game.'

Danny nodded, then clocked Andria at the bar.

She rounded on him. 'Oi, tell your dad, if he ever talks to me like that again, Archie won't take it lying down. You know the crack, don't you? Make sure you pass the message on to him and save me from getting my Archie involved.'

Danny sensed an opportunity as he paced over to her. His dad might be past it, but he wasn't. This was the perfect way to show it – to send a message to Archie that *he* was the Johnson he needed to worry about. He gripped Andria by the scruff of her neck and spit sprayed from his mouth as he delivered what he had to say. 'Never mind my dad. I'm here now. If your husband wants a pop at me, then bring it on. I don't know who you fucking Bennets think you are, but me and my boys are going to show you.'

He shoved her against the bar, and she wasn't as bold as before as she stumbled and broke free from his grip. 'If you want war, you prick, then so be it. I have sons who will eat you alive. Once I've told them what you've done to me, you'll be a dead man walking. Come on, Donna, let's get out of here.' Her heels clipped towards the door but, before she left, she shouted back at him. 'You've only got yourself to blame now, dickhead.'

This was a threat, and one he shouldn't ignore. Danny watched her leave. He could have easily run after her. But was that what he was about, beating a woman? No, he had bigger fish to fry.

Chapter Seventeen

Rachel couldn't focus. It was her lunch break and she kept checking her phone and searching through her messages. She tried Niall's number again and held the phone to her ear: nothing, no reply. Hannah was ordering her food and waiting for her to join her.

'So, from start to finish I want to know all the juicy goss. And, don't be leaving anything out. I want to know all the dirt. This is like a big moment for you, and I want to know everything.'

Rachel should have been happy, but anxiety pulsed through her.

Hannah pulled a chair up next to her and clocked she didn't seem herself. 'What's up, Rach? Come on, don't lie to me. I can tell by your face that something is wrong.'

Rachel turned away. 'I've not heard anything from Niall since we slept together. I've sent him endless messages and tried ringing him, but nothing.'

Hannah moved her arms out of the way so Katie could put her food on the table. She started to dig in. Chips, pudding and gravy. She popped the thick suet pastry with her fork and watched as the meaty gravy spilled from it. But Rachel seemed like she'd lost her appetite. Hannah checked Katie was back behind the counter and that no one could hear her – she loved a drama. 'Honest, the times that a guy has let me down, it's untrue. At first, they're all over me like a rash and then, once I've dropped my knickers, I never hear from them again. Trust me, Rach, lesson learned.'

Rachel quickly turned to face her. 'Niall is not like that. I would have known if he was a player. He said things to me. We shared time together. I know it's real.'

Hannah spoke with her mouth full of food. 'He's had you right over. I know you think he's all sweet and innocent, but you don't know guys like I do. I could have written this, Rach. He's a dirt-bag after a quick shag, another name to add to the long line of girls he's bedded.'

Rachel was fuming. 'I'm not daft. I know when some guy is chatting shit to me. Niall wasn't – isn't – like that.'

'So, where is he? Where are all the replies to your text messages? Go on, Mrs Know-it-all, why has he not been in touch?'

Rachel looked to the door, hoping Niall would walk through it and prove her worries were nothing. 'It is what it is. I'm sure he has a reason why he's not been in touch.'

'Yeah, whatever. Good luck with that one. Cut your losses and move on.'

Hannah carried on eating and Rachel shook her head. Why was her best friend not supporting her here, telling her everything was going to be alright? Was she jealous?

Hannah reached for her drink. 'So, what's the plan for tonight? It's the weekend and I fancy a night out clubbing, if you're up for it? Best way of getting over one guy is getting under another, after all.'

Rachel was still annoyed. 'I'm going to see Dot. She's not been well and I've already told her I am coming to see her after work.'

'Wow, you're a young girl. Leave the old coffin dodger alone. You should be out in the mix with your bezzie. It's not like she's your family, is it?'

'Have a heart, for crying out loud. You've got to understand what she's been through.'

'I understand that I want my mate to come out tonight and strut her stuff. Dot should be at bingo or something. Surely they have stuff like that where she is?'

Rachel sighed. What was the point in falling out? 'You are so bad, Hannah. Honest, the things you say sometimes. It's a good job I know you're kidding, otherwise I would think you were a heartless bitch.'

Hannah roared laughing. 'You know me, I say what I see. I can't help it.'

The atmosphere seemed to have lifted, and the two girls agreed that a girly night out was on the cards. Maybe Hannah was right, and Niall had played her, but in her heart she was struggling to believe he could ever do that to her. Once bitten, twice shy.

Jenny sat watching Charley from the corner of her eye. He seemed to be lost in thought. He'd lost his mojo and all he did lately was mope about, lethargic.

Charley knew Jenny was watching him. His marriage was on the rocks and all the plans he'd had in his head for when he got out of jail had fallen apart. His empire, and the world he knew before, were a million miles away now. What the hell was up with him? He needed to get a grip. All talk and no action had never been something people said about Charley Johnson, but he could feel he was losing his edge.

Jenny folded her legs underneath her and flicked the TV channel over. There was no way she was losing any sleep over her husband's problems; he could deal with them on his own, like she'd always had to. Where'd *he* been when the car had broken down? When the kids were playing up and doing her head in? Correct, nowhere to be seen. It was time for the soaps, anyway. Time for her to take herself away from her own miserable life and watch other people dealing with issues in theirs. The intro music started.

Charley let out a laboured breath and rolled his eyes as he scratched his chest. 'For fuck's sake, do we have to watch this load of shite again?'

Surprisingly cocky, she replied, 'It's what I like. If you don't like it, go to bed or piss off down to the pubs like you usually do.'

His face froze: even his wife didn't respect him anymore. Years ago, he would have bolted out of his chair and given her a slap, made her apologise for the way she spoke to him. He closed his eyes slowly to calm himself down. Aggression was not the answer here today and he had to change his tune if he wanted her back on side. 'Jen, I don't want us fighting all the time. You can see I'm struggling, and I need you supporting me, helping me get back on my feet. I'm nothing without you, you know that, love.'

'I supported you through thick and thin. Even through all the beatings you gave me. I was still there by your side, like an idiot. Did you think you could carry on treating me like that and I wasn't going to do anything? Come on, you're not that dumb.' Jenny sat forward and made sure her words were loud and clear so he got the message. 'Everyone thinks you're this big bleeding gangster, a person they can trust, but I know the real you, Charley. You're a weak, lying, wife-beating bastard. I've lost all respect for you and, no matter how much you hurt me, you won't change my mind.' She let out a sarcastic laugh and shook her head. 'You were my world, my everything, and you are the one who ruined it with your paranoid mind. And your fists.'

'We can fix this, Jen. At least let us try. If *we're* alright, everything else will fall back into place. We're like Samson and Delilah. I have no strength without you. Help me get back to me. I'm lost without you. Nothing makes sense anymore.'

She could see his eyes welling up. But he'd cried to her before, promising he'd change. He never did. Once bitten, twice shy. 'Charley, I think that ship has sailed. I've changed.

I want to do things that I enjoy before I'm too old to do it. I want to travel, educate myself more.'

'We can travel together, and what education do you want? You know everything you need to. You've run the brass gaff for years and that place would have fallen apart if it wasn't for you. So, there you go, you are a success. A businesswoman. And the money I've brought in has dressed you from head to toe in labels. Has it really been all bad?'

'I want to be a success and buy my own fucking dresses, Charley. I've never known how it feels to receive a wage slip, to have money that I've earned and worked hard for.'

He chuckled. 'Are you having a mid-life crisis? Where has all this come from?'

She folded her arms and sighed. 'See what I mean. Everything is a big joke to you. Well, *you're* the real joke – everyone's laughing at you behind your back.'

Suddenly Charley dropped the nice guy act. He stood over her, grabbed her, dragging her up with one hand from the sofa. But before he could do anything else, the living room door opened and in walked Paul, head bent over his phone. Charley let go of Jenny and quickly returned to his seat, his throne.

'Where's our kid, Mam?'

Jenny took a deep breath. She didn't want to bring her kids into her fight. She pasted on a smile. 'I'm not sure. He was in earlier, but only a flying visit. Why, what's up?'

'Nowt. Just wondered where he is, that's all. I've tried belling his phone but he's not answering.'

Jenny was still recovering and kept her eyes on the TV.

Charley chipped in. 'Pass me my phone from the table and I'll give him a try. Knowing him, he's probably at the gym.'

Danny still wasn't answering. Charley placed his phone on the arm of the chair and a few seconds later it rang.

It was Jezz from the big house. He smiled and answered the call. 'Alright, my man, how's it going?' He started laughing. Jezz would be a free man at the end of the week, and he couldn't wait to see him. Maybe he would lift his spirits, get him back in the game.

A king needed his court.

Chapter Eighteen

Niall opened his eyes slowly. His vision was blurred. Head pounding with pain. Every movement he made, his body creased with pain. Where the hell was he? Footsteps were nearing him, heavy breathing, voices nearby.

'Get the kid sat up,' a man's voice said. Niall's body was dragged from the floor, flung onto an old car seat. Silhouettes, pain surging deep in his body.

'Hello, pretty boy,' Marzy hissed.

Niall's eyes flickered, getting used to the light. He could see them now. He struggled to stand up but a clenched fist hitting the side of his head made sure he was going nowhere.

Danny and Tomo sat watching Marzy. He had this under control; this was his shout.

'Not such a big-mouth now, are you?'

Thick blood trickled from Niall's nose. He used his coat sleeve to wipe it away. Today was not the day to be cocky. He was playing a losing hand and had to decide quickly how he was going to beat the odds. 'What's going on? Why have you got me here? I don't have beef with any of you, do I?' But now he clocked Danny and gulped. 'Danny, what's the problem, Bro? Is that what this is all about – our dads' ancient fucking vendetta?'

Danny was calm as he spoke, nodding slowly. 'The problem, mate, is your fucking family. Did you think we would sit back and let you pricks take what we've worked hard for? Rumours have it your old man set my dad up and, for the life of me, I can't think why my dad hasn't ended him, the fucking grass.'

Niall had to put this to bed, sort it out. 'Dan, you know my dad doesn't work like that. It's not in his make-up to be a snitch. The law of the streets and all that.'

'That's what we've heard. We lost our old man for three years because some twat set him up.'

'Nothing to do with us, honest. On my mam's life, my dad is not a snake.'

Marzy was losing patience, pacing one way then the other. Ready to give Niall a proper beating, to shut him up permanently.

Niall shot a look over at Danny. 'Our family is just like yours. We all earn a crust the way we know how. Sure we scrap, but we don't bring the dibble in where they're not wanted. You run your ends, we run ours. Simple.'

Danny snapped. 'No fucking more. This is all our patch. Any of you fucking Bennets step in our way again and you'll be in a body bag.'

Niall swallowed hard; this wasn't looking good for him. Danny stood and strolled over to him with evil in his eye. He bent down slowly until he was eye-to-eye with him.

'I'm only going to ask you once and then this shit will get real if you don't tell me what I want to hear. Do you get me?'

Niall nodded. This was the do-or-die moment and he wasn't taking any chances: his life was in danger. Fuck the law of the land, or even the law of the street, he was doing what he had to do to stay alive.

Marzy walked away and came back holding a petrol canister, his eyes dancing with madness. Tomo stood with them both now, and Niall knew he had no choice. Marzy sprinkled petrol over his legs with a menacing laugh. 'Just say the word, Dan, and this dickhead will be torched.'

Danny revelled in the moment, ready to deliver his next sentence. 'Where's the grows? I want to know where they all are and who's babysitting them. Before you answer, make sure you're telling me the truth because, trust me, mate, this is not a fucking joke.'

Marzy flicked his lighter, a bright-yellow flame. This was serious. Niall saw this guy was out to hurt him. Any excuse and he'd touch the flame to the petrol. He spilled out a list of addresses.

Danny listened to the information, Tomo typing it straight into his phone.

Niall tried to regain his cool. 'So, are you letting me go now? I've told you what you needed to know.'

Marzy swung another punch at Niall, sending his head flying into the headrest. 'Who the fuck do you think you're talking to? You're going nowhere, you're staying put. I've not even decided if I'm letting you walk yet. If it wasn't for Danny, I would be burying you now.'

Tomo smirked. 'He's sick in the head, mate. You're lucky we're here, otherwise he would have tortured you.'

Danny backed off and sat down again. His plan was all coming together and, once he'd given his boys these names and addresses, they would boom the doors down on every house or warehouse where the Bennets had a grow and take the lot. Easy money, and it would cut the supply to the Bennets higher up the chain. Danny's phone rang. He pulled it from his pocket. His old man's name flashed up. He let the call ring out.

He rubbed his hands together. Power felt good. His dad might be past it, but he was ready for action.

Rachel sat in the club with Hannah, dejected. All night long, she'd been checking her phone, but still nothing.

Hannah leaned in closer. She'd had a few too many. 'Stop looking at your phone, Rach. The guy is a muppet, a rat. If he wanted to be with you, he'd have phoned or texted you. Do you see those two guys over there? They're asking if we want to go to a party with them? Decent they are, too. Have a look.'

Rachel lifted her head up and looked straight in front of her. 'It's not for me, Hannah. You know I'm not up for all that.'

'Boring,' she slurred. 'You have to move on, Rach. What's makes you ill makes you better, right? Come on, for once in your life throw caution to the wind and let's have a good night.'

Rachel looked at her phone one last time and dropped it into her leather handbag. Maybe her friend was right, why on earth was she sat waiting around for some guy who couldn't be arsed even replying to her messages? She looked over at the two guys and stood up as a tune hit the speakers. She picked up her drink and necked it one. 'You know what, let's go to the party. Who does Niall Bennet think he is, anyway?'

Charley Johnson had fallen asleep in his armchair and when he woke up he was alone. The TV was still on, and it was half past one. He stood up and walked over to the window, looking out at the night sky. Pitch-black with only a sprinkle of stars tonight. Charley stood there gazing out for a few minutes.

Finally he sprang into action. 'Fuck this.' He grabbed his car keys and stormed into the hallway. A quick look up the stairs and he was gone.

Jenny heard the door slam shut, jumped up out of bed and ran to the window. She stood back in the shadows and watched Charley get into his car. What did she care? He could go take a run and a jump if he thought she was bothered where he was going. She used to worry about where he was. Now, it felt like a weight was lifted every time he left the house.

Charley walked into Blossoms and smiled when he met Jackie's eyes.

'It's late for you to be here. To what do we owe the honour of this visit?'

He dropped down on the sofa and sighed. 'I thought I'd come and check on you girls, make sure everything is above board. I told you I would look after you. So here I am, doing just that.'

Jackie looked at him a bit longer than she needed to. She was weighing him up.

'Do you fancy a drink, Charley? I was just going to have one myself.' She draped her white silken dressing gown over her shoulder, revealing lightly tanned flesh.

Charley didn't have to think twice. He had nothing to go home for, he was in the doghouse. 'Go on then, make mine a double. I could do with something to take the edge off, the way I'm feeling.'

'Oh, is Mr Johnson not feeling too good? Do you want Jackie to fix you?' she murmured, her voice low and sexy, just how she spoke to her punters. Most of the men she slept with had wives or partners. And they all had similar stories. *'My wife doesn't give me sex anymore, she's always tired. My partner used to love sucking my cock but I'm lucky to get a gobble once a year now.'* The excuses were endless, all trying to justify why they needed to use a working girl to fulfil their sexual needs.

She poured two large vodkas and sat down next to him. She passed Charley his and sat back, holding her glass in her hands. The silken dressing gown slid from her leg and he could see the top of her thighs.

'So, come on, Charley, speak to me. What's on your mind?'

He sniggered. 'Fuck me, are *you* a therapist now?'

'I can be whatever you want me to be, darling. I'm a good listener. I've had years of experience.'

Charley gulped a mouthful of his drink. He did need somebody to talk to and maybe this woman was the answer to his prayers. She didn't know him; she wouldn't judge him. 'It's all gone a bit pear-shaped since I got out of the big house. My marriage is fucked up and everything I thought I wanted when I was lay behind my door in jail doesn't mean shit to me anymore.'

'Things change, life changes, Charley.'

'But I've always been able to pull it back. Honest, I was the top dog around here and I was ruthless. I don't feel like that anymore. I feel weak. I should be out there smashing doors in, popping caps in people for taking the piss, but I don't have the drive or strength for any of it.'

Jackie patted his knee. She rubbed it with a soft, gentle movement, her eyes glued to him. 'It happens sometimes, love. You've just got to get back on the horse, so to speak. There was a time in my life when I felt the same, felt like shit, you know when you just can't shake it off?'

He nodded. This woman really got him, she knew what he was talking about. 'And how did you get back to normal?' he asked eagerly.

'I know it sounds silly, but I looked in the mirror one morning and gave myself a good talking to. I looked at my reflection with my eyes all puffy through crying. I said, "Jackie, sort your bleeding head out. People are out there with no homes, no food, and no money, and you're crying over some waste-of-space bloke."' She blushed; she'd not meant to share her life story.

Charley touched her shoulder to comfort her. 'Go on, I'm not here to judge. This stays between us.'

'It was some man I had been seeing. I fell for him hook, line and sinker; he was everything to me. You would not have recognised me back then, Charley. I was wife material. I cooked, cleaned. He said jump and I said how high,' she laughed.

'Bloody hell, I wouldn't have had you down as a woman like that, Jackie. You look as hard as nails.'

'It shows you to never judge a book by its cover then, doesn't it? Life made me hard. I wasn't born this way.'

'Yep, me too,' he agreed. 'I often wonder how my life would have been if I'd been born on easy street. A nice family, raised to have a simple life, you know, a nine-til-five job, and all that?'

Jackie chuckled. 'Sometimes our life is set out for us. We don't get to make choices. When that fella broke up with me, I had to start working, do what I do to put food on the table. I lived with my mother at the time, God bless her soul.' She crossed herself. 'She was always ill, so there was no money coming in from her. I had to look after the both of us. Loan men come knocking on the door, bills not getting paid and every night I lay in bed worried about what the next day would bring,' She took a drink before she continued. 'Then I met Renée, same age as me, always dressed up to the nines and flashing the cash about. She lived down our road. I suppose she could see I was on the bones of my arse and one night while we was talking she told me about the job she did. I was gobsmacked, honest. I knew she had a few boyfriends and men were always coming to her house, but I never had her down as a brass for one single minute. She opened my eyes, I can tell you. The money that woman earned was untrue. Anyway, to cut a long story short, she introduced me to a few punters. Kinky, one of them was, you know the ones who want you to smack their arses and tickle their balls?'

Charley howled laughing as he necked his drink and poured them another one each. She continued, 'So now you know. I fell off the horse and got back in the saddle, and did what I had to do to get me out of the shit. So, what will get you back into the saddle?'

He held his head to one side and had a few seconds to himself. 'I need to fight again and get strong. My boys think I'm past it, but I'm far from over. I need to stop fucking stressing about the mrs and sort out what puts food in our mouths.'

'There you go, problem solved. Get back in the gym, get your team back together, word them up and go tackle whatever or whoever it is that is stopping you being top dog.'

What the hell had he been thinking? He was still Charley Johnson. He clenched his teeth together. It was all making sense now, a revelation. 'You know what, Jackie? You're right. Fuck her at home. If she doesn't want me, fuck her. I'm taking back what's mine and I'll show fucking Archie Bennet what I'm all about. Why the hell have I been sat behind my door planning and putting things off instead of getting out there in the mix snapping jaws and putting people in their places?'

Jackie smiled and fluttered her long dark lashes. She flicked her hair over her shoulder and moved closer to Charley. 'I'm glad you've realised what you need to do. Sometimes the answer you're looking for is right in front of you all the time and you just don't see it.'

Charley's eyes met hers. He cupped his hand around her neck and pulled her in closer until their lips met. This was more than a quick snog. This was a man seeking affection, someone to care about him, to make him feel special. Jackie pulled away from him and slipped her dressing gown back over her shoulder. Her voice was low. 'Not here, Charley. Too many eyes. Meet me downstairs in ten minutes.'

Charley stood up from the sofa. Jackie was right; this was his business, and he didn't want any of the girls telling Jenny. He hadn't really been a womaniser in the past. Yes, he's had a few drunken kisses, and there was a time when he'd slept with a handful of women, but his marriage was going through a bad patch, and he wasn't getting any at home. What did Jenny expect? This was his time now, time to get his head together, time to look at his reflection in the mirror and tell himself he was strong, powerful. He was Charley Johnson.

Chapter Nineteen

Jezz stood waiting outside Strangeways Prison with his bag slung over his shoulder. He was speaking to another con, talking about what his plans on the out were. The usual promises spilled out: how he was going to change his life and never end up in this shit-hole again. A car pulled up across from the prison. Jezz clocked Charley and said his goodbyes to the man. He was smiling from cheek to cheek as he yanked the car door open.

'Fuck me, I thought you wasn't coming. I've been stood out here for over twenty minutes. Get me to the boozer and let me get a few beers down my neck to calm me down. My heart is beating like a speeding train. I think I'm going to have a heart attack.' He flung his bag over the seat into the back and closed the car door.

Charley was smiling. 'I know that feeling, Jezz. Nothing better than being a free man. I'll take you for a few scoops and then, if you need a woman, I'll nip you to the brass gaff for a quick sack-emptier, if you want?'

Charley looked different today. No doom and gloom, he had a twinkle in his eye. Jezz punched him in the arm. 'You know me so well, a bit of action and a few beers is just what the doctor ordered. It's all I've thought about for the last few months. The touch of a woman is definitely what I need.'

Charley pulled off, leaving the prison in the rear-view mirror. Jezz opened his window. 'Freedom!' he roared like Braveheart. Charley chuckled.

'So, how's the mrs? Is she still playing up or has she sorted herself out?' Jezz asked.

'Can't be arsed with her anymore, Jezz. She's changed. Fucking too much mither for me at the moment. She's cooking and cleaning still and washing my clothes, and that will do me for now. But she's getting ideas beyond what she is. Women, eh.'

Jezz looked puzzled. 'You've changed your tune. The other day you was telling me how much you love her.'

'Things change, Jezz. Since when has Big Charley needed a woman to make him happy? I need fuck-all from no one. The only way is up for me from now on.'

Jezz reached over and grabbed a cigarette from the packet on the dashboard. 'Oh, a real ciggie. The luxuries you miss when you're behind bars. I'm sick to death of smoking roll-ups. Look at my yellow fingers.' Jezz sucked in the biggest mouthful of smoke. He'd sure missed a normal fag. 'Am I still alright for getting my head down at yours, Charley? I don't want to put you out, especially if you and Jen are at loggerheads.'

'No worries. You can sleep in the box-room. I told Her Indoors the plan last night and she never said a word, so everything is cushty.'

Jezz pulled the mirror over towards him. 'I need a trim, for sure. I look like one of them spice-heads in Piccadilly Gardens.'

'I'll take you now and get you sorted out, if you like. I'm going to get mine done, too. Honest, since I've been out, I've been a right lazy bastard and I've done fuck all. No gym, no runs, no nothings.'

'Well, your point man is here now, and we can soon sort you out. So, fill me in: where are we up to with the Bennets?'

Charley moved along in the traffic and tapped his fingers on the steering wheel. 'I've not been ready for anything until now. Sometimes you have to sit back and get your head together before you go rushing in. Anyway, you're out now. We can get our shit together and put a plan in place. We need a few more heads with us. My lads have stayed loyal, but Archie is working with the Malones and a few others from off our patch, so we need some decent man-power before we go in all guns blazing.'

'Yep. First things first, though. Haircut, shave, shit, and a shag, and I'll be raring to go.'

Charley picked up speed and headed to the barber's where he'd been going for over ten years. He was like that, Charley; he didn't like change.

Soon Jezz looked fresh. A trip to Manchester town centre after the haircut saw him in new clobber and decent trainers. He looked the part now. He still looked thin and could have done with a sunbed course, but he'd just come out of the chokey, what did he expect? He was back to his old confident character, putting aside the quieter persona he'd adopted in prison to get his time done without trouble. But that confidence also meant he was like a dog on heat. Two minutes he'd been out of the slammer and already he was hitting on anything in a skirt. Charley loved the way Jezz made him feel. He lifted his mood and could always get him laughing.

Jezz walked into Blossoms with Charley at his side. He was like a kid in a candy shop when he clocked the working girls. He nudged Charley as one of the girls walked past. 'Fuck me, mate. Get her lined up for me. I might have two, but give me her for starters.'

Charley rolled his eyes. As if Jezz could deal with two women. All men said it when they were having a few pints with the lads, but come on, reality was one and they were gone. Jackie walked into the room and nodded at Charley, no words spoken. She smiled at Jezz and stared at him a lot longer than she needed to, looking him up and down. Paige came back into the room, and it was obvious she was ready for this punter, too. Time was money and she sat next to Jezz, making small talk with him.

Jezz didn't hang about. 'Right, sexy, let's me and you go for a talk.' He winked at Charley and gripped Paige's hand.

Jackie glared at her. Charley could see she was annoyed the younger woman had bagged the punter. But this was water off a duck's back to Paige. New customers brought in by the boss were worth trying out. Maybe this man would be a good tipper, one who might send her presents, perfumes, clothes. She'd had all kinds of gifts from men in the past. It went some way towards making up for the lousy clients. The best gift she'd ever had was a Chanel clutch bag. It was her pride and joy – and had lasted a lot longer than the client.

Left in the front room, Jackie looked tired and yawned. 'Did you get any sleep last night, Charley? I've had about half an hour; I just couldn't nod off now.'

'I had a few hours. I had to be up to get Jezz from the nick this morning.'

Jackie put on her low, seductive voice. 'Just for the record, I enjoyed your company last night. It's been a long time since I've entertained anyone like you.'

Charley smirked. 'Me too. If you're up for it, we can do it again some time.'

'Give me a shout and I'll check my diary,' she giggled.

Jezz walked back into the room around twenty minutes later. He looked like he'd been for a run. He grinned at Charley. 'Class act, that one is. Well worth the money.'

Charley stood up and stretched. 'Right, as long as you're happy, we can get down to the boozer now and celebrate you being home.' He shot a look over at Jackie. 'Catch you later.'

As soon as they got into the hallway Jezz asked, 'Are you slipping it to that one, or what?'

Charley carried on walking down the stairs. 'Just good friends, that's all. Jackie is a nice woman, a good listener and all that.'

Jezz followed closely behind him and patted his shoulder. 'Yeah, whatever, mate. I'm not daft, I saw the way she looked at you.'

'Friends, like I said.'

———

Jezz walked into the pub and John the landlord stood clapping behind the bar. 'Welcome home, Son. Come on, the first drink is on me. What do you want, something from the top shelf?'

Jezz unzipped his coat and hooked it over his shoulder, revealing his new clothes, knowing he looked fresh. 'I'll have a Jack Daniels and coke, John. Throw me some ice in it, too.'

The whole pub stood for him and each man in turn came up and shook his hand. Most of these men had been to jail themselves over the years and they knew how it felt to be home after lying in a cell for years screwing about coming home. Charley's crew, Barry, Sam and Larry were there. Barry picked Jezz up right off the floor and squeezed him in a bear hug.

'Welcome home, mate. Me and the lads have got a few quid for you to help you out until you get back on your feet.'

This was the code of honour around this area; they all looked out for each other. If one of them went to jail, the rest bunged his family some money – not loads, just enough to keep them ticking over until their man came home – and then made sure he was set up with enough to get him on his feet when he was out. Of course, no favours came without strings.

Jezz felt like he was going to cry. He didn't have any family, that he spoke to, and these men had been like his brothers for a long time now. His own family lived out of Manchester and, after a fight with his older brother years before, his mother had flung him out and told him never to darken her door again. It had been no ordinary scuffle. Jezz was wild when he was younger and he'd put his brother in hospital, bit part of his ear off and left him half-dead. He tried to make amends with his family, but he'd pushed them too far. They were good people, worked hard, and there he was having the dibble at the door all the time for the life he'd chosen. It showed him that it doesn't matter what background you come from, you can never predict how your children's lives will turn out. Jezz had always been attracted to danger, crime and the fast money that drugs offered. He had turned his back on the safe world his family had raised him in and told them straight he would never be a nine-to-five kind of guy. And once you'd chosen this path – turning away from it was nigh on impossible.

The men held their glasses up and clinked them together. 'Welcome home, Jezz,' Charley cheered.

Jezz sat down and necked his first drink in one. He was a lush for sure and he'd missed his beer.

Charley waited a few minutes before he placed his pint on the table. It was time to talk business. 'Lads, let me put it out there that I'm ready now to sort things out. As you all know, my head's been mashed since I come home.' He paused. 'But I'm more than ready now to do what I should have done weeks ago. Archie Bennet is a goner. I need to front the cunt and see what he's saying. I think a trip to the gym is in order, lads, to start the ball rolling. He's in there every day, I hear, and I think it may be the best place to catch him off guard.'

Barry asked, 'What's the plan? Are you going to tell him straight, fight him one-on-one, or what?'

'I like to think I'm an honourable guy. I'm going to give him the choice: he can do things the easy way or the hard way. If he wants a straightener, then so be it. A winner-takes-all fight. That way, we don't spill the blood of anyone else on our way to the top.'

Jezz rubbed his hands together and sat back in his seat. 'We could put a purse on the fight, make it a bit more interesting.'

Barry agreed. 'Yes, let's do this the old-fashioned way. A fight, out of the way but with his boys there and yours, you know, like the travellers do. Fair and square.'

Charley liked this. 'Let's go and see him, find out what he wants to do. I'm easy. We can arrange a fight, like the old days, or we can all go to war. It means fuck all to me that he's got the Malones on side because we can all pull in heads if needs be. If I win, I take the area back, and if he does, then I'll step back.'

Jezz scowled. 'Sod that, Charley. If he wins, I'll cut the fucker up myself and feed him to the pigs. This is our area, always has been. What, you expect us all to fall in line and sit back while Archie rolls in the cash?'

'Jezz, nobody wants to go back to the pen, do they? Let's put this to bed once and for all. I'll train hard, I'll get in shape. Nobody will be knocking me on my arse. This all started because of me and Archie – and we're the ones that need to end it.'

Chapter Twenty

Danny put his foot on the gas as they speeded down Rochdale Road. Tomo and Marzy were in the car with him and the music was booming. They pulled up near Moston Lane and Marzy jumped out of the passenger side. Danny followed him to the car boot. Tomo was with them now.

Danny lit a cigarette up as he scanned the area. 'We'll throw him over there. Just let me have this cig and we'll drag the prick out.'

Marzy was pacing up and down. If it had been left to him, he would have kept Niall for a few more days and really worked him over. He felt like he'd let himself down, not lived up to his reputation.

Danny could see he was upset and waited until he come near him. 'Stop scowling, Marzy, we all know what you can do. I only wanted this to be a message sent out to them twats to show them what could have happened.

Once they find him, they'll either back down and our job's done or, if they come back at us, you can get the shooters out and all the rest of your tackle. Just breathe, and trust in me.'

Tomo agreed. 'Correct. Listen to Danny. We need to make sure we're ready if they come. From now on, we don't go anywhere without each other. We stick together, because we're sitting ducks if we're on our own. The Bennets will want revenge, I bet, and any of us could be targets.'

Danny flicked his fag and inhaled. He opened the boot. They carried Niall Bennet over to a grass verge and threw him onto it like an old rolled-up carpet. The lads knew there was no hanging around. Curtains would be twitching, residents trying to get a description of them; they had to be quick. The three of them ran back to the car and in seconds they were gone. Job done.

———

Niall was as good as lifeless. But the cool air slowly brought him round. His eyes flickered. Then his hand reached out. Every time he moved, his face creased with pain. A woman walking past clocked him lying on the grass. At first, she just gawped at him. Was he pissed? Drugged out of his head? She wasn't sure. It wasn't the first time she'd seen someone off their rocker lying on the floor around this area. Drugs were big in this neighbourhood and spice-heads were everywhere, looking for a quick fix. Even when she went shopping in Harpurhey they were outside the local supermarket, begging for money. Only the day before, she'd witnessed a security guard in the store wrestling with one of them, trying to get a bottle of gin from his coat.

Most people hurried past scenes like this. But she looked down at the little Salvation Army badge pinned neatly on her collar. She approached the man with caution, still not sure if he was in the land of the living. She walked one way then the other, trying to get a better view of him.

'Excuse me, are you alright?' She bent down. 'Excuse me, do you need any help?'

Niall moved, his eyes swollen, dried blood all over his face. 'Please, help … get me home … please.'

The woman had made the right choice. She was happy now that she had not walked by. 'What's your name, where do you live?'

Niall was mumbling now.

She couldn't make out what he was saying. 'I'll ring for an ambulance, and the police.'

Niall reached up and squeezed weakly at her fingers. 'No … a taxi.'

This was not what she was expecting: this man needed urgent medical help. 'You need to go to the hospital. What has happened? How did you injure yourself?'

Niall crawled along the grass, thick brown mud lodging under his fingernails. He made it to an oak tree. With all his might he scrambled to his feet, his legs buckling as he tried to walk.

The woman was right behind him, and offered a helping hand. 'Come and sit down. Look at you, you're bleeding all over the place. Have you been stabbed?'

Niall patted his stomach, and his hand came away wet. 'Can I … phone please? One call?'

The woman was apprehensive, not sure if this was a blag to nick her mobile phone. But he needed help and she was the only person here. She dug into her pocket and pulled out her phone. 'It's not a modern one, but it does the job. Tell me the number and I'll press it for you.'

Niall was struggling to breathe, chest rattling. He held the phone with shaking hands and waited until he heard a voice. 'Nat, it's Niall … get to Moston Lane … back of shops … I'm done in … hurry …'

He managed to hang up, and looked over at the woman. As quick as he could, he deleted the phone number he'd just rang. He passed the phone back. His head dropped, bubbles of blood coming from his nose. 'Cheers … you go now … thank you … I'm OK … people coming.'

The woman hovered. She wanted to wait with him until he was safe, but Niall stared at her, eyes burning into her. He unsettled her, and she knew she had better be on her way. Maybe she would hide away at a safe distance and watch what happened.

A black Audi screeched down the street. Nathaniel Bennet jumped out of the car and sprinted over to his brother. Three more men jumped out from the back. Nat gripped his brother's face in his hands and roared from the pit of his stomach, 'Who the fuck has done this to you? Give me their fucking name. Tell me who did this to you!'

The other brothers knew the score: they had to move Niall from here as soon as possible. They helped him into the car and got going. Niall lay across his brothers' legs in the back of the car. His eyes kept closing and Cruz did his best to keep him awake.

Arlo's voice was tight with fear. 'What's the crack? Do we take him to the hossy, or what?'

Cruz pulled Niall's t-shirt up to see where the blood was coming from. His mouth dropped open. 'Yep, get him straight there, he's been cut, I mean proper cut.' He caught Nat's eye in the rear-view mirror.

Niall was struggling to breathe as Cruz held his head on his lap. 'Give me a name. Tell me who's done this?' But Niall was in too much pain, unable to speak. His eyes closed. This was life or death. 'Nat, put your fucking foot down, we're losing him.'

The four brothers carried Niall into A and E at North Manchester General Hospital. Cruz yelled, 'It's my brother, he's been stabbed, he can't breathe, please, he needs to see a doctor.'

The receptionist took one look at Niall and knew he couldn't wait to see the triage nurse. Everybody in the waiting area was looking – hungry for the drama.

Arlo screamed, 'He needs help! Please, somebody fucking help him!'

A medical team came flying in through the double doors and took Niall straight away. The brothers tried to follow them but were told they had to wait where they were. The doctors had a job to do and there was nothing worse than family members crying and shouting. The four brothers came together and held each other. Nat was white and rushed outside. The brothers followed him.

Niall was the baby of the family and, even though he came from a notorious family, he was more laidback than the rest of them. He'd been shielded from the worst of the family business. Of course he had a criminal record, like his brothers – no Bennet didn't do at least a bit of dealing – but he wasn't violent, never carried guns and knives like his brothers did. His older brothers knew as much, and tried to keep him out of the nasty stuff. And yet here he was, bleeding out.

Nat stood in a corner of the car park and, when his brothers came outside, he was spewing his ring up. He lifted his head and wiped his mouth. Slumped against the cold brick wall, he sucked in mouthfuls of air. Nobody spoke for a few minutes. They were all digesting what had happened.

Nat took control. 'Who the fuck has done that to him? I swear, once I get a name, I'll make sure they are in a fucking body bag. How dare they think they can do our brother in and get away with it. How has this happened, why the fuck didn't we know he had beef with someone? Has he spoken to any of you about anything? Think, fucking *think!*'

They had no reply. Too shocked to think straight.

Nat sighed. 'Someone better phone my dad. He'll go ballistic when he finds out. I pray to God Niall pulls through. Please God, don't take our baby brother.'

Nat crossed himself and his brothers followed suit. They were a Catholic family and each of them had attended a Catholic school, even if they didn't go to Confession these days. They had more on their consciences than any priest could absolve. The Bennet family were part-traveller, and proud of their heritage even though they'd always lived in a house and none of them spoke with anything other than a true Manc accent.

Arlo pulled his iPhone from his pocket. 'I'll bell him and tell him what's happened.'

They all huddled around and listened as Arlo rang his father. Nat's eyes filled with tears, the vision of his baby brother in the doctor's arms too much to bear.

'Dad, it's me, Arlo. Niall has been done in. He's in a bad way. We're at North Manchester General with him.' Arlo held his phone from his ear, shouting, screaming audible from the other end. He ended the call, and they went back inside to wait.

Not long after, the double doors of the waiting room swung open and in rushed Archie Bennet with Andria at his side. Their mother was hysterical. She screamed, 'Where is my baby? Nat, is he alright? Tell me he's going to be alright?'

Nat rushed straight to them. He kept his voice down: this was family business and he didn't want other people hearing what he had to say. 'Dad, he rang me, told me he was at the back of the shops on Moston Lane. I got there as soon as I could. He's too far gone to tell us who did this to him.' He choked up and had to take a few deep breaths to continue, tears falling now. 'He was hurt, Dad. Stabbed in the stomach. Black and blue, his face was.'

Archie held his head back and gritted his teeth. No words.

Archie stood over his son's bedside. The doctor was shocked to see him there. 'Sir, you need to go back into the waiting room. No family and friends are allowed back here.'

Archie glared at him. 'This is my son. Don't fucking tell me what I can and can't do.'

The doctor was in a panic, ready to raise the alarm, get the security in. 'I can understand you are worried, sir, but you need to let me do my job. Your son is not in a good place and the next few hours are critical.'

Archie touched the top of his son's head softly and said quietly, 'Come on, Son. You are strong. Pull through this.'

The doctor gave him a few more seconds, then repeated himself.

Archie left the ward and walked back into the waiting room. Andria ran to him, her legs buckling. 'Archie, is he alright? Tell me my boy is going to be OK?'

Archie found a chair and plonked down on it, head held in his hands. His family gathered around him. It was going to be a long night, for sure. The Bennets sat together in the waiting room, each praying silently. Niall was in God's hands now.

Chapter Twenty-One

Rachel was rushing around the house as per usual. Jenny stood at the front door waiting for her. Rachel just had a call from the care home telling her Dot had taken a turn for the worse. She'd never properly recovered from that last beating, and now a bad cold had turned into pneumonia.

Jenny was driving and she kept reaching over to pat her daughter's knee. 'Are you sure you want to go and see her, love? Things aren't always easy at the end, and she's getting good care now.'

'Of course I'm sure, Mam. If she's not got long left, she will need somebody she knows by her side.' Rachel's eyes filled up, and she cried, 'I don't want her to die alone, Mam. She only used to see her family occasionally. That's if you don't count that bastard of a son. I don't know how it came to this. She's a lovely lady.'

Jenny carried on driving. Watching somebody die was not easy. She was with her own nana when she died, and it had that stayed with her. Her Nana Ethel was eighty-two when she passed. All of her family were by her side when she took her final breath. Yet it had spooked Jenny. Her nana seemed wide awake, talking to somebody that nobody else could see.

'Wait, I'm not ready yet,' she had muttered to an empty chair.

Everyone in the room looked over at the chair and then at each other in disbelief. Ethel definitely thought she was speaking to someone. She spoke again. 'I'm saying goodbye and then I'll be ready. Hold your bloody horses, don't rush me.'

It wasn't long after that she passed. It was like somebody had come for her. Jenny didn't like to admit it to anyone but, ever since, she'd worried who'd be coming for her when her time was up.

The care home was quiet. It was nearly nine thirty and the place was dimly lit. Rachel walked to the reception and Alison, the carer who knew her, rushed to her side. 'I'm so glad you could come; she's been asking for you.'

Rachel followed Alison down the corridor and hesitated outside the door. Jenny came to her side and gave her a hug.

'I'm ready now, Mam. I'm ready.'

The room had a small light on in the corner. At first Rachel couldn't see Dot's face, only her hands. Slowly, she edged into the room with Jenny closely following her.

Alison spoke in a soft tone, 'She keeps drifting in and out of sleep. I'll go and get an extra chair so you both can sit down.'

Rachel thanked her and sat at the side of Dot on the chair that was already there. She looked around the room and shook her head. 'It's such a shame, Mam. Why are none of her family here with her?'

Jenny shrugged. 'All that matters is that you are here with her, love. She's not alone.'

Dot's eyes flickered at the sound of Rachel's voice. Her eyes opened suddenly, and Rachel bent over the bed so she could see her face.

She took Dot's hand and held it as she sat back down. 'Hello, Dot. How are you doing today?'

The old woman's chest was rattling, fluid flooding her lungs. Her voice was so low, Rachel could hardly hear her. 'Not too good, sweetheart.'

'You just need to rest, Dot. You've had a really bad chest infection and it will take time for you to feel one hundred percent again.'

The old woman closed her eyes again and she was back asleep. This was going to be a long night.

At ten minutes past twelve that night Dot woke up for the last time. She sat up in her bed and smiled at Rachel as if there was nothing wrong with her. 'Remember what I told you. You need to make sure you do what it takes to make you happy. Never live your life for somebody else.'

Jenny choked up. Dot's words hit her hard.

Rachel held Dot's hand. 'I will, Dot. I always listen to your advice.'

'You're such a kind-hearted soul. Thank you for all you have done for me, I'll never ever forget it. I've had a long life, some ups and down, but I'm not complaining. Just be happy, Rachel, and never forget who you are. Sometimes life takes over and you forget your hopes and dreams. Don't ever forget yours.'

Jenny rushed out of the room and stood with her back against the wall. She held her hand to her neck and rubbed it up and down. She was having a panic attack, she could tell. She needed to get some fresh air, control her breathing. She headed outside and round the side of the building, out of sight. Her phone was quiet tonight: no text messages from her husband, no phone calls. Ever since Jezz had been staying at her home, Charley was like a new man, life and soul of the party, always laughing and not on her case about where she was. Her breathing was calming down now. Slow, deep, breaths. She reached in her pocket and grabbed her fags. Head held back against the wall, she lit up. She knew Dot's words had been meant for her daughter, but it was as if she was being sent a message, too.

Rachel stroked Dot's hand. Alison was with them now, and a few other staff members. Dot slipped away comfortably, in no pain. She was even smiling at the end. Rachel lifted the old lady's hand up to her warm lips and kissed the end of her fingertips.

'Goodnight, god bless, Dot,' she sobbed.

Getting to her feet, she brushed wet strands of hair from her cheek. She looked down at Dot one last time and wrapped her arms around her own body, hugging herself tightly, rocking slightly.

Alison came to her side. 'Come on, let's get you a nice drink of tea. It's always sad when a loved one passes. All I can say is she's at peace now.'

Rachel sucked on her bottom lip. Even though she knew Dot wasn't well, she'd thought, hoped, she would pull through. She wasn't prepared for this.

As Rachel left Dot's room, Jenny was on her way back in. She studied her daughter and knew without asking what had happened. She should have stayed with her, forgotten about her own problems. 'Come here, love. I'm so sorry.'

Rachel cried like a baby, sobbed her heart out. 'Mam, it's so unfair. Why do people have to die, to leave people behind?'

Jenny didn't have the answers for her. She hugged her and kissed her.

Charley looked concerned when his wife and daughter walked into the living room. It was late by the time they got home, but he was still sat drinking with Jezz. Jenny opened her eyes wide at her husband to let him know something was wrong before he started to crack jokes.

'Dot has just passed, Charley. Rachel was with her.'

Charley stood up and wobbled as he walked to Rachel's side. 'Oh, princess, come here.' He wrapped his arms around her and kissed the top of her head. 'I'm so sorry, love. I have no words that will take away the way you must be feeling.'

Rachel tried to hold a stiff upper lip. 'I'm going to make a hot chocolate and get in bed.'

Jenny walked up behind her daughter. 'Do you want me to finish making your drink? You can go and sit down.'

Rachel nodded and, as she turned around, said, 'Mam, it seems that everything I love is being took from me. First my boyfriend, now Dot.' She realised too late that she'd said too much.

Jenny was right on her; this was the first she'd heard about a relationship break-up. She added the cocoa powder to the hot water and chose her words carefully. This was a touchy subject, she had to tread carefully. 'Rachel, I didn't even know you were having problems with Jack. You never said a word. I thought it was going smoothly?'

'So did I. I must have *dickhead* written across my forehead. How did I not see he was a player?'

Jenny finished making the drink and sat down next to her. Her back was up now, and she wanted to know more details. Or to go and find the lad and give him a piece of her mind. How dare he hurt her princess. 'Go on, tell me more about this Jack, because let me tell you something for nothing: if he's laid a finger on you, I'll have his guts for garters and I'll make sure he never breathes again.'

'No, you've got it wrong. He's never hit me, he's just …' Jenny reached over and patted her arm, urging her to continue. 'He's ditched me, never returns any of my calls or texts. It's like I never existed.'

Jenny shook her head slowly. 'What a coward. You're gorgeous, baby girl, and this Jack the lad will regret losing you, for sure. Mark my words, men will be queuing up at your door soon and you'll laugh about this Jack guy one day.'

Rachel picked up her hot chocolate and blew on it. Maybe her mother was right, and Niall would regret not getting in touch with her.

Jezz walked into the kitchen and smiled softly at them both. 'I'm not too good with emotional things like this, but I'm sorry about your friend, Rachel. I'm going to order a pizza to be delivered if either of you want some?'

Jenny sat up straight and flicked her hair back over her shoulder. 'Yes, Rach, have something to eat. I bet you're starving. Just have a few slices with me.'

'No, Mam, I'm going to take my drink upstairs to bed with me now. I just need a good sleep.'

Rachel kissed her mother on the cheek and headed to the door. Jezz came and stood behind Jenny. His large hand rested on her shoulder. 'Death puts everything into perspective, doesn't it? I mean, I know you and Charley have your ups and downs, but it's all going to be fine, Jen. Trust me, everything will be OK.'

Jenny didn't feel too sure. 'I hope so, Jezz, I hope so.'

Chapter Twenty-Two

Charley woke up, turned on his side and stretched his arm out. The space next to him was bare, his wife gone. He sat up, listening. Voices downstairs. He picked up his phone and started to read through his messages. He could hear Rachel in the next room and her friend Hannah's voice in there, too. Their voices were raised now, and then he saw Rachel rushing past the bedroom door.

'Whoa, what's the rush, where are you going?' he shouted after her. The footsteps stopped and he watched as the bedroom door opened fully. 'What's up?'

Hannah was by Rachel's side and they stood at the doorway looking lost for words. Then Hannah said, 'Oh, it's only drama with some of the girls on the estate. Bitches, they are, Charley, always stirring shit that doesn't concern them.'

'Bloody hell, I thought you lot had grown up now and got past all that stuff?'

'We have, but you know what they're like. Jealous cows with too much to say.'

That was enough for Charley to relax. His daughter bickering with her friends was nothing for him to worry about. He had more on his mind.

The girls left the house together, but Rachel rushed ahead.

'Wait, will you?' cried Hannah. 'Your dad might have bought that story, but you can't go running into the hospital when they don't even know about you.'

'I don't care, Hannah. This is Niall. My Niall. This is why he never rang me, he was in hospital on his death bed, and I didn't know a thing about it.'

Hannah led her friend to a nearby wall and sat her down; she wasn't thinking straight.

'Tell me again what you heard?' Rachel asked urgently. She was still trying to make sense of it all.

'It was gobby Charlotte from the Two Hundred estate. She gets to find out everything, right News-of-the-World, she is.'

Rachel knew who she meant and urged her friend to continue as she sat biting her fingernails.

'She said Arlo Bennet was in the boozer and he was heartbroken, crying over his brother. All he said was he was in a bad way. No clue who did it. He's on a life-support machine, drips, and all that.'

Rachel rubbed her arms, eyes filling up. 'Who would do such a thing? Niall is an alright guy and he doesn't give a shit about the family business. He's not into the gang life. If he is, he's never mentioned a thing to me.'

'Rachel, give your head a shake, will you? He's a Bennet. God knows what they get up to. I bet he's had someone over or something like that.'

'No way, he's not involved in all that shit with his brothers. I do know him, and we have spoken about stuff.'

Hannah let out a sarcastic laugh and looked at her directly. 'Are you having a laugh? Take your head from up your arse and listen to what you're saying. Niall is involved in all the crime his brothers are. Guilt by association, even if he's not got his hands dirty himself. Don't let him pull the wool over your eyes. Don't you remember when Karl Denvon got done in the other month and he was in a bad way?' Rachel rolled her eyes. 'Well, I heard that was Niall. He's no angel, Rach. He's ruthless like his brothers. This is probably a comeback from what he done to Karl, because, trust me, he messed him up big time.'

'I want to see him, make sure he's alright. I love him, Hannah, he's not just a passing thing. I've fallen in love with him.'

'For crying out loud, Rach, you don't even know the guy properly. You've been on a few dates and shared a kiss here and there. That's not love, it's lust.'

'Fuck off, Hannah,' Rachel growled. Her back was up now. 'You've never had a good thing to say about Niall since the moment I met him. Go on, admit it, you don't like him.'

'Oh my god, have you heard yourself, Rach? I have always spoke my mind with you and if the truth hurts then deal with it. Niall is a Bennet. Get that into your thick head and realise he'll never change just because he's with you.'

Rachel sprang off the wall, and faced Hannah, hands on hips. 'Just because nobody treats you with an ounce of respect don't take it out on me. For your information, I've had lots of dates with Niall. Not only a few, like you're making out. He told me he loves me. Go on, say that's a load of lies, too?'

'Believe what you want, Rach. I say what I see. You watch; maybe one month down the line, maybe two, but he'll show his true colours. You're just another notch on his belt, you'll see, just another girl he's added to his list. He probably gets a sick thrill from knowing he's shagging the little Johnson girl. Maybe even doing it just to wind up your brothers.'

That was it. Rachel twisted her fingers into Hannah's hair and dragged her to the ground. A side to her she tried to keep under control, she was her father's daughter right now. Red mist, rage she couldn't control was pumping through her veins. 'Don't ever say I'm just another girl to him. You've always been jealous of what me and Niall have got, jealous that nobody stays with you longer than it takes to get into your knickers.'

Hannah was wriggling to break free and when she did she made sure she kept her distance from Rachel to say what she had to. 'Deluded, you are, don't even bother calling me your friend anymore. We're done, Rachel. The truth hurts and just because I have told you straight you think you can rag me about like this. You deserve everything that's coming your way. I might even let the cat out of the bag and tell your brothers you're banging Niall, eh? Yeah, let's see how that goes down, shall we? Book me a ticket because I'll be watching and laughing my tits off.'

Rachel sucked on her gums as she watched Hannah storm off. She could still hear her shouting in the distance. She stood in the same spot and drew in large mouthfuls of fresh air. 'He does love me, I know he does,' she sobbed.

Danny sat in the living room watching TV. Charley and Jezz were sat talking and he couldn't help but listen.

'You need to get training, Charley. We can go and see Archie, set up the fight and set a date. You have to remember Archie still tans the gym every day. You've been locked up and don't have the eye of the tiger like he does. You need to train, and fast, before he makes a show of you.'

'I'll be in the gym every day, don't you worry about that. Archie Bennet is all show. He looks the part, that's all. We've been on the inside – prison trains you to fight tougher, faster, harder than any gym. And you're forgetting we've come to blows before and I knocked the chancer spark out.'

'Sure. But how long ago was that?'

Charley laughed. 'I've been waiting for this fight for years.' He sat up straight. 'Let's not wait any longer. Get Larry to arrange a meeting with Archie, and have the boys ready to come, too. We'll sort this war out once and for all. It's winner takes all.'

Danny squirmed. What the hell was he listening to? Here he was getting shooters ready, and the machetes, and his old man was talking about a fist fight to solve the feud between the two families. Did he not realise fist fights belonged to the past?

'Am I hearing things right, Dad? Did you say you're setting up a one-on-one with Archie?'

Charley nodded, proud that he was finally going to sort this out his way. 'You heard me right. I'll knock the prick out and put this to bed once and for all. That's if he's up for it. If he's not, then we'll go down another route and see what happens, but he'll have lost face. He's old school like me. I can't see him turning down a one-on-one showdown.'

Danny let out a sarcastic laugh. 'What a load of crap, Dad. Things don't work like that anymore. Jezz, come on, pal, word him up and put him straight, for crying out loud.'

Jezz fidgeted in his seat, unsettled that the young lad had put him on the spot. 'It's whatever Charley wants to do. I stand by whatever he wants. If he wants to knock the prick out, then I'm there with him. If he wants a full-on war with the Bennets, bring it on. I'm ready, willing and able.'

'Well, good luck with that,' scoffed Danny. 'You do things your way and I'll do things my way. The Bennets are running scared now and, trust me, in a few days the lot of them will be lying in the hossy being fed through a fucking drip. Not taking bets on a fist fight,' he sniggered.

Charley was up in arms, ready to have a go at Danny, but his son stood up and walked to the door before he could get a word in. 'The winner does take it all, Father. Just remember that.'

With that, Danny was gone.

Jezz shot a look over at his pal. 'Hot head, that one. But he's right, Charley. These young ones are up and coming, and they do things differently. It's all about firepower now, not honour. Come on, you know that, don't you?'

'It's like I'm an embarrassment to him, like he wants my place before I'm ready.'

'He's a man, Charley, not a fucking kid. He's bound to have ambition. Let him do his thing and you do yours. He's a chip off the old block, if you ask me.'

'He's a gobshite, Jezz. Honest, I've had to bite my tongue with him lately. He doesn't think about stuff, he goes rushing in leaving himself vulnerable.'

Jenny walked into the room and sat down with a fag hanging from her mouth. She'd heard the conversation from the kitchen and she wasn't in the mood to stay silent anymore. 'Grown men fighting. What next?'

But, as usual, Charley didn't want to hear what she had to say. 'Come on, Jezz, people to see, places to go.' He snatched his car keys from the table and stormed out, just as Gina bustled in.

Jenny could tell by Gina's face that she had gossip. It was always the same when she'd heard something on the streets. She folded her arms. 'I've just heard the news, Jen. I don't know how you are sat there as calm as you are. It's a wonder Archie and his mob aren't here smashing this place up already.'

'What on earth are you going on about?'

Gina froze. 'What, you've not heard? Archie's youngest is in hospital on life-support and it's touch and go if he makes it through. Everybody's talking about it. Andria is on her knees with worry.'

Jen tried to work out the consequences of what her friend was saying. 'So what has that got to do with me?'

Gina reached over for one of Jenny's cigarettes. 'The word on the street is your Danny put him there, him and his boys. Marzy has told his girlfriend and she's shouting it from the rooftops. Jenny, you know Archie – he won't let this go by without heads rolling.'

'My Danny has put a Bennet in hospital?' This was a code red. She needed to get her ship in order, ring her son and ask him what the hell was going on. She had an awful feeling that this was Danny going solo. She'd have heard Charley ordering the hit, if he'd planned it. She stumbled as she stood up and reached for her phone. Her hands shook as she tried both her sons' numbers. No answer. What the hell was she going to do?

Jenny stared at Gina. 'Are you absolutely sure of this? Our Danny is so different to his dad. I mean, I know he's no angel, but I'd have thought he'd want to carve his own path – use his head not his fists. I never figured he would hurt someone enough to put them in hospital.'

Gina raised her eyebrows. 'I suppose the apple never falls far from the tree.'

Chapter Twenty-Three

Charley had been trying to arrange a meeting with Archie Bennet all day long, but nobody was able to reach him. He was probably hiding, the coward. Charley was in the pub now, already claiming it as a victory.

He was shouting the odds to his boys who were sat around the table with him. 'He's not making contact because he knows Charley Johnson will kick ten bags of shite out of him. You never lose it, you know.'

Jezz was fuelling Charley with drinks, and, as always, it was Charley's money that bought the beer. Jezz was a freeloader, but he paid his way in loyalty.

The shouting died as Nat Bennet walked into the pub with a few of his boys.

Charley couldn't help himself. 'Oi, Bennet boys, where's your old man? Does he know Big Charley is looking for him? Is he hiding away somewhere, the shit bag?'

Nat turned his head slowly and clocked where the voice was coming from. His crew were at either side of him, whispering into his ear. One was holding him back by his arm.

There was no way Nat was letting old man Johnson shout the odds to him. There were a few punters in the boozer today and one man in particular who seemed to being taking notice of what was being said, but Nat loved an audience. 'Look who it is, lads. Charley Johnson. All washed up, everyone's saying.'

Jezz held Charley down and replied for him. 'Oi, fucking Charlie Big Spuds. Keep that mouth shut before I put you over my knee and give you a smacked arse.'

The other men chuckled and Jezz flicked the invisible dust from his collar.

Nat was chomping at the bit, ready to deal with Jezz, to put him on his arse, but his boys were still holding him back. 'We're ready when you are. Now your sons have made the first move, watch this space. And now you've brought me and my brothers into it, you can forget about you and my dad sorting it out one-to-one. This is a family affair now.'

'We've made no moves yet, you dickhead. You would know about it if we had.'

Nat was louder than before to make sure everyone heard what he had to say. 'My dad is at the hospital watching his kid fight for his life. Don't tell me you don't know it was your lads who put him there. They've been shouting it about, proud of taking our Niall down.'

This was all news to Charley. He looked around the table at his boys with a blank expression, waiting for someone to fill him in. 'I don't know what you're talking about, mate.

You've got your wires crossed; my boys have done Jack-shit.'

'We'll see about that. An eye for an eye, and all that?' Nat booted the chair nearest his foot and tried to run at Charley, but his boys made sure he never got near him. This was neither the time nor the place for the big showdown. 'Watch your back, you old twat, and tell your sons I'm all over them.'

Nat was dragged out of the boozer by his mates, still screaming the odds.

Charley looked around the table at his men and could see they knew nothing. Had Danny and Paul really taken things into their own hands, not listened to a word he'd said? Charley's fists flexed. 'Someone get Danny on the blower, now, or I'll smash this fucking pub up.'

Chapter Twenty-Four

Rachel hid in the shadows. She'd been waiting in a doorway at the hospital for more than an hour. Waiting for everyone to leave Niall's bedside. She pressed her body against the cold wall and closed her eyes. She pretended she was playing hide-and-seek with her friends like when she was younger, hoping nobody could see her. Shit, Niall's family were leaving; she'd seen them around Niall's bed when she peeped through the window minutes before. Andria was sobbing her heart out, heartbroken, and Archie was trying his best to hold it together. Bloody hell, they'd stopped right near her. Taking a long, deep breath Rachel strained to hear every word they said.

'If he doesn't make it, Archie, what the hell are we going to do? He's our boy, our baby.'

The woman was almost on her knees and Rachel nearly stepped out from her hiding place to put her arms around her. Here was someone who cared about Niall as much as she did.

Archie's voice was deep, shaking. 'I'm putting a stop to this once and for all.'

'It's too late for all that, Archie, it's gone beyond that. For crying out loud, my son is on his death bed. If anything – and I mean *anything* – more happens to my son, I will go to jail for him. I'll find out who has done this to him, and I'll put a bullet right through their head. I'm not joking, Archie, I will blow their fucking head off.'

'Andria, calm down. I'm going to sort this out. I'll find the bastards and I'll cut them up, hurt them good and proper.'

Rachel covered her mouth with her hand, trying to quiet her breathing. She needed to get out of here, she needed air. Eventually, Andria and Archie moved away. She popped her head out from her hiding place and saw them walking through the double doors at the end of the corridor. She looked around. She had to make a move before her chance was gone. With speed, she hurried down the corridor and walked onto the ward where Niall was. The nurse was with the patient next door and she took her chance.

As she opened the door, the beeping of machines echoed in the silence. Even before she saw Niall, she saw the tubes, the needles in his arm, the bandages. He was a mess. At death's door. Tears streamed down her face as she sat down on the chair next to the bed. The nurse popped her head inside the room and looked at her suspiciously. Rachel had to think on her feet. 'My mam and dad have just left. I'm going to sit with my brother for a while until they come back.'

The nurse rolled her eyes. She had a job to do and checking visitors in and out was not on her list. 'Your brother needs rest. If anything changes with his condition, I will give your family a ring.'

Rachel sensed that what she really wanted to say was *'piss off and let me do my job properly without distractions'*. 'I'll only stay for five minutes, then I'll go home. He's my brother, and our family is heartbroken. We need him to be alright.'

The nurse realised she'd been rude. She could see how upset this young girl was. But she'd worked a double shift, hardly had any sleep, and she was more than ready to go home herself. 'He'll pull through, I'm sure he will. He's in good hands here. I can assure you that he's getting the best medical care possible.'

Rachel smiled softly as she dabbed a crumpled white tissue into the corner of her eye. 'Thank you for helping him. I won't stay long.'

When the nurse left, Rachel couldn't help but stare at Niall. His head was swollen like a watermelon and she had to look twice to make sure it was him. 'Oh, Niall, what the hell's happened to you? I thought you'd carted me, left me, but you didn't, you were in here all the time.' Rachel sobbed as she took his hand in hers. 'I've missed you so much, babes. Who would have done something so bad to you? I love you, Niall. I need you to pull through. You're my world, I can't stop thinking about you every second of every day.'

His eyelids flickered, his body stirred. She sat up straight. 'Niall, can you hear me? If you can, nod your head, anything, just let me know you can hear me?'

Niall groaned, his mouth moving but no words coming out. Rachel didn't have much time. She quickly looked around the room and got to her feet. 'Niall, I have to go before someone finds me here. Please, get better, please pull though. I'll tell the nurse you're waking up.' Her warm lips kissed his fingertips. She stared at him a few seconds longer and then left.

Chapter Twenty-Five

Danny watched the old building facing him. Marzy, Tomo and Tez were sitting in the car with him. There was another car parked up at the side of him with more of his lads inside: Ethan, Steve, Pat and Jack. Something was going down, men dressed in black, hats pulled over their eyes, shifty-looking. Danny reached under his seat and pulled out a package wrapped in an old towel. He placed it on his lap and unwrapped it with caution. He smiled over at Marzy in the passenger seat. 'This shit is real now. It's time to show these little shits that we are a force not to be messed with. I reckon there are about six of them in this gaff. We're taking the fucking lot: money, drugs, and anything else these pricks have got behind them doors.'

Marzy patted his coat pocket. 'I'm tooled up and ready to go. There's a large amount of sniff behind them doors and I'm not leaving without it.'

The Bennets didn't only have a stake in all the cannabis farms, but were well known for dealing in class A drugs.

This was where the real money was. Heroin, crack, and cocaine were all up for the taking today.

Danny twisted in his seat and spoke to Tomo and Tez in the back. 'You know this is not going to be a walk in the park, right? So make sure you've got everything you need to take these bastards down. This is the job that will put us on the map. We're not dealing with kids and a few rooms of weed anymore. These are men, big fucking tanks who will fight us.'

Tez swallowed hard and pulled a small bag of white powder from his jacket pocket. He dug a silver key into it and held it up to his nostril before he snorted the sniff from it. It took a few seconds before he replied to Danny, his head back, eyes closed, as the drug rushed through his body. 'A nice bump always sorts me out before a job like this. I'm fearless, I am. Anyone else want a quick sniff before we go and boom these fucking doors down?'

Tomo sniggered and declined the offer. His head needed to be in the game, no room for mistakes.

Danny smiled at them through the rear-view mirror and shook his head. Yes, he'd had cocaine in the past, but there was no way he was having a fix right before a big job like this. He needed to be straight-headed, aware of everything that was going on around him. His phone buzzed in his pocket. He'd put it on vibrate and, the last time he looked, he'd had over twenty missed calls from his dad. Now was not the time.

Tick tock, tick tock. It was time. Danny jumped out of the car and gave the nod to his boys in the other. They looked like a group of ninjas, all dressed in black, identity hidden.

Danny addressed them all. He was already tripping on the power. 'Right, no fuck ups. We do what we have to do to get the job done. There's a lot of money and drugs to be had in here and, if we pull this job off, we will all line our pockets. Which means,' he paused, 'doing whatever we have to.'

The men shuffled, ready to get stuck in. Each man who stepped up today knew they could be stabbed, or even lose their life, from the moment they tackled the guys inside. It was all about greed and power.

And Danny Johnson was fixated on power. He wanted to be the top man, feared by all who knew him, like his father was back in the day. He clutched the silver pistol in his hand and gave instructions once again to his boys. This was a night when only the strong would survive.

Jenny was worried sick. Her husband had come home from the pub, and she could tell by his face that something was lying heavy on his mind. Jezz was still in the boozer and this was the first time they'd been alone for a while. She could have cut the atmosphere with a knife. The TV was on low and, although they were both staring at it, neither of them was watching it. Charley kept picking his mobile up and checking it. Jenny hadn't told him what Gina said – she needed to hear it from the horse's mouth first. She wondered if Charley had heard the same rumour – he was pondering something, that was for sure.

So they both sat in deep thought, in worlds of their own. Both waiting for Danny to come home so they could tackle him about what they had heard. But it was Rachel who walked into the room. Her eyes were red raw from crying. She flopped down on the sofa next to her mam and rested her head on her shoulder.

'Are you alright, love?'

She whispered, 'Not really, Mam. But what can I do about it?'

Charley joined in the conversation. 'Dot is at peace, sweetheart. Remember that we all have to meet our maker one day.'

'I know, Dad. I've got a lot on my plate at the moment and Dot dying has knocked me for six. I'm going back into work tomorrow. Hopefully that will take my mind off it all for a while.'

Jenny stroked her daughter's cold cheek. 'It will all turn out fine, love. It's a shock, that's all.'

Charley grunted. 'Have you seen or heard anything from Danny or Paul, Rach? I've tried ringing them both but they're not answering.'

Jenny fidgeted as if the truth was trying to spring out of her mouth. 'Danny will be at the gym. God knows where Paul is. I think he's got a new girlfriend because he's constantly on that bloody phone sending messages.' Jenny's cheeks blushed slightly as she changed the subject. 'Have they said when the funeral is yet, love?'

'No, but it should be in the next few days. Alison from the care home rang me and asked if she could give my phone number out to some lawyer who's been looking to get in touch with me. It's probably about John, Dot's son. I gave a statement but I don't want to go to court.' Rachel looked grey with anxiety. But it was time for the local news and she was glad of the attention shifting away from her. They all turned to the TV as *News Northwest* came on.

The newsreader spoke about an attack on a young male in the area and gave a phone number to contact if anyone had witnessed the attack. The reporter stressed that anyone could report tips anonymously. But it was all too often said in Harpurhey that snitches got stitches. Nobody in their right mind would grass, not if they knew what was good for them. As the item finished, all three Johnsons seemed unable to meet each other's eyes.

'Fuck this for a laugh,' Charley mumbled under his breath and left.

Jenny watched him drive off and paced the room. She was restless, couldn't settle. She reached for her phone and stared at the screen for a few seconds before she sent a message:

Where are you?

She put her phone down and resumed pacing.

Charley headed to Blossoms with his head spinning. He picked up speed.

There was a strong northerly wind tonight that bit into his skin as he stood in the doorway of the gaff pressing the silver buzzer and waiting for someone to answer.

'It's Charley,' he grunted. And that was all it took for the door to open.

The stairs were dimly lit as he made his way to the top. Once he opened the door, he looked around cautiously. Jackie appeared from the side corridor and smiled at him. Her cheeks were flushed and judging by her eyes she was half-cut.

'Where are the girls?' he asked.

'Paige is with a client, and I think a few of the other girls have guys in with them, too.'

'Has it been busy tonight?'

Her words slurred. 'Not really, we don't usually get a lot in through midweek. It's more towards the weekend when the men get paid, that's when we get busy.'

Jackie wasted no time in getting Charley a drink. He relaxed more when he had a drink in his hand. She looked around the room and when she knew the coast was clear she touched his warm hand and stroked the tip of her tongue along her top lip. 'I've been thinking about you a lot, Charley. You've got under my skin for some reason. We could be good together, you know?' He didn't answer but she continued, 'I enjoyed myself with you and I'd like to do it again.'

There were no flies on this woman; she said exactly what she thought. Charley liked that about her: what you saw was what you got. No chase, straight to the point.

'I enjoyed our time together, too,' Charley said, taking in every inch of her. 'I am married though, Jackie. I don't make a habit of sleeping about, and I'm not leaving the missus any time soon.'

Jackie rolled her eyes. 'Oh, don't tell me Charley Johnson has a conscience now. Bloody hell, just when I thought I'd found something special.'

For Charley, she was a shoulder to cry on when he was down, and she helped him out: nothing more, nothing less. No promises had been made, and he didn't want a repeat if she was getting ideas it could be more than a leg-over. 'Jackie, don't be like that. We had a good night and that's where we should leave it. If my wife ever found out about this, she'd have us both done in. I was at a low the other night and it should never have happened. Gutted, I am, that I've let myself down – and let you down and all.'

Jackie's grip tightened on her glass. He'd fed her a sob story and got into her knickers and, now he was done, he was flicking her away like a fly that had landed on the end of his nose. 'The story of my life, Charley. More fool me for thinking you was any different from the pricks who come calling here. You owe me money then, if it was only a shag. If you are acting like a punter, then I'll treat you like one. Never mix business with pleasure, Charley. You should know that.'

He was lost for words, not sure whether she was joking about the money. He laughed, trying to lighten the mood. 'Jackie, button it. I'll make sure you're taken care of.' He couldn't let it get out that even his brasses didn't respect him anymore. There was no way he was having Jackie calling the shots here today. 'It was a shag. We're both adults and we can keep it civil. Or, and trust me on this, if you carry on with that mouth of yours, you'll be out of here on your arse.'

Jackie flicked her hair. The girls had told her he could be an evil bastard and up to now she hadn't believed them. The buzzer rang and she jumped up to answer it, glad of the interruption that stopped her saying something she'd regret.

Her back was well and truly up, and Charley didn't like the cunning look in her eye as she answered the buzzer.

'Yes, come up,' she replied to the caller.

Charley walked over to the window, and looked out at the night sky. Things had to change in his life, he needed to be back at the top. The door opened and in walked the punter Jackie had buzzed in, looking embarrassed to be paying for it. Fuck this. Charley gave one last glance at Jackie and left. Once again, he was running away from his problems. It was time to face them. Only he needed a drink in him first.

Jenny had been asleep for over an hour when she heard banging, glass smashing, and loud voices coming nearer. Her bedroom door was booted open, and a shadow stood over her, though she couldn't see her attacker's face. His warm, sweaty hands dragged her up from the bed and she strained to make out the face in the darkness.

'Where the fuck is he?'

'Who, who?' Jenny gagged as her breathing was restricted, and realising they could be after any of the men of her family.

'Fucking Charley, that's who.'

Jenny was kicking and screaming as another man appeared on the landing. As he came closer, she could see he had Rachel in his grip with his hand over her mouth. The man spoke. And this time Jenny would know that voice anywhere.

'I want Charley, where the fuck is the wanker? Does he think he can take my boy down and nobody will bat an eyelid?'

Jenny's eyes were wide open now as the first man pinned her up against the wall. Light from the hallway sprayed into the room and she could see properly for the first time. 'Archie, get your goon to get his hands off me, and you had better get your filthy fucking hands from my girl, now!'

On Archie's nod, Jenny was thrown onto the bed. She was nothing to him, no real danger. He stood over her and stared at her for a few seconds. Then he bent right down to her and whispered something into her ear, her eyes widening in fear.

Rachel was flung next to her mother, shaking from head to toe. 'Mam, tell them to go. Where is my dad? Where's Danny? Or Paul? Where the hell are they?' she cried.

Archie's voice was chilling as he spoke. 'Tell that cunt I'm ready when he is. My son is lying in hospital and your sons are responsible for it. He wanted a war and now he's fucking got one. He knows where to find me.' His eyes were dancing with madness but his words were slow and chilling. 'Look how easy it is to get to the things he loves. If he thinks he can come for my youngest, then I think that makes you fair game, darling,' he said, winking at Rachel.

Jenny held her tighter in her arms and rocked her slowly. 'Leave us alone, Archie. Get out of my bleeding house before I do something I might regret.'

Archie laughed. 'You could have had it all, Jenny, but look at you now, a nervous wreck with a wanker of a husband. Go on, where the fuck is he when his family needs him? If he doesn't come and find me within twenty-four hours, I'll be back.' He paused, 'And next time I'll do more than just rough you about.'

The man behind him had finished checking the other rooms and came back to Archie's side. 'Just these two in the gaff.'

Archie backed out of the room. 'Easy-peasy, isn't it, Jen? I'd sleep with one eye open if I was you, love. Trust me, this is far from over. Your family will be wiped out if anything happens to my boy, and I mean all of you. Now sleep tight, ladies.' He was gone.

Jenny and Rachel stayed where they were until they heard the sound of a car screeching away. Then Jenny jumped off the bed and sprinted down the stairs. The front door was hanging from its hinges, and she could see sharp shards of glass sticking up from the grey carpet. Where the fuck was her family? Danny, Paul, Charley, even Jezz? Archie was right. Charley had left them as sitting targets. What kind of man does that when he knows something is kicking off? Jenny turned to the cupboard in the hallway and flicked the light on, returning with something in her shaking hands which she hid in her fluffy white housecoat. She whispered under her breath as she climbed back up the stairs. 'I'll show them, I'll show them all.'

Rachel was bent over the toilet seat, spewing her guts up. Jenny ran into the bedroom and hid the thing away before she went back to attend to her daughter.

'I'm so sorry, Rachel. This should never have happened. I swear to you now, over my dead body, this will never happen again. Your dad has let us down, left us to deal with his shit, but we're going to have to step up. We can't wait around for a white knight.'

Rachel lifted her head from the toilet bowl. She was whiter than white, like she'd seen a ghost.

'Mam, I don't want any more trouble. Please tell me there won't be any more trouble?'

Before she could answer, Jenny froze as she heard footsteps coming up the stairs, her heartbeat doubling once again. Who was it this time?

'Mam, where are you? What the fuck's happened to the door?'

Jenny ran out from the bathroom half-relieved, half-furious. 'Where were you, Paul? You left us. They've been here looking for your dad. Where is he?'

Paul ran to her and gripped her in his arms. 'Mam, breathe, just tell me what happened.'

She was sobbing now, tears streaming. 'Archie Bennet and his firm boomed the door in looking for your dad, but he wasn't here. They dragged your sister from her bed and flung me all about the bedroom. Go and find Danny and your dad. Trust me, if they don't sort this mess out, I will.'

Rachel stood at the toilet doorway, still shaking, eyes wide. 'Paul, is it you who put Niall in hospital? The man said it was you and Danny. Please tell me it's not true?'

Paul rushed to her side and tried to console her. His poor sister. This should never have happened. 'On our mam's life, Sis. I know nothing about it. I knew he was in hossy, but it's fuck all to do with me. All sorts of stories are flying about him but defo nothing to do with me.'

'What about Danny, does he know anything about it?'

Paul shrugged. 'If he does, he's said nowt to me. I've not been chilling with him lately. I've been doing my own thing with my own boys.'

Rachel stared at her brother, examining every inch of his face for signs that he was lying: no eyebrow twitching, no sniffing. He might be telling the truth.

Paul huddled his mother and his sister together and a large lump formed in the back of his throat. 'Sorry, honest, from the bottom of my heart, I'm so sorry. You're right, you should have been protected. I swear to you both that this will never happen again. Archie Bennet is a dead man walking, and if Dad doesn't sort the twat out, then I will.'

Jenny swallowed hard and broke free from his arms. 'Go and find your father. Tell him what's happened. He's probably had a lock-in down the pub. Jezz must be with him. In fact, tell your dad not to bother coming back here at all. Tell him to stay wherever it is that he's been all night, the no-good bastard.'

Jenny could hardly believe she'd said the words out loud. There was no going back now.

Chapter Twenty-Six

Danny was hurt, his face creased with pain. His hand was covered in blood from a deep gash. He dragged his t-shirt over his head and wrapped it around the wound. A few of the lads were wounded too; cuts, black eyes. Marzy had been shivved in his chest and he was the main cause for concern here today, bubbles of red blood pumping from the wound. Danny tied the grey t-shirt tightly around his hand and went to Marzy, who was slumped in a chair. 'You're going to be fine, lad. We'll get you to the hossy as soon as. But eh, we showed them, we took them down, we done good. A few scars, and blood was spilled, but we got the job done. Well done, lads. Nobody will mess with us again.'

Tomo was struggling to stand up, pain in his face as he spoke. 'Get on the blower and get rid of this gear. Get it out to the dealers, get it out of county, get it sold. Just get good money, and fast. The sooner it's gone the better. The word will be out now and those pricks will be getting heads together.'

Tomo spoke wise words and Danny knew he didn't have long. Tonight had been a good hit, the best one ever. He'd never seen so much drugs and money in one place. The men lay about the room like injured soldiers. None of them had got off scott-free, each of them with wounds. Danny looked at his hand. The blood was still gushing from it. 'The twat caught me off-guard and sliced me up with that machete. Did any of you see it? It was fucking massive.'

Marzy blew out his breath, beads of sweat forming on his forehead. 'It was a hard one tonight, Dan, I'm not going to lie. Them geezers were fucking tanks. The one who gripped me in the bear hug was like a gladiator. I nutted the prick twice and he never flinched.'

Tomo agreed. 'This is the big league, Danny. Fuck knows what they will come back with. But one thing for sure is that once I get my cut from this lot I'll be on my toes. Yep, a few weeks in Ibiza for me. Sex, drugs and rock and roll.' He forced a smile, but he was in bad pain.

Danny inhaled deeply and his nostrils flared, adrenalin still rushing through his veins. 'I'll bell Ricky and see if he can shift this lot. I bet them bastards are fucking gutted. There's at least seventy-grand's worth here, lads.'

There was no cheering today, even though this was a big parcel they'd landed. Each of them knew that there would be repercussions. Big repercussions.

Jezz staggered down the garden path and turned around to watch Charley wrestling with the garden gate. Drunk as anything, both singing. Jenny stood in the wreckage of the front door and glared at them both. Paul clearly hadn't delivered her message.

Jezz looked at her and burst out laughing. 'Aw, Jen, don't be kicking off. Charley wanted to come home, but it was me who kept him out. I had a little win on the gee-gees and treated him to a few beers. Go on, blame me, it's my fault.'

Jen remained silent and watched her husband swaying down the garden path. She could smell him from where he stood, he stank of beer. 'You're a bleeding disgrace, Charley. Look at you, you're a drunken mess. Look at the bleeding front door. Archie Bennet is the one who booted it from its hinges, if you are wondering what happened. Yes, he's been in here and ragged me and your daughter all over the place. You took your eye off the ball and left us vulnerable. Rachel is a mess and look at you, her father, her protector, pissed out of his head.'

Charley tried to register what his wife had said, but he was past all reason, his body swaying, eyes rolling, lips dry. Jenny stood aside to let him through where the front door should have been, and heard a crash behind her as he fell head first into the side cabinet in the hallway. She didn't even turn to look. Instead she watched Paul coming up the path.

'Mam, I found him, but he was too rat-arsed to listen to a word I said. I'll wait here until the door is fixed and Dad's sobered up.' His gaze shot to his old man, who was dead to the world at the bottom of the stairs. 'I didn't say it earlier, Mam. But you're right. He needs to man up or fuck off out of our lives. Danny was right, he's a has-been, he's lost his bottle, otherwise why is Archie fucking Bennet coming through? Once I get hold of Danny, I'll make sure we have a few of the lads on watch here every night. I'll make sure nobody gets to you or Rach again.'

Jenny stepped over her comatose husband, marched into the kitchen and sat down at the table. Paul was close behind her. 'Pop the kettle on, Son, and make me a coffee. Black, no sugar.'

Her son did as she asked and searched for the right words. 'Mam, this is going to get worse before it gets better. If one of the Bennets is in hossy, and they think we put him there, it's going to kick off big time. That's not the kind of thing you let slide. And our Danny's head's too far up his own arse to want to keep the peace. He's all about making a name for himself, but he's forgotten about his family.'

Jenny nodded. 'I know Archie means business, Son. The look in his eye told me this is far from over. He wants blood. I only hope his boy is alright, because I dread to think what will happen if he doesn't make it.' Jenny closed her eyes. 'Maybe I should go and see Andria Bennet. She must be as bad as me – no mother wants to see her kids hunted down. We can sort something out, surely. If we're leaving it up to Archie and your dad, nothing will ever get sorted. If we do it Danny's way, half of Manchester will burn.'

'Mam, I know you're trying to help,' Paul ventured. 'But Andria Bennet can't stand you. How many times have you been nose to nose with her?'

'Well, I have to do something, I can't sit here twiddling my thumbs, can I?' Jenny held her cup, steam from it hitting her face. She checked nobody could hear her and said quietly, 'I suppose I could always go and talk with Archie himself. I've known him a lot of years and maybe I could talk some sense into him if I got him on his own – not acting the hard man in front of his heavies.'

Paul shuddered. 'Whoa, I can't believe you would even say that. My dad would shit a brick if you were liaising with the enemy.'

Jenny snapped and smashed her flat palm down onto the table. 'No one else is coming up with anything, are they? That idiot is constantly pissed, and Danny is nowhere to be seen. So, come on then, know-it-all, tell me what we can do?'

Paul swallowed hard. She'd put him on the spot. Danny was the one who always made the plans, not him. 'We'll go through their door, like they've done to us.'

Jenny chuckled and rolled her eyes. 'Like that's going to do anything. Bloody hell, Paul, no wonder Danny doesn't ever leave you in charge.'

Paul screwed his face up. 'Listen to me, Mam. I can step up when I need to. I'll go and get a shooter. I'll find Archie fucking Bennet and blow the old man sky high. Don't underestimate me. I'll do anything for my family, and I mean *anything*. Go on, where is golden boy Danny now, eh?'

Jenny realised what she'd said and tried to back-pedal. 'I'm not saying you don't step up, I'm saying we need to sort this out – a one-and-done thing, not another chapter in the same bloody vendetta.'

Paul stood up from the table and looked down at his mother. 'I'm going out to find Danny. He should be here with us sorting this mess out together. And if it's him who's took Niall Bennet down then he's got a lot to answer for. Why the fuck has he not told me about it? I'm his family, his blood.'

Jenny was still now, quiet.

'Mam, go to bed, let's sort this out in the morning. I can't think straight with you sat there. Go to bed and let me find Danny and work out what we do.'

Jenny lifted her head to look at her son and a single tear fell from her eye. She twisted her gold wedding band around her finger. 'Sleep? What's that, Son? Since your dad's come home from prison there has been nothing but trouble in this house. No rest for the wicked.'

Chapter Twenty-Seven

News started to filter through the streets that Niall Bennet was making a good recovery. He was home now and being cared for by his family. But healing wounds didn't mean healing feuds. As soon as they were no longer on hospital watch, the brothers were on the rampage, taking things into their own hands. Fuck the police and doing things by the book. They had their own law and if anyone broke it there was hell to be paid. Danny and Paul Johnson both had a price on their heads now, and everyone was on the hunt for them. Marzy was nowhere to be seen and Tomo seemed to have gone missing from the face of the earth, as had the rest of Danny's boys. Nat was gunning for the Johnson brothers and he'd use anyone to get his hands on them. He put the word out in the area: if anyone was hiding them, they were involved, too. No one in their right mind would harbour the Johnson boys when they were dead men walking. Even Jenny didn't have a clue where they were staying now. Danny was a marked man, and not only by the

Bennets. He'd upset quite a few big men in the area and they'd be only too pleased to grass him up to the Bennets.

But not all the Johnson men were AWOL. Charley sat in his armchair, looking around the living room. He'd lost weight and his cheeks seemed sunken. He looked over at his collection of boxing trophies. He clutched his favourite one with both hands and held it tightly to his chest.

Jenny walked in and gave him a resigned look. He'd done nothing regarding Archie booming his door in. He'd sat there in his chair, wallowing in his own self-pity.

His eyes moistened as he spoke. 'I was at the top of my game back in the day, Jen. How different my life would have been if I'd chosen boxing as my career instead of the one I did. Look at me, Jen, what the fuck is up with me? I've got no fight left in me. My family is falling apart around me, and I'm sat like an old man in my chair, doing fuck all about it.'

Jenny shook her head. 'You should have taken the advice of your trainer and carried on boxing. But you thought you knew it all, Charley, and greed and power took you over. Just like Danny, the same story is repeating itself.'

Charley gripped the trophy tighter in his hands. 'I did what I did for us, Jenny. We had fuck-all, no work, we barely had a roof over our heads. I got us money – lots of it and fast.'

'We could have managed. Waited until your boxing brought in some more cash. Coped without the dirty money.'

'What, and watched Archie Bennet raking all the cash in? Over my dead body. He'd have stolen you back off me in no time.'

'Look at us, Charley. It's game over. It's only you sitting here, waiting for the end. The boys are in hiding, Rachel is a nervous wreck, and still you're stuck on ancient history with Archie. It's gone on for too long. Both our families are being destroyed because of it. Just end it, for crying out loud, end this bloody feud and let us live our lives in peace. Even if it is too late for you and me.'

Jenny had wanted to stay true to her word after the night of the attack. She'd stuck around until Charley sobered up and they got the door mended, then she decided, if Charley wouldn't leave, she would. She'd even packed a bag. But where could she go? There was nowhere safe round here. She needed a better escape plan than a dingy bedsit a few streets away.

Charley sucked hard on his gums and held back the tears. Maybe he was going soft in his old age. He sat thinking a while then jumped up, still holding the trophy. Jezz walked in and shot a look at Jenny. He sat next to her and both of them watched Charley with eager eyes. Charley didn't say another word, he rushed out and slammed the front door shut. The house shook.

Jenny sprinted over to the window and peered from behind the blinds, talking to Jezz over her shoulder. 'Where the hell is he going now? On my life, the man is doing my head in. You should have heard him before, Jezz, still talking about when he was younger, when he was a boxer. He's losing the plot. Whatever the hell is going on inside that man's head is beyond me.'

Jezz moved closer to Jenny and swept her hair back from her neck. His warm, wet lips pressed deep into her skin.

'Get up them stairs and get in bed. I've been dying to have some time with you.'

Jenny twisted her body to face him, and their lips met. She looked guarded as they shared a kiss. She broke away from him and gazed into his eyes. 'Jezz, when will this all be over? I want to get away from here, start again. If you can get me out of here, like you said, maybe we could be a thing. But not here. This place is poison.'

'Sshh, I've told you everything will work out for the best. We just have to sit pretty for now and watch the story unfold. I might not have to do anything; Archie Bennet will do it for us. You'll get your freedom from Charley, and I'll get you.'

Chapter Twenty-Eight

Rachel looked around the solicitor's office. She'd received a letter to attend an appointment here today at nine forty-five, regarding Dorothy Jenson's last wishes. Rachel had slipped out without a soul asking where she was going. There was so much going on in her house lately that she may as well have been invisible. She wanted to get this morning out of the way so she could do right by Dot, but her thoughts kept leaping ahead. After her appointment she was finally going to see Niall again, for the first time since the attack.

Getting a message to him hadn't been easy, let alone finding a time he wouldn't be surrounded by his family. She'd tried setting up new accounts online, finding ways to reach him, and all the time wondering if he was suffering, if what had happened to him meant he wouldn't want to see her again. She eventually got a message to him, and he confirmed he wanted to see her, too, but she was full of nerves. Did he only want to see her to dump her to her face? Or what if it was a set-up? Maybe he regretted the day he ever got mixed up with a Johnson. Or maybe, and she hardly let herself hope this, maybe he was like her, thinking of that night in the hotel. That night it had been only about them, not their families. It was the thought of that night that kept her going through everything that happened recently.

Rachel turned in the black leather chair and looked around the reception. Through the window, the Manchester weather was shocking today. Rain, rain, and more rain. Big grey clouds hanging down from the sky. There was a young girl behind the reception desk. She was dressed in a crisp white blouse and knee-length pencil skirt, black shiny shoes and her hair clipped back neatly. Maybe Rachel should have concentrated more in school. She could have had the career she wanted instead of working in a café where she'd never escape her family's reputation. There was a bowl of sweets on the glass table in front of her and, up to now, she'd eaten five of them. As she pushed another sweet into her mouth, she smiled over at the receptionist.

'I'm starving. I've not had any breakfast this morning.'

The girl smiled back at her, but Rachel could tell she wasn't happy. She picked all the silver wrappers up from the table and pushed them into her pocket.

A door opened and a middle-aged man walked out, holding a brown file in his hands. Grey hair, oval-shaped gold-rimmed glasses perched on the end of his nose.

'Rachel Johnson, is it?'

She quickly chewed her sweet and tried to reply with her mouth full. 'Yes, that's me.'

'Do you want to follow me to my office?' The man didn't wait for her to answer. He opened the door and waited for her to come through.

Rachel surveyed the office and watched the man step behind his long wooden desk. She smiled when she saw he had photos of his family placed neatly at the side of his computer. She took a closer look and raised her eyebrows. This guy was punching above his weight with his wife, for sure: she was a beauty.

'Take a seat,' he said, as he scrolled through his messages on his computer screen.

Rachel was indignant. Here she was making sure she was on time, and here he was thinking she had all the time in the world. He reached over and filled his glass with sparkling water from the small fridge at his side. Bloody hell, why didn't he just drink tap water like everyone else? But she guessed with him it was all about show.

He coughed slightly to clear his throat. 'My name is James Coby. I am the solicitor dealing with Dorothy Jenson's last will and testament.'

Rachel wasn't looking forward to listening to him drone on. She guessed she'd been asked here to discuss what to do with Dorothy's things. The care home had already asked her about the personal effects Dorothy had with her when she died. Rachel had suggested they bag everything up, ready for when her extended family finally bothered to show up. But she didn't fancy having to sort out all the crap from Dot's house – she remembered the stink of the place and how awful John had let it get. In fact, she had already decided that if they wanted her to sort it out, she would tell them to donate it all to charity. Anyway, where was John? Should *he* not be sitting here making these decisions? He was probably lying low, feeling lucky he'd escaped a charge of assault and battery for everything he'd done to his poor mum.

James took a small sip of his water and turned to Rachel. He rolled his silver parker pen about in his hand and opened the file in front of her. Reading, wobbling his head from side to side. He picked up a white letter from his desk. 'Dorothy thought a lot of you, Rachel, and she left this letter for you. Do you want me to read it out to you, or do you wish to read it?'

She was touched, aware that whatever was written in the letter was most likely going to make her cry. Maybe she should have brought someone with her, someone to hold her when she broke down crying. 'Yes, please, can you read it?'

James pushed his glasses up his nose. He took a deep breath, sat back in his black leather chair and began in a surprisingly soft voice:

Dearest Rachel,

Firstly, let me thank you from the bottom of my heart for all that you have done for me. You are such a kind, caring person and you have been my angel in disguise. When my world was full of darkness you brought me light, and when I had nowhere to turn you welcomed me with open arms. I've never really had friendship like this in my life and you have brought me so much happiness in times of trouble. I loved our talks each day at the café and I can never thank you enough for all the tea and toast you gave me – but most of all for your time.

James lifted his head, peered over his spectacles and smiled at her. She felt a warmth rising through her body. He continued:

You have been like a daughter to me, and I wish you all the happiness in the world. Life is for living, Rachel, stop hiding in the shadows and let the world see what a beautiful and strong person you are. Follow your heart and don't listen to whatever anyone else says. Live your life for you and not your family. Take chances and go on that adventure. I don't know if I ever mentioned the cottage in Devon? I probably didn't, but it's a place I often spent time with my husband when we were younger. You brought me so much happiness and now I want to try and return it back to you. Thank you again from the bottom of my heart and I'll never be far from your side. I'll only ever be a whisper away. Go and be happy, Rachel. Thank you, my Angel. Love Dot xxxxx

Rachel twisted her fingers rapidly, overcome with emotion at Dot's kind words.

James folded the letter neatly and passed it across the desk to her. His voice was soft as he spoke again. 'That was such a lovely letter. Dorothy thought a lot about you. And she wants you to have happy memories of her.'

'Yes, I didn't quite follow the middle bit,' said Rachel. 'The part about Devon. It sounded like she wanted me to go there and have a holiday in the same place she did. Is that what her last wish was? I don't mean to sound cheeky, but has she left me the money for a holiday? Because she didn't have enough money for the gas, let alone to give me money for a coach trip.'

He opened the file in front of him and then dug his hand deep into his briefcase. He popped three keys into a white envelope and placed them on top of some paperwork. 'I don't think you understand. The place in Devon isn't a village – it's a cottage. Dot's cottage. It's small but really rather charming.'

'But if she had a house somewhere else, why was she living like she was up here? I mean, she had no money for the meter, the fridge was bare, and her thieving bastard of a son, excuse my language, wouldn't even give her a couple of quid for a slice of toast.'

'I think you've hit the nail on the head, Ms Johnson. The other parts of the will make it clear that, even when Dot was well enough to come here and make her will, she was already starting to distrust her son's motives. The cottage belonged to her husband's family – I gather Dot's late husband was John's stepfather – and it seemed Dot didn't trust John not to sell it and spend it all on booze. The cottage is lovely. I've printed you some photographs of it and directions how to get there.'

Rachel sat forward in her seat, still puzzled. 'Does this really mean she has given me a house in Devon? I don't even know where Devon is. I've only ever been to Blackpool, is it far from there?'

James smiled. He folded the paperwork and slid it into a large brown envelope. 'If you've never been to Devon then you're in for a treat. The fresh air is heavenly, the coastline is beautiful and everything about the place is a little slice of paradise.'

Rachel took the envelope from him and placed it on her lap. 'What about her John, does he not have a claim on the cottage?'

'That's another story, Ms Johnson. All you need to know is that he was looked after too, despite how he treated his mother.' James shot a look over at the clock on the wall and stood up. He walked around the desk and held his hand out to Rachel. 'If you need anything else, please don't hesitate to contact me. Good luck with your new home. I hope it means as much to you as it clearly did to Mrs Jenson.'

Rachel stood up, still trying to make sense of everything as she walked out of the office. The receptionist narrowed her eyes at her as she walked slowly through the reception area. Rachel stopped, reached into the sweet bowl, grabbed a handful of sweets and rammed them into her pocket.

'I'm celebrating. I'm a homeowner now,' she chuckled as she left.

She stood outside the offices and lifted her eyes to the sky. It was still raining, but suddenly Manchester's grey skies didn't bother her. 'God bless you, Dot, and thank you so much. I'll never forget you.'

She zipped her coat up and placed the large envelope in her black leather bag. It was time to meet Niall.

Rachel pulled up in the taxi and saw Niall in his car across the road. She picked up her bag and paid the fare. She hurried across the main road and down the side street. Her heart beat faster than normal: she was torn between hurrying to the car and running away in fear. With shaking hands, she approached, opened the passenger door and got inside. She could feel the warm air as soon as she sat down, but one look at Niall's face and her blood ran cold. He wasn't even looking at her, but straight through the windscreen instead.

Refusing to give in to her fears, Rachel tried her best to sound upbeat. 'I'm so glad you're alright, Niall. I came to see you in hospital, you know. I sat by your side and held your hand, you probably don't remember. I've been worried sick about you, about us.'

He looked thin, grey, no colour in his cheeks, his hair overgrown. She reached over and touched his lap. He squirmed, moved her hand away.

'Rachel, this isn't easy for me to say, but you do know it was your brothers who put me in hospital, don't you? Your Danny and his cronies?'

'I've heard stories, but I don't know what to believe anymore. I'm only glad you are alright. I've missed you so much. My heart's been broken into a million pieces at the thought of you hurt, whoever did it.'

'I'm telling you it was your Danny. He may be your big brother, but a twat is what he is, and once I'm healed I'll settle that score myself.' He sniffed, looked straight ahead. 'So we're done. It's over,' he said abruptly.

Rachel froze. All her fears were coming true. He turned to face her and more in sadness than rage he said, 'Look at the state of my fucking boat-race. Look what your brother did to me. Do you think I could ever be with you after this? No way. Once them bastards are found I'll make sure each of them gets exactly what I did. Look, four stitches under my eye, three under my chin, ten in my head, and seven near my ear. I want fuck all to do with the Johnsons, beyond revenge. And that means you, too.'

Rachel covered her mouth with both hands as he revealed his scars. But she hadn't let his words sink in. She still hoped she could talk him round. 'I thought you loved me, Niall. You said nothing would ever come between us.'

'That was then. Things change. After what Danny did, I want revenge. I want to see them tossers on a drip like I was. My mam's been on her knees with worry and so has my dad. I could never be with a Johnson. This isn't Romeo and bleeding Juliet. You're all rotten to the core.'

Rachel swallowed hard, digesting his words. Was he for real? She sat back in the seat and tensed her jaw. Why was she still sat here when he'd just spoken to her like that?

He gripped the steering wheel. 'I wish things could have been different between us. We could have been good together.'

That was it, she'd heard enough. She snapped. 'Niall, our families have been fighting for like forever. You knew that at the start and told me you didn't care about anything but us. Was that all lies?' She never gave him chance to reply. 'Do you know what? if you can't see past my surname, you can do one. I thought I meant more to you than that. Here's me sat about crying, when all along you've never give a shit about me. You can sling it, Niall Bennet. You're not the man I thought you were.'

She opened the car door and bent forward to pick her bag up from the floor.

Niall gripped her arm. 'You meant the world to me, but family comes first. You know how it is.'

Rachel had to fight all her instincts not to collapse into his arms, and instead dragged her body away from him.

'Tell someone who gives a fuck, Niall, because I don't. Don't you ever darken my door. Lesson learned for me. Big lesson. I'm a Johnson and proud of it.' She slammed the car door. 'Fuck you, Niall Bennet, fuck you all.'

Chapter Twenty-Nine

Jezz stood by Charley's side as Archie Bennet walked into the room with one of his heavies. Jezz focused on the heavy: he was a big fucker, over six foot tall and solid as a rock. Archie was bigger than he remembered, too. A giant. Jezz pulled his shoulders back and his nostrils flared. Fuck that. If this kicked off, he was steering clear of this beast. Charley could deal with him. Jezz patted his coat pocket, made sure his tool was still there. He coughed nervously. There was no way he could have a fair fight with this monster. No way. He was getting stabbed up, brought down in seconds, if he came anywhere near him.

Archie paced over to the table and sat down first. His eyes drilled into his opponents, scanning them from head to toe. Charley followed him, constantly checking over his shoulder too, none of them trusting each other. Charley was carrying a bag in his left hand and dropped it to the floor before he sat down. Archie had aged, but his eyes still held the same determination and envy they always had. Jezz pulled his chair out and sat slightly away from the table. If it kicked off, at least he would have a few seconds to pull his blade out from his jacket pocket. Archie looked trim, in great shape for his age. You could see he'd spent hours at the gym lifting weights, running, rowing. His t-shirt fitted him like a glove. Charley was not in the same league as this man anymore, no way. Chippy-tits and chub-rub rather than muscle and sinew. All those pints and takeaways had caught up with Charley.

The conversation began with Charley speaking first. He was the one who'd called this meeting and Archie was only here out of curiosity, barely even acknowledging Charley as a serious threat. Charley sighed and licked his lips before he spoke. 'I'm here to sort out this shit between our families. It's gone on for years and we need to put a stop to it before someone ends up on a slab in the morgue.'

Archie smashed his clenched fist on the table. 'Do you think it will stop just like that? My son was at death's door and it was your son who put him there. This feud won't be over until the score is settled. You know the dance, pal, an eye for an eye and all that.'

Charley said, 'I had no idea what they were up to. I don't work like that. You know me better than that. They will have me to answer to when I catch up with them both. It's not my way, as I said.'

'You think your Danny will listen to you? Let's face it, pal, you've got fuck all anymore. And, for the record, stop telling people I stitched you up. As you know,' he stressed, 'that's not my game, either.'

Jezz was on edge, watching Charley, watching Archie for any sudden movements. It was like a game of tennis.

Charley bent down, picked up a bag from near his legs and banged it onto the table. Archie sat back and folded his arms, curious as to what was inside it. Charley slowly dug his hands inside and pulled out a trophy. The one he'd had in his home all these years. Archie's eyes lit up and a smile filled his face. He knew what it was before anybody told him, still had memories of the night he was on his arse watching this prick facing him holding it up in the air, celebrating. He nodded before he spoke. 'The Collyhurst and Moston trophy, the one you robbed from me.'

'I won it fair and square, but you never got over it, did you?'

Archie looked to his heavy. 'He told everyone he won fair and square, but nobody saw the low blow he gave me in the nuts. He stole one on me then and got declared the fucking winner. He's always been a lying rat.'

'That's a load of shite, Archie. I won, end of. And you know it.'

Archie frowned. 'And your point is?' He shot a look at the trophy. 'What has that got to do with our beef?'

Charley sat back in his seat and folded his arms over his beer belly. 'Simple. Let's settle it once and for all. Me and you back in the ring, winner takes all. If you win, I'll back down and let you run the area, if I win, same. Plus, the winner takes the trophy home.'

Archie couldn't believe what his old rival was saying. But he was interested, Jezz could tell: his eyes never left the trophy. Charley must have been right; the title still meant something to him. Archie sat thinking, stroking his chin. Jezz tried not to look at him. He was uncomfortable with the offer on the table, but this wasn't his shout.

Archie swallowed hard, cracking his knuckles. 'I'll fight you, but not in the ring. Nah, fuck that, I want you to feel every punch. A bare-knuckle fight. And the same with our lads, my eldest versus yours.'

Charley smiled over at Jezz. 'A bare-knuckle fight, I can do that. You say when and where, and I'll be there with my boy.'

Archie nodded and chuckled. 'I'm ready when you are but, looking at you, you're going to need a bit of time. Plus, we'll put a purse on the fights to make it that bit more interesting.' He winked and smiled over at his wingman. 'It's not my normal way of doing business but, eh, I like a bit of variety.' His fingers glided slowly over the trophy. 'Plus, I want my name and the date putting on this when I win.'

So Charley was right after all. Archie did still care about the boxing match. Archie picked the trophy up and pressed the cold metal to his lips. 'I'll see you soon. You'll be back where you belong, where you should have been all these years.'

Charley acknowledged the meeting was over when Archie stood up. As he walked away, he shouted, 'Two weeks, twenty grand purse, Charley. I'll get my lads to sort out where and get back to you. And mind you make sure your eldest is there too because our Nat is going to knock ten tons of shit out of him.'

Jezz was horrified. He stood up and paced about the room. 'Fuck me, Charley, why this way? We could have settled this on the streets, the way we usually do things. We have the man-power to do the job proper. Take out their foot soldiers before going after the generals.'

Charley stood. 'I do things my way. If it's a bare-knuckle fight, then so be it. I've delayed too long. That's why Danny went rogue.'

'What, and you think Danny will go along with this? The guy hasn't showed his face around here for I don't know how long and you think he's going to listen to you and turn up here while there's a price on his head?'

Charley roared. 'He'll do as I say. He's not been home because he knows what he's done, going behind my back. And, for that, he'll have me to answer to.'

Jezz muttered under his breath. 'Like he'll be bothered.'

Charley froze. 'What did you just say?'

Jezz tried to get away with it. 'I'm only saying Danny is a young one, pal. They don't do things this way anymore. They go to fights tooled up. Shooters, mate. You know the score.'

But, as ever, Charley wasn't listening. 'I've got some serious training to do.' He grabbed the trophy, picked up the bag from the table and marched out of the room.

Chapter Thirty

Jenny sat in the small office at Blossoms, counting the takings, when Jackie came out into the reception area. Jenny could feel her eyes on her through the small window and she lifted her head. The door opened slightly.

'Are you alright, Jackie? You after something?' Jenny clocked her eyes on the cash as she walked to the door, and quickly folded it up and tucked it into a large white envelope. She looked at the monitor in front of her and switched off the CCTV footage she was viewing. There had been a few nutters hanging around in the car park lately, and Jenny was making sure nobody was lurking in the shadows. Jackie stood in the doorway with her hand resting on the wooden frame.

'Yeah, I'm good. It's been quiet tonight and I'm just debating getting off home early.'

Jenny raised her eyebrows. Since when had these girls took it upon themselves to pick and choose when they worked? As far as she was concerned, they were here until the early hours. Men loved to call in after a night on the town when their mrs was fast asleep in bed. There was even a man – been coming for over a year now – who every night told his wife he was taking the dog out in the midnight hour so it wouldn't fight with other dogs. He was never questioned, he said, and he'd often leave his four-legged friend tied up in the car park whilst he came into Blossoms for his guilty pleasure. His wife was none the wiser.

Jenny sat up straight in the black leather chair and eyeballed Jackie. 'It doesn't work like that, love. I thought you would know that more than anybody else?'

Jackie flicked her hair over her shoulder, walked into the office and sat down facing Jenny. She poured herself a drink and Jenny carried on with her paperwork. But she could feel her Jackie's eyes all over her. She stood and walked from behind the desk. If this girl had a problem, she needed to put it on the table and sort it out.

'Pour me a large one, love,' Jenny said. 'It's been a crap day and I need a nice drink to help me unwind.'

Jackie unscrewed the red lid from the vodka and poured some into a glass. She passed it over to Jenny and watched her neck a mouthful of it before she sat down on the small white leather sofa. The two women sat watching each other drink. Jackie tried to make small talk. 'Is Charley not calling in tonight?'

Jenny shook her head. She had never really sat down with Jackie and spoken to her before. Of course, she was the one who'd recruited her, but that was while her husband was banged up and she was desperate for new staff. Jezz knew her and said she would fit in well, but Jenny had never got to know her. She was not in the habit of making friends with the brasses that worked here. Most of them were here one minute, gone the next. There was no point. Their worlds were so far apart.

Jackie poured herself another drink. She was well on her way and her eyes looked glazed. Jenny knew that most nights Jackie had something to take the edge off her work here. She could never have done what she did with a straight head. No, a few lines of cocaine and some vodka were on a lot of the girls' menus before a shift. They blocked out the things they allowed these men to do to their bodies for money. Jackie offered Jenny another drink, but she declined. 'How are you getting on with the other girls, Jackie?'

Jackie licked her cherry-red lips. 'It is what it is, love. They stay out of my business, and I keep my beak out of theirs. I'm not into making new friends and all that. I'm a lone wolf.'

Jenny agreed. 'I get where you're coming from. Friendships are hard to come by. You can't trust anyone these days; nobody has an ounce of respect. Right, it's home time for me. I hope things pick up in here. I bet you're bored waiting around?'

Jackie clocked the time and chuckled to herself. 'I usually get old Frank in on a Thursday night. He's a dirty old bleeder for his age. He waits until he gets his pension money and spends the lot of it here with me. Pervert.'
Jenny reached over the back of the chair and grabbed her red coat. It was cold tonight. Winter had well and truly kicked in. All she wanted to do now was go home and put her pyjamas on. She watched Jackie walk out of the office,

flicked the light off and followed her out. As she left, she called, 'Tell the girls I'll see them tomorrow. Have a nice evening, and be careful when you're leaving. It's been on the news again about a man attacking women in the area. So be vigilant, and tell the others, too.'

Rachel felt weak as she stood over the stove making beans and toast. Her appetite had vanished lately and she was finding it hard to keep anything down. Losing Dot had been bad enough, and now she had the heartbreak of losing Niall on top. It had left its mark on her. She'd not told anyone about her inheritance. She didn't want it tarnished by all the crap going on round here. The house from Dot was her secret. When she felt better, she was going to get a train down to Devon and see the place for the first time. She needed to sort her head out first, though. Get some cash together and book time off work. She stirred the beans and watched them bubble.

A voice behind her made her jump. 'Hey, Sis. If you're making something to eat, bang me something on. too. I'm Hank Marvin. Where's my mam, anyway?'

Rachel turned and faced Paul who, as ever, looked like he'd just woken up. 'What are you doing showing your face round here, Paul? Have you got a death wish?'

'Dad summoned me and our Danny back home. He rang and told me the Bennets know it was Danny who done Niall in, so I'm out of hiding for now. Are you going to eat that, or what?'

'I've lost my appetite.' She pushed the plate towards her brother. Paul rubbed his hands together and sat at the kitchen table. It was rare that Rachel spent time with Paul, and she was glad to see him sober for a change. She dragged a chair to sit down next to him.

He tucked into the meal and spoke with his mouth full. 'It's going to kick off big-time when Danny finally comes through that front door. He went behind Dad's back. I'm so glad I wasn't involved with it all this time. It's usually me who's getting a bollocking, not Danny.'

Rachel stared at her brother. 'That attack was a low blow. The lad was innocent and nothing to do with all this crap that's going on. It was shady and, when I see Danny, I'll be telling him that.'

'Oi, Sis, since when have you cared about the Bennets? Sure, Danny should have got Dad's blessing, but the Bennets have had this coming for a long time, so don't feel sorry for them fuckers. Do you think they gave us a second thought when they moved on our patch while Dad was in the slammer? Did they fuck. So yeah, it might have been over the top what Danny did to Niall, but you live by the sword, you die by the sword. It could have easily been one of us lying there in that hospital bed.' Paul finished his food and sat back in his chair, rubbing his belly. 'So Dad's in there with a face on him. Has he been arguing with my mam?'

'Dunno, it's not helping, Jezz being here all the time. I thought it was only a short time he was staying. Didn't he say he was looking for somewhere else?' Rachel twisted her hair around her finger. 'The sooner the better for me, he gives me the creeps. He always seems to appear from nowhere. He freaks me out.'

Paul chuckled. 'Jezz is sound, a bit off his rocker when he's had a few, but he's harmless. He's the one guy who's always got Dad's back, I guess. Anyway, I'm going to jump in the bath before all the hot water is gone. If Danny comes in while I'm upstairs, give me a shout. I don't want to miss this for the world. At last, big boy will get his comeuppance.'

Chapter Thirty-One

It was well past midnight and Jenny had just got into bed. Charley was still downstairs waiting for Danny to come home. He'd finally told Jenny about the fights that had been arranged and she'd hit the roof, telling him to get his clothes and go to his bloody mother's house. But Charley was waiting it out – waiting for her to calm down like she always did. And, in the meantime, he was doing his best not to go into the fridge and get the four cans of Stella that were waiting there for him. He needed to get his body in shape for when he fought Archie. Strict diet. He'd done it before and he could do it again. But as much as he hated to admit it, he needed Danny by his side for this one. He kept checking his wristwatch and shaking his head. 'Where are you, you little bastard?' he mumbled under his breath. Finally, he heard Danny check for the key under the rock where the spare was always kept.

Danny fumbled with the lock, his hand still bandaged. The house was silent. He plodded into the kitchen and opened the fridge door looking for something to snack on. The light from the fridge seemed to fade, a shadow behind him. Turning his head quickly, he met his father's eyes. He'd seen this look many times before, a glare that told him this was serious.

Charley didn't even waste a breath before smashing him up against the wall, and speaking through clenched teeth, 'Do you think you can do whatever you want to do around here, and nobody is going to say a fucking word? *I'm* the fucking voice in this house, you prick, and you will listen. Do you hear me? You will fucking listen.' He dragged Danny across the kitchen. He tried to break free, but Charley was stronger than he looked – especially when he was angry. 'You took one of the Bennets down when I told you to wait.'

Danny retaliated, gasping for breath. 'Because I'm not sitting about waiting on you to get your shit together. For years me and our kid have kept things ticking around here, waiting for you to come home. Do you know how hard it's been for us all, watching them clowns taking half of everything we own? It's ours, Dad, not fucking theirs.'

Charley flung his son to the floor with one hand and stood over him. 'You could have gone to jail if that Bennet kid had kicked the bucket. Life in jail for fucking murder, you muppet. Go on, tell me how you would hack the rest of your life in the slammer?' He didn't give Danny chance to answer him. 'It's the worst place in the world to be. Nightmare. Look at me after jail. I'm fucked up in the head. I'm all over the place. And you think I can stand by and watch you, my first-born son, end up like I have? No way.

This time you will listen, and you will do as I damn well say. Your little kidnap and torture escapade has put us all in the firing line. Archie's been here. He's manhandled your mum and your sister. And now he's demanded you fight, too – all because you couldn't bide your time. So, no going off plan this time. We fight like men. No tricks, no gloves, no blades. Just fists and fury.'

Danny dragged his knees up to his chest with his back against the wall. There was no way he could tackle his old man while he was injured himself.

The door flung open and Jenny ran in, having heard her husband's words. 'Get away from him, Charley. He's not fighting anyone. You do whatever you're doing, but my son is not getting involved in it.'

'Woman, go back to bed and let us sort this out man-to-man.' Charley moved towards her, eyes bulging from their sockets. He meant business and she knew it. 'I said, go to bed.'

Danny shouted over to his mother. 'Mam, I'm fine. Leave us to it.'

'No, Son, not a chance. I've seen this man in action and I don't trust him, he's a shady bastard. A woman-beater, and a bully. Go on, tell your son how you beat his mother.'

She'd lit the touchpaper of Charley's temper with that. He stormed at her and rushed her out of the kitchen. He closed the door behind him so Danny couldn't see and held her up against the wall, her legs kicking in the air, her face turning first red then blue.

'Don't you ever try to come between me and my kids. The next time you badmouth me to them you know what will happen. Nobody will help you.' He let her go, her body falling to the ground like a sack of spuds.

She felt the air rush back into her body, her stinging lungs sucking in the oxygen greedily, her own hand now around her neck, feeling the tender skin. She scrambled on all fours up the stairs, never looking back.

Charley went back to the kitchen, held his hand out and pulled his son up off the floor. 'Sit down at the table and let's talk this out.'

But before they could speak, Paul ran in. 'What the fuck is going on? I've just heard all the screaming, and my mam is a mess, crying her eyes out.'

'Nothing you need to bother about, son. A bit of marital strife, that's all. What we need to have tonight is a man-to-man talk, if you know what side your bread's buttered on.' Charley shot his eyes to the other chair for Paul to join them. He waited til they were both seated.

'I've been to see Archie Bennet today and we've found a solution to end this shit once and for all. Me and Archie will fight each other, and Danny and Archie's son Nat will battle it out, too. Twenty grand purse, bare knuckles. Winner takes all. Both crowns are up for grabs, the younger and the older one. But it ends after the fights. If the Bennets win, we take it on the chin and walk away.'

Danny screwed his face up, fuming, cheeks bright red. 'What, and let them cunts have everything we've grafted for?'

Charley eyeballed Danny again. 'Are you deaf? I've just told you what is fucking happening. You fight the Bennet kid. If you fuck it up, it's down to me to make sure I snap Archie's jaw.'

Danny shook his head. 'This is a joke; I'll be a laughing stock. We don't do things that way anymore.'

Charley smashed his rounded fist onto the table, getting up in Danny's face. 'You fucking do now. So get training, and let's show them pricks that we are still the main name around here, not them.'

Paul rubbed his hands together, relieved that his name had not been thrown into the mix. He could fight when he had to, but to be put up against Nat Bennet was another story. The kid was into all that cage-fighting shit. Moves that made sure his opponent couldn't move: arm bars, a choke hold, kimura lock. He wondered if his dad knew that when he agreed to Archie's terms.

Danny let out a laboured breath and shot a look at his dad. 'If that's what is arranged, then so be it. I've never been one to walk away from a challenge. This area is run by us and the sooner everyone knows it the better. I'm in.'

Charley held his shoulders back with pride. This was more like it, his boys working together. 'We'll rip them apart.'

Chapter Thirty-Two

Rachel's shift at the café was dragging. Every time the door opened, she was still half expecting it to be either Dot or Niall. There were no customers in yet and the staff were enjoying the quiet before the storm.

Katie came out from behind the counter. 'So, fill me in. How's it going with Niall? I've not heard you mention him for a while?'

Rachel wanted the ground to open up and swallow her. 'Nothing to tell. We had a few dates. I've not rang him, and he's not rang me. It wasn't all that, if I'm being honest.' She was lying through her front teeth, and blushing.

'I thought you was mad for him. You used to fall to pieces whenever he came in here.'

Rachel picked up a small piece of burnt toast and nibbled on it. 'Be careful what you wish for, that's what I say. He wasn't the man I thought he was. I say love them, leave them. Break their hearts before yours gets stamped on.'

'So, what's next, Rach? Or rather, *who's* next? As my mam always tells me, you have to kiss a few frogs before you find your prince.'

'Give me time, Katie. I'm not ready to get out there just yet.'

'Book yourself in the hairdresser's, love, have a spray tan and get your nails done. It always works for me. You got to love yourself before anyone else can love you, darling.'

Rachel smiled and nodded. Yep, this was what she was going to do. Why should she sit here crying over some man? Katie was right: shoulders back, smile on her face and move on.

Jenny sat in the kitchen staring at the clock. Gina had not been over for a week now, and the last time she called it had only been for a few minutes. They'd made up after their last words, and Jenny could have done with a friendly ear; someone she could unload on. She picked her fags up from the table and her house keys.

Gina's husband's car wasn't outside their house and Jenny was relieved. At least now they could have a good natter and a catch up without anyone listening in. Jenny noticed the blinds at the front room window were still shut. Maybe Gina was having a lie in? She never knocked when she visited Gina, just let herself in, like Gina did at her house. She yanked the silver door handle down and walked inside. A quick walk into the living room and the kitchen:

nobody about. Jenny stood in the hallway, listening. Voices upstairs, but then the noise subsided. Jenny started up the stairs with caution. 'Gina, are you still in bed, you lazy cow? I've not seen your ugly mush for days. Where have you been hiding?' Still no reply. Jenny held her keys in her hand, silver key sticking through her fingers, ready if any intruders were here waiting for her.

She swung the bedroom door open and gaped. 'What the fuck, Gina?'

Paul scrambled out of the bed and fell about trying to put his clothes on.

Her friend jumped up from the bed and grabbed a blue fluffy housecoat. 'Jen, erm, Jen, it's not what it seems. . . '

Jenny roared and ran at Gina. 'You dirty slut, what is wrong with you?'

'Jen. I know what you must think about me, but my Dave is always working, and he's tired all the time. I needed some attention.'

'Fuck off, I'll give you some bleeding attention, you tart.' She lunged for Gina. 'He's my son, you dirty slapper. How could you do this to me? We had rules, you know the rules, you don't ever touch my boys.'

Paul was dragging his jeans over his legs now and helped free Gina from his mother's grip. 'I'm a man, Mother. Go home, will you? Wow, we are both adults here.'

'*Me* go home, are you having a laugh? I'm going to knock her teeth out, the dirty cow.'

Gina stood in the corner of the room now, hair all over the place, red marks on her cheeks where Jenny had clawed her. 'We was only having a bit of fun, Jen, hurting nobody.'

Paul stood in front of Gina, protecting her. 'She's right, Mam. It is what it is.'

Gina got cocky behind Paul and said over his shoulder, 'And don't tell me you've never had a bit of fun, Jen. Come on, people who live in glass houses shouldn't throw stones.'

Paul gripped his mother's hands and pulled her away. 'For crying out loud, it's not like I've committed a crime here. Ease up. Just go. Do one.'

Jenny stood at the doorway, hands on her hips, as she screamed at Gina. 'I thought you were my friend. I thought I could trust you. But you're nothing but a tart.' She ran down the stairs and straight out of the front door. She slammed it shut, nearly taking it from its hinges.

Paul sat down on the bed, bare-chested, head in hands. 'Well, the shit has hit the fan now, Gina.' She came over and plonked down next to him, tears streaming down her cheeks. Paul placed his warm hand on her bare knee and stroked her leg. 'For fuck's sake, did you see how angry she was? And what did you mean about people in glass houses?'

Gina was determined not to make a bad situation worse. 'Oh, nothing. I was shouting anything to get back at her. I'm gutted, Paul. Your mam has been a good friend to me.'

Paul jumped up from the bed. 'Nobody has died, she'll get over it. I'll go and see her, smooth things over.'

'Paul, she was livid. Leave her for a bit before you go near her. Tell her I'm sorry, and ask her not to tell my Dave. He's been stressed lately with work, and I don't want her adding to it. It would break him in two if he got wind of this.'

Paul was unbothered by mention of Gina's husband. In fact, he had a cocky smile on his face. 'Same time tomorrow, then,' he chuckled.

She pushed him away. 'It's alright for you, Paul. She'll throttle me when she gets her hands on me. She's always told me never to touch her sons.'

'Naughty girl then, aren't you? All the better for me,' he sniggered. 'I'm off, Gina, catch you later.' Paul motored down the stairs and out of the front door.

———

Jenny hadn't long been home when Paul popped his head in the door.

His mother was a woman of the world. Once he sat down with her and explained it was just a bit of no-strings sex then, surely, she would get over it and move on. Paul coughed to get her attention.

She glared at him through the cloud of smoke circling her face. 'Dirty bastard,' she hissed.

Paul walked further into the room and sat down. He knew he had to tread carefully here, choose his words wisely. 'Mam, bloody hell, it was only a bit of fun. Nobody got hurt.'

'That's not the point. She knows the rules. Liberty taker, she is.'

'Oh, come on. If it wasn't me, it would be someone else. The woman is a sex addict. Our Danny has slipped her one, too. Most of my mates have over the years. Gina's sound – she never gets all soppy – she recognises a screw for what it is. A little bit of fun.'

Jenny was gobsmacked. 'What, she's slept with Danny, too? Come on, you're having a laugh, surely?'

Paul grinned. 'It's true. Shagging Gina is a rite of passage round here. So don't be falling out with her and going to tell her husband. She's not hurting anyone.'

'She was my friend. I've let in my house for years. I trusted her. You'll be telling me your dad's had sex with her next?'

Paul played with his coat cuff. Jenny looked at him closer: he was going red.

'I know nothing, Mother. Stop going on about it. If it makes you feel any better, I won't be going there again.'

Jenny still glared at him but she was calming down. She probably realised she'd acted first and thought second. They sat for a while in complete silence. Paul started scrolling through his phone, deleting the dirty snaps Gina had sent him. That was all he needed, his mother seeing them; she would have wasted Gina good and proper.

Jenny gazed into the distance. 'I don't know what is happening to this family. On my life, I feel like packing my clothes up and going far away from all this crap. Nobody would even miss me.'

Paul lifted his head from his phone, aware his mother was tearful. 'Of course you would be missed, Mam. Once all this is over with the Bennets, we can all go back to a peaceful life.'

'It will never be peaceful, Paul, there will always be one more fight to win. What, when this fight is over, do you really think either your dad or Archie Bennet will just walk away?'

'That's what he's said.'

'Bullshit. He's a snake. I wouldn't trust a word that comes out of that man's mouth.'

Paul's phone started to ring and he seemed glad of the excuse to end this discussion with her. 'Yo, what's happening, bro?' Paul listened to the voice at the other end of the phone and replied, 'Yeah, give me ten minutes and I'll meet you there. Who's training with you?' He chatted away for a few more minutes and ended the call.

Jenny was straight on him. 'Who was that? Danny?'

'Yep, I'm going down the gym to meet him. The guy has to put a graft in now, doesn't he, if he's up against Nat Bennet. Personally, I think he'll get wasted, Mam. But I'm not the one calling the shots, am I?' He came to her and kissed her cheek. 'Sorry about all that with Gina. Like I said, it was a bit of fun. It's over now.'

She watched him leave. 'It's always only a bit of bleeding fun, Son, but people get hurt. Trust me, I know.'

Chapter Thirty-Three

Charley was in the gym, pounding the punchbag. One two, one two, one two three four. The black leather bag swung from side the side as he sank his clenched fist into it. This man was on a mission; fast, furious, barely recognisable from the drunk, lethargic guy usually sitting slouched on the sofa.

Jezz was standing next to Charley with a white towel hung around his neck, coaxing him on. 'One two, one two, body shot, up again, one two, one two.'

Charley was agile. The years had fallen away and he looked as if he could spin on a penny. He was ducking from side to side, sweat dripping from his body.

'Good lad. Rest time,' Jezz said.

Charley gave one last punch to the bag and sent it flying up in the air. This man had his power back. He took a bottle of cold water from Jezz and guzzled it. What was left he poured over his head. He looked leaner, more toned, thinner in the face. The fight was days away now and, every hour of every day, Charley could be found in the gym, training.

Jezz nodded as Charley slumped down on the floor. 'You're bang on the money, mate. I can admit it now: at first, I had my doubts you'd get your shit back together but, hats off to you, Charley, you are smashing it. I'd hate to be Archie Bennet. You're going to leather him.'

'I'm not taking my eye off the ball again, Jezz. No way. I feel amazing since I've been off the beer and not been eating shit. Our Danny is nailing it, too. I watched him training earlier and he's fast as fuck. Learned from the best, you know?'

'Yeah, the Bennets don't stand a chance, mate.'

Charley held his head against the cold wall, cooling down. 'Give it another ten minutes and I'll do another few rounds.'

Jezz slung the towel to Charley and sat down next to him. 'So, what's the plan after you win this fight? What next?'

Charley cracked his knuckles. 'I rule my empire like I have always done, never letting things slip again, never taking my eye from the ball. Always two steps in front of these fuckers. Because I know, despite what Archie says, they won't walk away honourably.'

'And your plans for me?'

Charley shot a look at Jezz and studied him more closely. 'We can talk about you after the fight. As you know, I always look after the people who look after me. I've got a nice treat coming your way, because you have stood by me, Jezz, haven't you?' Charley held his mate's eye.

Jezz pulled his shoulders back, proud that he'd been recognised. He jerked his head. 'I've got your back, Charley.

Told you that in jail. You've helped me out when I've been on my arse. Look at what you did years ago when that fucking ex of mine bin-bagged me. Without you, I would have been sofa-surfing.'

Charley sneered. 'Women, eh? They should never come between mates.'

His father was right. Danny had upped his game, too. Now he knew the kind of fighter Nat was, he was undertaking a crash course in mixed martial arts. He was having intensive coaching from Josh Jones, a kid he knew who had been doing it for years, even had a few titles. Paul watched his brother as the trainer put him in a choke hold.

'Tap out, man,' he yelled.

Danny kicked his legs frantically, wriggling about. There was no way out of this. The grip was locked and there was only one way to get out of it: to tap out. Danny knew he was beaten; he patted his opponent's arm. That's how easy it was to be released. But tapping out was admitting you were beaten. Part of Danny would rather pass out than tap out. These moves had to be precise, no room for error. Josh, the trainer, rolled on his side and flipped his body onto his feet. Danny lay still, deflated that he'd left himself open.

The trainer stood over him, offering a hand. 'It's all about speed, Dan, seeing a weakness and striking when you see it. No time to be pussyfooting around.'

Paul agreed. 'Yeah, our kid, you left yourself open. I spotted it straight away.'

Danny jumped to his feet and snarled over at his brother, 'Shut it, gobshite. Since when have you become a master of fucking martial arts?'

Paul smirked. 'I could be Bruce Lee's son, me, mate. I've got moves. *Cobra Kai.*'

Danny was still fuming, finding nothing to laugh at in his brother's jokes. 'Get in here with me then, and let's see what you can do.'

'Do one. I'm not the one in training, and my special moves only come into play when they're needed.'

'Bullshit. You're such a tool, mate.'

Josh was ready for some more grappling, and he clapped his hands. 'Right, you know the score, so don't let me get near you. Protect yourself, and only strike when you see your chance.'

Danny was concentrating, the tip of his tongue just touching the top of his lip. Boom, the two of them were at it again, pulling, dragging, rolling about, arms here, arms there, legs locking around each other's bodies. This was intense and, if Nat Bennet was everything people said he was, this was going to be a hell of a fight.

Jenny refused to watch her men training. She bided her time at home, planning her next move. Charley still assumed she was simply doing the washing and cleaning up as always. Rachel walked into the room and at last she had some company. All day her mind had been racing and, now she'd found out about Gina sleeping with her son, she'd had no one to talk things through with.

'Hiya, love, you're home early.'

Rachel's face looked as fed up as her mother's, the face of a thousand cuts.

'Yeah, it was quiet after the rush today so Katie said I could go home early. I'm glad really. I feel a bit rough. I'm sure I'm coming down with the lurgy.'

'Come and get on the sofa with me and we can watch a chick flick. Or do you want to talk stuff through?'

'No thanks, I'll go and get my pyjamas on and I'll come back down.'

Jenny smiled. She loved spending time with Rachel, even when she was sure she was holding something back from her – there was a guardedness in her eyes she never used to have.

Rachel was soon back down, dressed in her *Lion King* PJs. She had a grey chunky blanket wrapped around her shoulders and fluffy bed-socks on. She plonked down on the sofa next to her mother. Jenny looked at her and she could see her daughter wasn't well. 'There has been a bug going about, I bet you've got that?'

'Yeah probably,' Rachel moaned.

Jenny started flicking through films on Netflix. 'If you see anything you want to watch, tell me. I fancy a nice rom-com, something with a happy ending.'

Rachel let out a sarcastic laugh. 'Like anybody ever has a happy ending. Love is for fools.'

'Don't say that. Love is beautiful and special when it's with the right person.'

'Yeah, whatever.'

Jenny stopped scrolling, reached over and touched her daughter's warm hands. 'Are you sure you don't want to talk about anything, babes? I'm here if you do?'

Rachel pulled her knees up to her chest and rested her chin on top of them. 'Mam, don't you ever think of getting away from around here? I mean far, far away where nobody knows you and you could live your life without being judged.'

Jenny sighed. 'Every bleeding day, Rach. But where would I go? I mean, you've heard me to your dad – if he doesn't change his ways, then I'm gone. But I need time to plan – find somewhere I can get my head down. Somewhere where I'm not Charley Johnson's wife.'

Rachel was about to say something, but froze. This was her secret and, if she told her mother, she would no longer have a place where she could go alone, where nobody would find her. Her mother needed a safe place, too, but could she trust her?

Jenny kicked back and reached for her fags. 'With everything that's happened, I feel our time on this estate is over. Honestly, even if our kid and your dad cream this fight, is the prize worth having? I don't want to be a gangster's wife. I don't want all the hassle anymore. It's putting my family in danger and I don't have any real friends,' she sighed and rolled her eyes. 'I did have Gina, but she can go and take a run and a jump now, the hussy.'

Rachel giggled. 'Why, what has she done now?'

'I've only gone and caught her in bed with our Paul, bang at it like bleeding rabbits.'

Rachel looked aghast. 'Stop it, no way! Are you having a laugh? She's a married woman.'

'It makes no difference to a man that, love; sex is sex, isn't it? She should have known better, though. It makes me sick inside to even think about it.'

Rachel was shocked, but she couldn't help giggling. Her brothers were on another level when it came to choosing who they slept with. Any hole, they would fill it.

After laughing about Gina, Jenny and Rachel had cheered up.

'Mam, all this fighting with the Bennets, do you think it will put a stop to all this beef once it's over?'

'Honestly, love, no. This war goes back for years and years and none of them will ever back down. Even when Archie and your dad have retired, this will be a blood feud between the boys, I can see that much already. We're trapped in it, whether we like it or not.'

Rachel sat playing with her fingers, sucking on her bottom lip. 'I've lied to you, Mam.'

Jenny was immediately alert. 'About what?'

Her daughter took a deep breath, and slowly she revealed the truth. 'I told you I was seeing a lad called Jack, but he wasn't called Jack. It was Niall Bennet.'

You could have heard a pin drop. Jenny held her flat palm on her chest as if she was having a heart attack, colour draining from her cheeks.

'We were in love, Mam, or at least I thought I was. He told me I was the one, and – do you know what? – I believed him. But it's over now, done with.'

Jenny winced, her daughter's words like lashes across her back. 'No, love. I can't believe it, not one of the Bennets. Bleeding hell, when it rains in this house, it bloody pours down.'

'I think we always knew we didn't stand a chance, with our families at war, but there was something between us stronger than that – electric, it was. But then Danny put him in hospital, and how could we be together after that? Danny's the one who broke us up.'

'No, Rachel, Danny didn't break you two up. If that love was real, the Bennet boy would have stood by you, no matter what. Love conquers all.'

Rachel rocked her body to and fro. 'I thought it did once, too, but he thinks more about this bloody war between our families than he does me.'

'There you go then, enough said. The guy is a wanker like the rest of his lot. You had a lucky escape if you ask me. Bleeding hell, Rach, don't let anybody know about this. Please keep it under your belt. It would cause World War Three if your dad ever got wind of this. As if I need him kicking off about this on top of everything else. This is going to end in disaster – it's not like we're in the movies. There's no hero to walk on the save the day. We women have to save ourselves or get walked over.'

'There is something else I have kept from you, Mam, but I need you to promise me you will never breathe a word of it to anyone. Promise me.'

This was getting serious, and Jenny was scared, but eager to know what else her daughter was hiding.

'When Dot died, it broke my heart. She was such a lovely woman, and she was the only one who knew all about Niall.'

Jenny felt gutted that her daughter could not come to her and tell her about the man she loved. She'd let her down as a mother, but she knew she'd have told Rachel to can him. Dot was the only one who didn't have a stake in the fight. 'I know she meant a lot to you.'

Rachel welled up, emotions all over the place. 'I got a letter from her solicitor about her last will and testament, and they asked me to attend a meeting.'

Bless the old dear, she'd probably left her daughter a nice brooch or something like that to remember her by. Jenny smiled softly and waited for her daughter to finish. 'She left me a cottage in Devon, Mam. A beautiful two-bedroomed cottage.' Rachel reached down and found her handbag. She ruffled about inside it and pulled out a printed picture of the house. 'Number five, Buttercup Lane.' She passed the picture over to her mother and watched as she scrutinised it.

'Oh my god, are you having me on? I mean, a home like that in the countryside. It must be worth a lot of money.' Jenny passed the piece of paper back to her daughter in disbelief. 'I don't know what to say, Rach. I'm speechless.'

'I don't want you to say anything. This is our secret. This could be our new start away from it all. Dad will never change his lifestyle, and Danny and Paul won't either. It's in their blood, Mam. I thought Niall and I might change things, but it just showed me that even love isn't enough to end this. I can't live like this anymore, and the house Dot left me is my chance to change my life. I could live by the sea. No police, no dealing, no massage parlours, no fighting between you and Dad. It could be your chance, too.'

Jenny's eyes widened. 'What do you mean, fighting with me and your dad?'

Rachel slid her fingertips down the side of Jenny's cheek. 'Do you think I've not heard you crying? Seen the bruises you try and hide, the black eyes where you tell me you bumped into a cupboard? I've always known. Make a stand, Mam. Don't allow him to treat you like that anymore. You are worth so much more.'

Jenny swallowed hard as a ball of emotion filled her throat. At this moment, she realised how much she'd let her daughter down. She should have been teaching her that men should respect women, never lay a finger on them. But, instead, she'd been weak and hidden away the domestic abuse she was suffering.

Rachel held the picture of the Devon house in front of her mother and pointed at it. 'There is our answer, right there. I will never sit back and watch you get hurt again, Mother.'

Jenny wiped her tears. 'I'm sorry, baby. Sorry that I've allowed you to be involved in this shit life. I've let all my kids down – Paul, Danny, you. I should have kicked your dad to the kerb years ago, told him it was over.'

'Why didn't you?'

Jenny shook her head slowly. 'Because I thought he was the one keeping you all safe – but now I see he was the one bringing trouble to our door. But I'd married him and thought he was my happy ever after. I always thought I could change him, always forgave him. I listened to his lies for years, always promising me that he would never go to jail again, but he always did. You're right, Rach, I need to do something and sooner rather than later.'

Rachel smiled softly. 'You are the strongest woman I know, Mam; I love you.' They hugged each other with a tight squeeze. 'I'll make everything right soon, baby. Trust me, this will all stop.'

Chapter Thirty-Four

Jenny was getting ready when her bedroom door opened slowly. Jezz walked inside and sat on the edge of the bed. He looked her up and down. 'Sexy woman,' he grunted.

She turned away quickly and dragged her jeans on, covering her black lacy knickers. 'Jezz, you need to get out of here. Charley will be home soon, he's only nipped out.'

'Do you think I'm arsed anymore about him? If he loses this fight, he'll be over. You can ditch him and there's nothing he'll be able to do about it.'

'Jezz, I can't do this anymore. I'm done with it all. Me and you was a mistake. I can't keep making mistakes in my life. You were there for me when I needed a shoulder to cry on but, come on, we will never work. You live in the same world as Charley and I'm not willing to change one criminal for another.' Jenny had seen the light at last. The talk with Rachel had hit home, made her look at her life differently and believe escape was still possible.

Jezz sprang up from the bed. 'I knew you were getting cold feet; you've not been near me since the date of the fight was set. Jen, it's nearly all over, all this ducking and diving, and we can be together.'

Her words were firm, she knew what she wanted. 'No Jezz, it's over. Just leave me alone.'

He came at her with evil in his eye. She'd rattled his cage. 'What, you think you can piss me off, just like that? Nah, woman, it's not as easy as that. If you want me gone and to stay quiet about us,' he inhaled deeply, 'it's going to cost you.'

Jenny was dressed now. She kept checking out of the window for any signs of her husband. 'Cost me what?'

He sucked hard on his gums and pulled his shoulders back. 'A few grand I'll need to get out of your hair.'

Jenny let out a sarcastic laugh. 'Piss off, Jezz. As if I have that kind of money, and, if I did have it, like I'm going to give any to you.'

'We can do this the easy way or the hard way, it's up to you?'

'Do your worst, Jezz. Are you forgetting something here?' She went nose to nose with him. 'It's you who has been sleeping with your mate's wife. Charley will destroy you. And, as for me, what can he do to me that he hasn't done before? Go on, you barmy bastard, get your stuff together and fuck off out of here.'

He gripped her by the throat and spat in her face. 'Do you think you can just get rid of me like that, Jenny? I'm going nowhere.'

Jenny ran to the car and flicked the engine over. She screeched out of the drive and headed towards the main road. Her life was a mess and there was no longer any denying it. She needed a plan and quick. She pulled up outside the bank and dropped her head onto the steering wheel. Head banging slowly, up and down, up and down. She rummaged in her bag and found her purse. Clutching it closely to her chest, she got out of the car.

Jezz was on edge, looking one way then the other, checking his watch, agitated. He lit a cigarette and sucked hard on it. In the distance he could see someone approaching. He jogged to meet them. 'For fuck's sake, you're over twenty minutes late.'

The woman smiled at him. 'Oh, hello to you, too. Bloody hell, I had a late night, chill out. I do work, you know.'

'Jackie, things have gone tits up. Jenny's not playing ball anymore. She says it's over. Fuck me, this plan is falling apart. We were so close to the finish line, and it's gone tits up.'

Jackie gripped him by the arm and looked around the area. 'Come on, I'm not discussing our business out here. Let's get in the pub over there and get a drink.'

They found a quiet corner of the pub. Jezz fidgeted waiting for Jackie to come back from the bar. She was paying for the drinks: he still had barely a penny to his name. She set the drinks down on the table. He reached over for his and swigged a large mouthful, wiping his mouth with his sleeve.

'Jackie, we were so near to getting money from these fuckers. Fucking nightmare. She would have trusted me with everything given a bit more time. I could have taken every penny she had.'

Jackie gave him a told-you-so look. 'Shit happens. Charley carted me too. I never expected him to wife me up, but a bit of an affair could have been on the cards. Imagine what I could have got out of him if he was shaking my bones every now and then.'

Jezz was alert. 'You can still ask him for money, say you're going to tell his wife. He'll shit a brick with all the trouble he's been having with her lately.'

Jackie rubbed at her arms as a cold chill ran up her spine. 'Not a chance, Jezz. If we'd hit it off then I could have got money out of him that way, but there is no way I'm trying to blackmail him. The guy is a nutter. Sack that.'

Jezz sat thinking, his mind racing. 'The fight is next week. I have to stay around a bit longer and see how things pan out. He trusts me. I know I can get to his money.'

Jackie sat back and eyeballed Jezz. 'You still love me, right? You said if I slept with Charley we would be back together. I hope that hasn't changed?'

'Jackie, we work well together, don't go and spoil it. We have to take things day by day like I told you. When we were together, you were too much, too needy. And knowing you're sleeping with other geezers is hard to get my head around. It's a lot to take in, knocks me sick sometimes, you know it does.'

'Hang on. I put your mates onto that job at Blossoms when they nicked all the takings, and you still haven't given me a penny. What happened to my cut? Don't think you're having my eyes out on this, Jezz.'

'I had to invest it, darling. Speculate to accumulate, you know the dance.' He stroked her cheek with his grubby fingers.

'Jezz, I waited for you while you were in jail. I sent you money, ran around for you, got you parcels dropped off. And I've gone along with this daft bleeding plan of having Charley Johnson over.' She caught her breath. 'And up to now nothing has happened except I have to sit back knowing you've been sleeping with his wife. Don't take the piss out of me, because I'll sell you down the river if you are.'

Jezz pulled away from her, growled in her face. 'Turn it in, woman. I was sticking it up other women long before you come along.'

'I know that, but then we met and we fell in love, didn't we? Remember what you told me, Jezz? You said we would be together once this was sorted out. Don't be selling me out now, changing your bloody tune.'

He gulped the rest of his pint and sat with his arms crossed. 'Looks like it's Plan B then.'

Jackie necked her drink. 'What does that mean?'

He stood up and tapped the side of his nose. 'For me to know and you to find out. I'll be in touch.'

He walked out of the pub with his head dipped low. Desperate times called for desperate measures.

Chapter Thirty-Five

Charley sat in his car with Jezz and the boys, waiting for Archie and his lad to show. The referee had just turned up. He was experienced and it was all in a day's work for him. This was how beef was settled in his world.

Danny sat in the back with Paul. He'd not said a word all the way there. He was focused, head in the game.

Paul twisted around to look out of the back window. 'Showtime, lads, here they are. Let's have this.'

Charley flicked his eyes at the rear-view mirror and his nostrils flared. He gripped the steering wheel tighter. 'Right, ready as I'll ever be.'

Jezz zipped his coat up fully and got out from the passenger door. None of them said a word as they made their way to the car park.

Archie had parked up and stood waiting. He smirked as Charley approached. 'So, you turned up then. I thought you might have had second thoughts and stayed at home.'

'Wouldn't have missed this for the world,' Charley replied in a sarcastic tone.

Danny was eyeballing Nat. Bloody hell, they both had the cold eyes of a killer: this was going to be one hell of a fight. Paul nudged his brother as he clocked the Bennet brothers whispering to each other. 'You better take that prick down, and quick. If you need me to step in, give me the nod. I've got a blade on me and I'll stab the cunt up.'

Danny sniggered. 'Don't you worry about me, mate. I'm all over him. There will be two hits – me hitting him, and him hitting the floor.'

The referee came over to them. He was on the ball and went through the rules: when he said break, they broke away from each other, no snide digs. The purse was handed to him. He walked away and put it by a brick wall. Twenty grand. The trophy was with it. Archie smiled as he spotted it. His eyes lit up.

Charley was eager to get started, bouncing around now, keeping warm. 'So the younguns fight first, then us big boys?'

Archie jutted his head forward. 'Yep, I'm fine with that. It shouldn't be a long fight. My boy's all over this.'

Jezz was edgy, rubbing his left hand down the side of his coat, checking for something.

Charley stood with his son and moved everyone away from them both so they could have a quiet word, a father and son moment. He placed his arm around Danny's shoulder and pulled him in closer. 'Are you ready, Son?'

'Sorted. Let's get this over with.'

Charley studied his boy: he was psyched up, ready to rumble. Archie was having a similar chat with his son, and by the looks of things he was ready to fight too. Charley patted the top of Danny's head, just like he did when he'd won a race at sports day when he was younger. 'Let's do this. Destroy the fucker. Snap his jaw and show him what you're made of.'

Danny's ears pinned back, chest expanded. He was on his toes now, bobbing and weaving about. No more words needed. He went and stood next to the referee and Nat jogged over to join them. The onlookers had gathered now and formed a circle around them, eager for this fight to get started. The referee spoke to them both again, made sure they understood what he was saying. They agreed and he stood between them. 'A good clean fight, lads.'

Nat crossed himself and looked up at the grey sky. With that, the fight started. Danny was making sure he never left himself open. His guard was up and neither of them had swung a punch yet.

Archie roared, 'Give it him, Son! Steam in and put him on his arse. Remember what he did to your brother, make him pay.'

Whack, Danny's head went back, a good blow that connected. It was clear from his reaction that he'd underestimated this kid. Nat was fast and powerful. That was it, they were blow for blow, blood soon spraying from both bodies, heads flying back, blood being spat out. Danny's training plan went right out of the window, no time to think.

Charley was playing it cool; there was no shouting or screaming from him. No, he stood tall and clenched his jaw as he watched his son giving it all he had. This was a top contest. The onlookers were getting a good performance from both fighters tonight. The Bennet boys were cheering, shouting. Paul swallowed hard; this could go either way, but Nat Bennet seemed to have the edge.

The referee pulled them apart when they clung to each other. 'Break!' he shouted. 'Fucking break when I say.'

Danny backed off and licked the bright-red blood landing on his lips. He blew hot steamy breath from his mouth. Straight away, they were back at it. Danny was clever now, making his opponent do all the work, protecting himself. And here it was, an uppercut right under Nat's jaw. He wobbled and crashed to the floor. Good night, Vienna.

Charley punched his clenched fist into the air as he saw the Bennet lad knocked out for the count.

Danny roared at the Bennet clan, blood dripping down the side of his head, eyes swelling by the second. 'Any of you want some too?'

Archie made sure his sons stayed back because there would have been a line-up to fight him in seconds.

Danny danced about with his hands in the air. Paul was at his side now, hugging him, shouting over to Nat Bennet as he was coming round and being lifted from the floor. 'Told you our kid was the man, fucking told you all!'

Archie was bright red, steam practically coming out of his ears, as he walked over to the referee. He was ready. Charley turned to pass Jezz his tracksuit top, but Jezz was nowhere in sight. Paul was by his dad's side now with

Danny. 'Well done, my boy. You done us proud, now it's my turn.' Charley punched his fist into his chest like a gorilla getting ready to attack. His t-shirt was off. He would fight bare-chested. It wasn't only vanity; having a top on meant his opponent could drag him about by it, pull it over his head.

This was the main event; the fight everyone had come to see. The referee worded them both up. He wanted a good clean fight, no fucking about. Charley looked in great shape. The last two weeks had treated him well and he was lean, toned. Archie was slightly taller than Charley and built like a tank. They locked eyes and there it was.

'Fight,' the referee shouted.

The sound of the grey gravel crunching under their feet as they moved about, weaving and bobbing. These men knew their shit, not like the young ones rushing in. They had a game plan. Charley started goading Archie. 'Come on, soft lad, this is what happened the last time, too scared to steam in.'

Archie wasn't biting though. He kept schtum, waiting to see an opening so he could knock this prick out. A few punches now, body shots, kidney punches. All eyes were on the fight, everyone shouting. And here it was: right hooks, left hooks, body shots. Both of them going for gold, fighting for the power, the empire.

The fight had been going on for over fifteen minutes. Both the men had cuts and swelling on their faces. This was a test for sure and only the strongest would survive. Paul danced around on the spot. 'Come on, Dad, finish him, take him down.'

This was anyone's game, they were blow for blow, Rocky and Apollo Creed. They were both tired now, resting on each other. But the referee was all over them. He dragged them apart. Archie swung a right, Charley swerved and came back up with a combination. His moves were faster than they had been all the fight. He'd saved his energy, left some fuel in the pipes. He landed the sweetest punch possible.

Archie gasped for breath, legs buckling under him. The referee pulled him to one side and spoke to him; Archie could barely reply.

At last, Charley had showed them all that he was still the man. The fight was over.

Tears streamed down Charley's cheeks as he staggered to his boys. 'It's all ours again. I told you. I fucking told you,' he roared up to the sky, eyes closed.

But before his boys could celebrate with him, there was shouting from behind him. Charley fell to the floor as the trophy was smashed over his head, one, two, three times, bludgeoning him.

He was still, silent on the ground.

Danny and Paul were targeted too, blows raining down on them. They'd been double-crossed – all talk of a fair fight vanished.

The referee sprinted to his car. This was a blood bath, and he wanted no part of it.

Paul was on his toes, hurt but trying to see who was behind this. He scrambled down a path. Someone was behind him, hot on his trail. For crying out loud, it was Arlo Bennet. Paul twisted around quickly, trying to get his blade from his pocket with shaking hands. Arlo wasted no time, he was straight on him, punching and kicking, biting. But Paul was strong, getting the better of his opponent. Then arms were getting in between them, splitting them up, dragging at them both. Paul tried to focus, his vision poor. He stumbled back and saw Archie Bennet in front of him. The guy was a mess, blood all over his face.

'You two don't need to fight!' he screamed. Paul had nowhere to run. Arlo was doing his best to get at him, but his dad held him back. 'I said turn it in.'

'Dad, let me at him, I can take him down.'

Paul was forcing his swelling eyes to stay open, his breathing laboured, when Archie screamed, 'He's your blood, Arlo! Paul is your brother.'

Arlo froze, not sure if he'd heard right. 'What do you mean, he's my blood? He's a fucking Johnson, a dirty no-good Johnson, the scum of the earth.'

Archie licked his lips slowly and turned to Paul. 'Your mam should have told you years ago. She always said she would, so don't look at me like that. I wanted to tell you. I loved Jenny. We could have been so good together. Instead, I had to settle for a few nights here and a few nights there when your old man was in nick.'

'Fuck off lying. You're lying,' Paul yelled.

'It's the truth. Ask her, go on ask her.'

Arlo was white, colour drained from his skin, disgusted. 'I'm out of here, Dad. This is some sick, twisted shit. You better tell my mam too, because don't think I'm keeping something like this from her. Nah, no way. I'm fucking ashamed of you.' Arlo turned on his toes and ran off.

Paul charged at Archie, fighting him, trying to bring him down.

'It's no good, mate. I'm still your dad, you can't change it.'

Paul broke free and ran. He never turned round once. He ran and ran.

Chapter Thirty-Six

Charley Johnson lay on the tarmac, lifeless. Eyes wide open, the trophy lying by his side. Alone in death, except for the animals of the night – foxes, rats – going about their business.

An old man appeared from the bushes, the same man who had been in the pub the day Charley kicked off. He bent to look at the body on the ground. His voice was low. 'So, Son, you are like me after all. You beat your wife like I beat your mother, and look at you now: you have nothing, just like me. Like father, like son, eh?' Saxon Johnson gazed down at his son for a few more seconds, then straightened up. Shaking his head, he walked away into the shadows of the night.

Paul stormed into the house, running into each room, yelling, 'Mam, where the hell are you?' Nobody was home. The house was cold, no lights switched on, no TV on. Paul fell to his knees and cradled his body in his own arms. 'It's not true, it's not true.' He trudged up the stairs and switched the light on in his mother's bedroom. It looked so bare, perfumes all gone from the dressing table, drawers emptied. He sat down on the edge of the bed and his head dropped into his hands. 'I need you, Mam. Where are you? I need to know the truth.' His eyes shot to a white envelope on the dressing table. He picked it up. Across the front of it was Charley's name. Paul had always been a nosey parker, and the letter wasn't sealed, so why shouldn't he have a sneaky look at it? It was probably more secrets she'd kept from him, dark secrets she didn't want anyone to know about. He opened it slowly, still unsure if he wanted to read it:

Charley, I have finally done it. I've left you. I feel free already, like a dark cloud has been lifted from over my head. Like a bird who has been let out of a cage. I want a life, to find me again. To do all the things I've wanted to do. I will never ever let a man treat me like you have. I owe it to myself to be a stronger person in the future. You are no longer my jailer. Oh, and I know about you and Jackie. Come on, I manage the CCTV at Blossoms for crying out loud, don't ever take me for a fool. We both have secrets, Charley, but the last laugh is on you, because you'll never know mine.

Rot in hell.

Jenny.

Across town, Jezz left the train station in a rush. He was carrying a black sports bag and constantly checking over his shoulder. He was a Judas. The lowest of the low. He'd betrayed his friend, the man who'd helped him out when he had nothing. And for what? Money. The sky was pitch-black. What he'd done meant he'd be looking over his shoulder for the rest of his life. He clutched the bag closer to his body, and walked down an alleyway. It stank of bin-juice, empty beer bottles everywhere. Rats ran in front of his feet. Noises behind him, rubbish being stood on. Jezz squinted into the shadows.

He quickened his pace: someone was following him.

'Yo, who that?' There was no reply. Coming out of the alleyway, he trudged across muddy wasteland. He spun around and still nobody was there. His nerves were all over the place as he reached a brick wall. He needed a fag. His mind must have been playing tricks on him, he was so jumpy. He lit his cigarette with shaking hands and sucked in a large mouthful of nicotine.

The cigarette was still in his hand when he went crashing to the ground. A trickle of blood slowly rolling from the side of his head. He struggled to move: he could see the silhouette of his attacker.

'Jenny? What the fuck?'

She stood over him, aware he could strike at any second. She never took her eyes from him as she picked up the bag he'd dropped. 'I think this belongs to me, eh, Jezz?'

He saw she was holding something in her other hand. He tried to move, but as soon as he spotted the silver pistol, he froze. It was over. 'Jenny, I did this for us. I was going to phone you when I got settled, on my life.'

She let out a sarcastic laugh. 'Do I look green, or what? I knew what you were up to all along. I saw you on the CCTV in the gaffe car park, talking to Jackie. It's not rocket science to work the rest out, is it? Don't think I don't know you planned that the Bennet boys would jump my lads if Charley won. You could have had my sons killed all for a few poxy quid.'

'Jen, come on, love. I wouldn't do that. Alright, I've made a few mistakes, but come on, I love you.'

She chuckled as her grip tightened on the gun. These were her words, the ones she'd practised in her mind. But she had to be quick before she lost her nerve. 'You all piss in the same pot, Jezz. You treat women like they are nothing. Poor Jackie really thought you cared about her, but be at peace knowing I've been to see her too.' She smirked as she continued, eyes dancing with madness, 'Oh yes, Jezz, gone are the days when I let people take the piss out of me. I've spent my whole life being underestimated. Today I stand tall. Today is the start of the new me. You men can kiss my arse.'

She pulled the trigger.

Jenny walked over to the body and kicked at it. No movement. She squatted and un-zipped the black bag. Yep, it looked like it was all there. Twenty thousand pounds would help her set up her new life with Rachel. She looked down at the body one last time and sneered.

'You can break down a woman, but we will always pick up the pieces and rebuild ourselves. And when we do, we come back stronger than ever.'

Chapter Thirty-Seven

Rachel was sweating as another wave of pain surged through her body. Jenny was by her side, holding her hand, mopping her brow. 'Come on, Rachel, you can do this.'

The midwife lifted her head from between Rachel's legs and looked at her directly. 'I can see the head. Come on, a few more good pushes.'

Jenny brushed her daughter's hair back and rubbed at her back with a flat palm. Screaming, groaning, Rachel grabbed her mam's hand and squeezed with all her might until it turned white. She strained, eyes bulging.

'Push, come on, push,' said the midwife.

Jenny was all over the place, tears streaming down her face, as she heard a baby crying. Exhausted, Rachel collapsed back onto the bed, eyes barely open.

'Rachel, you've done it. You are so brave,' Jenny sobbed. This had been a hard labour.

Rachel wiped sweat from her eyes. 'I did it, Mam, I did it! Thank you for being here with me.'

The midwife passed the baby, wrapped in a cotton blanket, over to Rachel who choked tears back as she met two beautiful blue eyes. 'He's a lovely baby boy, Miss Jackson. Do you have a name for him yet so I can fill out his name tag?'

Jenny peered into the blanket and looked at her grandson for the first time. 'Oh, he's beautiful, Rach. So precious, so innocent.'

Rachel played with her son's little fingers, just staring at him, mesmerised by him. 'I want to name him Niall.' She paused and closed her eyes. 'Niall Charles Jackson.'

The midwife jotted the name down and carried on about her business.

Jenny waited until they were alone, then stroked her daughter's hand. 'This is a fresh start, love. Are you sure you want that little boy to carry those names? I've loved living down here as a Jackson not a Johnson. But Niall Charles? That's some legacy. This is new life. Have you ever seen anything more innocent?'

Rachel lay with her baby on her chest, smelling him, holding him against her warm, pink flesh. 'Mam, I'm sure of it. Dot once told me three things that can't be long hidden: the sun, the moon, and the truth.'

Jenny nodded. They had a new life now, even a new name, but the past was hard to outrun.

Paul and Danny had been remanded in Strangeways. A big operation had linked them with supplying drugs, and with gun and knife crimes. They were both looking at a ten-stretch. Charley's demise had been all over the news alongside his sons' imprisonment, and the police had charged Archie Bennet with his death. He too was looking at life imprisonment – for the murder of both Charley Johnson and Jezz: gangland crimes that the police didn't look too closely at. With Archie convicted and Charley dead, that took two big names off their patch. But it wouldn't take long for the police to be getting familiar with the new names on the street.

The Bennet sons were a wildcard. The brothers were be busy for now taking over the Johnsons' turf. But Rachel and Jenny both knew the day would dawn when they'd start looking for the loose ends.

It was hard to think of that though when, only a few months in, Devon was such a beautiful place to live. Not a soul recognised them. Dot's cottage was small and clean and, most importantly, free of the ghosts of the past. The police had bought their tears when they were questioned about Charley's death. They'd assumed the women couldn't have had anything to do with the darkest side of the vendetta.

By the point Rachel had realised she was pregnant, their old life already seemed like a bad dream. This was their new life, the one they had both craved, peace at last. Nothing was going to ruin it. The baby was a fresh start. They would be hard to track down – but not impossible. For now though, they woke up every morning to quiet and contentment – no one telling them what to do or how to spend their time, time which felt precious, time to plan. Somewhere inside they both knew one day a knock on the door would come.

When the knock came, however many years in the future, they'd be ready.

Acknowledgements

Thank you to all my readers for all your support.

Thank you to HarperNorth: Gen, Megan,
Alice and all the team there.

Thank you to Empire Publications.

My journey as a writer continues and after 23 novels to
date I still pinch myself to see if it's real. I write for
everyone who has not had the best start in life and for all
those people who thought they were not good enough.
I hope my stories shine light on a lot of subjects we rarely
speak about and help people realise that they are not alone
in whatever they may be facing.

Thank you to my husband James and my children:
Ashley, Blake, Declan, Darcy and all my grandchildren.

My last thanks goes to my mother Margaret for the hours we spent discussing story lines.

To all my family and friends this book is for you.

Love Karen xxx

Harper
North

Book Credits

HarperNorth would like to thank the following staff
and contributors for their involvement in making
this book a reality:

Hannah Avery
Fionnuala Barrett
Claire Boal
Charlotte Brown
Sarah Burke
Alan Cracknell
Jonathan de Peyer
Anna Derkacz
Tom Dunstan
Kate Elton
Mick Fawcett
Simon Gerratt
Monica Green

CJ Harter
Megan Jones
Jean-Marie Kelly
Nicky Lovick
Oliver Malcolm
Alice Murphy-Pyle
Adam Murray
Genevieve Pegg
Agnes Rigou
Florence Shepherd
Emma Sullivan
Katrina Troy
Sarah Whittaker

For more unmissable reads,
sign up to the HarperNorth newsletter at
www.harpernorth.co.uk

or find us on Twitter at
@HarperNorthUK

Harper
North